THE AMERICAN GIRL

THE MAUREEN RITTER SERIES
BOOK 1

EOIN DEMPSEY

This book is for Julian Mittman.

1

New York City, Friday, April 28, 2006

Amy Sullivan sat in the *New York Times* newsroom, fingers poised over the keyboard, trying to focus on Iraq and not on her boss, Ryan Smith, the foreign editor she'd been seeing in secret for months. Ryan glanced in her direction from where he was standing in the corner, but she kept her eyes on the screen in front of her. It was tough not being able to touch him, even smile at him, but he'd assured her many times it wouldn't always be this way. His children weren't ready for another woman in their lives, and newsrooms were notorious for gossip. Keeping their secret had been fun at first, but the longing to go public with him was becoming hard to bear. She had to walk past him or his office every morning on her way to her desk and whenever she went to lunch or the bathroom.

She'd only been here a year when he had taken her to Iraq. He was going through a divorce, and she was fresh from a breakup of her own. They stayed in the foreign reporter hotel in the Green Zone together. He was her mentor, and she flourished under his tutelage. Within weeks she was writing more and more of her own stories. He even talked about changing her contract so she could reclaim the copyright on her articles from *The Times* and collect them as a book under her own name.

They'd spoken of it one night as they lay entwined in each other's arms in the Baghdad Hotel, the sound of shots crackling in the distance.

She'd felt so happy and grateful. A collection of her war stories could launch her career.

"You worked on them too, Ryan," she said. "Hence the joint by-lines."

"Yes, but it was your heart, Amy, your perceptions."

They returned to New York with a plan to reveal their love to the world and for her to have what he described as "her incredible work" published under her own name. But neither of those things had happened in the almost 11 months since they'd been back. It seemed he'd been stringing her along with promises lately, and he was more distant. His handsome face and sparkling eyes were in her mind all the time. It was difficult.

She endeavored to focus on work. Memories of her time in Iraq flooded her mind but only as a jumbled mess. Conversations with officers, soldiers, and the people begging on the street. Riding in utility vehicles with a helmet strapped to her head with six soldiers and her cameraman. The car bomb she witnessed and the dead on the street in its wake – she'd written about the same things for *The Times* repeatedly—violence, shooting, bombs, and war. She needed a different angle.

She took a deep breath and brought her fingers to the keys on the laptop. Perhaps if she started writing about...

His name was Adnan, and he came to the firebase each day to sell cans of coke or candy to the soldiers. He arrived each morning with a bag slung over his shoulder filled with sugary treats and a smile just as sweet. His huge brown eyes danced with every word he spoke, and he strutted around the camp as if he owned the place. New nicknames for soldiers and guards sprang from his lips every time he walked through the gate. He even had one for me. I was "Julia" after Julia Roberts, a movie star no one else had ever compared me to, and to whom I bore no resemblance. But delivered with the charm and confidence that Adnan exuded as a matter of course, it stuck. And I always greeted the name with a grin as the little boy shouted it across the dusty parade ground. The ten-year-old treated every soldier like a friend in a country where they found few.

I was in Iraq for only a few weeks when I first met him, and like everyone else, I took to him in seconds. He had a fearsome charm and an exuberance that drew people to him. His English was better than most, and I soon learned he hadn't spoken a word a year before. Everything he knew was from talking to the guards, and his appetite for learning was insatiable. Between jokes and made-up handshakes, he would ask about America and what it was like there. He wondered why so many came to Iraq if the US was as wonderful as it sounded. The thought of baseball, beaches, and all the food he could ever dream of just sitting there on supermarket shelves was almost more than he could comprehend. In a country where so many of us grumble about trivialities, Adnan taught us all to appreciate the wonder of what we'd previously thought of as the mundane.

On the 4th of July, some of the soldiers invited him to a cookout and watched with glee as he ate hamburgers and hot dogs with them. The next day he returned with fresh bruises, but his smile remained intact. His father beat him for breaking Muslim halal rules on the base, but Adnan declared the experience worth it. I guess we all have to take a beating once in a while.

By the time I left the base, Adnan was spending most of his time there, learning English from the guards and working on the engines of the Humvees with the mechanics. I bought his entire bag of candy and soda on my last day in the country so he could play soccer with the soldiers, guaranteed to bring home money for his family that night. I bid him goodbye with a hug, sure I'd hear his name again someday.

He died two weeks after I left, killed along with his sister and 30 others by a suicide bomber who blew himself up in a crowded market on a Sunday morning—Adnan's one day off. The heavens cried for him as much as the soldiers when a monsoon poured on the day of his funeral, and I've thought about him many times since.

I wonder what ideology in that suicide bomber's mind could have been worth the life of someone who shone so brightly. That little boy's essence stayed with me. I just wish his life wasn't a lesson to others, and he could have lived it on his own terms. It was the least he deserved.

The idea of preserving Adnan's memory was comforting. That little boy should never have been a lesson for others. He'd just wanted to be a kid. Amy thought of his mother. Men started wars, but women picked up the pieces.

Politicians might have been the ones who made the decisions to send men and women to war, but they weren't the ones who suffered the most. She wanted to write about the cost of political decisions rather than the would-be kings who made them.

Working here wasn't always her dream job. She'd have been horrified if someone had told her fifteen years ago she'd end up a war reporter. It was strange how her ambitions and desires had morphed over time. At age four, all she'd wanted to be was a princess. At 15 it was to be a famous actor. But she drifted into student journalism in college and then local radio. Now, at age 34, her dream was to be one of the world's most famous and trusted news reporters, the ones to whom the public turned when they got sick of celebrity gossip and the sports pages. Someone who made a difference.

Amy hit send.

The call came ten minutes later while she was chatting to her friend, Sara, the Washington correspondent. They were planning what bar to visit after work.

The newsroom was still busy, though most of the reporting and feature staff were preparing to head off, leaving the subs and editor to put the paper to bed.

The low hum of her desk phone interrupted their conversation. Sara walked away as Amy picked it up.

The bright smile on Amy's face melted as soon as she heard the voice on the other end. Nicole Frost from HR was inviting her for a "quick huddle in one of the meeting rooms before the weekend," and Amy's heart sank. Why were they calling her last thing on a Friday? Nothing good ever came of a call from human resources at this time on a Friday.

She thought about saying she was busy on a story and running out of the office. The more reasonable side of her mind told her to calm down. This was probably nothing—just a technical matter.

"I'll be right down," she said.

A few deep breaths calmed her a little more. She'd never been fired from a job in her entire life. Why would management dump her now? Her name was in the paper almost every day. Ryan had her back. The irrational feelings coursing through her were a sign of stress. Her contract was up for renewal soon. It was probably about that. *But of course*, she thought, and her heart lifted. This was about amending her next contract to give her copyright over her articles for a book, just as Ryan had promised her.

He looked up as she passed him. He was in a gray Givenchy suit that cost more than most junior reporters made in three months. His ice-blue eyes met hers.

"I'm off to HR. I think it's about my book. Do you know anything about it?"

He shook his head and didn't ask any follow-up questions, returning to his screen. "I'm sorry, Amy, I'm swamped."

"Did you like my story?" she asked though she hadn't much time.

"Yes, I worked on it for a while, added some factual stuff. It'll go in tomorrow, both our by-lines, yours first of course."

She loved the joint by-lines. They made her feel like they were married, signing Christmas cards together.

"Thanks, Ryan. We're all off to Gallagher's later, Sara and the gang."

She waited for him to offer to join them. He just continued flipping through his notes.

Ryan looked up from the papers in his hand as she left his side.

"Amy, I just wanted to say—"

"I have to get to this meeting. Are you running off?"

"No. I'll be here."

"I'll come back," she said with a smile.

He winked. "Okay."

Several people were crowding into the elevator, and it wasn't until she was inside that Amy noticed it was going down.

Mike Nugent, a junior reporter, was standing beside her. He flashed her a smile disguised as friendly, but men had been grinning at her like that since she was 13, and she knew the intent behind it.

"You coming with us?" he asked. He had sandy brown hair and a thin layer of stubble covering the sallow skin on his face. He was handsome in a safe, hometownish kind of way. He was from somewhere in Pennsylvania she'd never heard of before he told her one night at the bar. She'd meant to look it up on a map but kept forgetting. He was probably working up the courage to ask her out or make a move, but she was in love with Ryan, and he was waiting to talk to her, maybe to apologize for being so distant.

"Sorry," Amy replied. "I just have to go see HR about something."

"On a Friday?" he said and seemed to stop himself.

She didn't know what to say next and was relieved when the elevator stopped on the first floor.

She stayed behind to go up as the others got out.

"We'll be in Gallagher's—" he said. The doors closing cut him off.

Alone, she pressed the button for the seventh floor and stood back as the elevator ascended the first of the five stories she'd have to travel. Amy looked up at the numbers above the door and then pushed out a breath as the doors opened.

She stepped out as soon as the doors were wide enough to squeeze through.

Amy strode toward meeting room seven and saw Nicole Frost sitting at the table waiting for her. Someone Amy had never seen before was sitting beside her, and both greeted her with a handshake as she sat down. This wasn't about amending her contract. This was the end.

"This is Jennifer West," Nicole said. "Jennifer is the new assistant editor starting next week."

Nicole shuffled some papers and opened her mouth to speak. Amy beat her to it. She was damned if she was going to make this easy for them. "How's Ainsley?"

Nicole spluttered a little. "Very well. Sleeping through the night now."

"Was it this time last year I was at the baby shower? That was a fun time, wasn't it?" She turned to Jennifer. "Nicole had it out in her parents' house in Commack. They put on quite the spread. She and her husband had been trying for such a long time. I remember hearing the news when she got pregnant. We were all so happy for her."

Nicole's face was sour, dispelling any lingering doubts in

Amy's mind that this was an execution. The blood in the water was hers.

"That was a wonderful day," the HR manager said. "But we didn't bring you here today to talk about the past."

"Do you have children of your own?" Amy asked Jennifer.

"Three boys," she answered. "All in college now."

"You must be proud. I don't have any in case you're wondering. I've dedicated my life to my work."

"It's come to our attention that you're considering releasing a book of copyrighted material," Jennifer said with ice-cold eyes. Perhaps delivering this news was the last test of her management skills before she began.

"I wasn't the one who came up with that plan." She wanted to bring up Ryan's name but held her tongue. Then she realized it was all a setup. He'd grown tired of her or was getting back together with his wife, or both. Ryan Smith was an important man around here. She was just another junior female reporter. "Are you firing me? Is that why I'm here? I met my boss on the way up here. He didn't breathe a word about this meeting, but it's becoming clear now—"

"As you know, your contract is coming up for renewal in four months," Nicole said, cutting Amy off.

"And you're giving me a raise for all my good work?" Amy said.

"We've come to the decision not to renew your contract," Nicole said. "I'm sorry, Amy."

The fact that Amy thought it might be coming didn't make it any less painful. This job was her whole life. She had no husband or children. This was all that mattered, and now it was gone.

"Why? What's the reason for letting me go?"

"As stipulated in your contract, we're not bound to provide you with a reason," Nicole said.

"You're not even going to give me that much?" Amy said with an incredulous smile.

Jennifer sat forward with a smile on her face. "In light of the service you've given the organization, we'd like to extend the offer of paying out the remainder of your contract without the need for you to come into the office."

Nicole pushed a piece of paper across the table. "There is a non-disclosure clause in the letter of resignation."

"Resignation?" Amy said.

"Don't make this any harder than it needs to be," Jennifer said.

"Was this on Ryan's orders? Or is management trying to keep the talent happy?" Neither woman answered. "The goose that lays the golden eggs must be protected. Maybe he wants my work for a book of his own—to win another Pulitzer maybe?" Nicole's stony glare showed signs of cracking, but Jennifer looked ready to be on Mount Rushmore.

"Do I have to sign this?"

"If you want us to pay out the remainder of your contract. It's for the best, Amy," Nicole said as a glimmer of her humanity shone through.

"I should have known this was coming," Amy said, shaking her head. "It was only a matter of time."

A tear rolled down Amy's cheek. She wiped it away in milliseconds. She imagined herself tearing up the offer to pay out her contract and throwing it in their faces.

"I'd love to rip this agreement into a thousand pieces, but the truth is I need the money."

Amy signed the paper and pushed it back across the table.

"You've made the right decision," Nicole said. "I'm so sorry." Her poker face was cracking now.

"We wish you all the best," Jennifer said, taking up the slack. "This gentleman will escort you back to your desk and then from the building."

A security man was standing by the door, his hand crossed in front of him. Amy knew him.

"Not leaving anything to chance, are we?" Amy said. She tried to be flippant in her tone, but the words caught in her throat. The pain was too much to brush aside now. All she wanted to do was not cry in front of these two. With nothing left to say and the well of her pride tapped out, Amy Sullivan stood up and walked to the door with her head low. Nicole said something else as she left, but she couldn't hear her now.

"Didn't expect this, Tom," Amy said to the security guard.

"I'm sorry. I swear sometimes I think these people have no souls," Tom said.

"I've been here a while; can I at least walk around and say my goodbyes?"

"No can do, Amy. It's not my call."

The elevator arrived before she could respond, but she knew none of this was on the security guard. The tears came in earnest as the elevator doors closed, and her head dropped as she wept. She never cried. This wasn't her.

"I'm so sorry," Tom said. "You didn't deserve this."

She managed to pull herself together enough to stand up and walk out of the elevator when it reached the second floor. This was the last time she'd ever be in this place where she'd spent so much time, and she looked around as if her eyes were recording every detail for her memories. A cardboard box sat on her desk, ready to be filled.

No one was around to say goodbye. Sara and the rest of the reporters were gone, and Ryan was nowhere to be seen.

"Had it all ready, didn't they?" Amy said.

"It ain't right."

She shoved a few journals, magazines, and a framed photograph of her with her parents into the box. She lifted her head up as Tom escorted her to the elevator. They rode down together, and he showed her through the glass door to Fifth Avenue, wished her the best, and she was alone. She reached for her phone and called Ryan, but just as she suspected—no answer. Her fingers trembled as she texted a question to which she already knew the answer. *I was fired! Did you know anything about this?* She waited for a response for a minute or two before realizing none was coming.

It was a fine evening in the city. Amy drew a deep breath into her lungs and started to walk, carrying the box. She so wanted to call her mother. The image of her appeared like an apparition in her mind. Picturing her wasn't hard when Amy saw almost exactly the same oval face, light-brown hair, and green eyes every time she looked in the mirror. It was a constant reminder not only of her mother but of the pain of losing her. Another tear rolled down Amy's cheek. It was hard to know if she was crying because of being fired or at the loss of her parents. She felt a deep chasm inside her. They'd only been 15 years older than she was now when they'd died in that accident. She'd been on her way home from work at the time. She remembered the flashing light on her answering machine and her brother's quaking voice. And her grandmother in the South of France, widowed herself, the toughest woman she'd ever known, blubbering on the phone.

Being an orphan felt like she was adrift in a turbulent ocean without a compass or a map. Her parents had always been there for her until they could no longer be. Her mother would have found the perfect words to soothe the open sore within her, but now she had no one.

She forced herself to keep going. The only other choice was to collapse on the sidewalk. Ryan didn't respond to another call and still hadn't texted back. Her anger toward him drove her onward and lent her the strength to keep putting one foot in front of the other.

It was a 20-minute walk home to the two-bed apartment her

great-grandfather, Seamus Ritter, had bought back in the 30s for his son Michael and his new wife.

Sitting on the couch by the window in the empty apartment, Amy let her emotions flood out. She was never usually one to cry in public. Not for years, anyway. It was best to do embarrassing things like that behind closed doors where such displays of weakness went unnoticed. The buzzing of her cell phone on the couch beside her brought her back into the moment. It was Sara—probably wondering where she was. Amy wiped the tears from her face and cleared her throat before she flipped the phone open.

"Where are you?" her friend asked.

"At home," she said, trying to disguise the pain in her voice.

"I left work. Did you not see the email I sent you? We're at Gallagher's."

Realizing that neither Sara nor anyone else knew what had happened, Amy stood up. "I'll be there in 30. Who's with you?"

"The usual suspects."

Amy said goodbye and snapped her phone shut. Taking a few minutes to do her makeup, she retreated to the bathroom. The silence of the enclosed space unnerved her. She was thankful for the constant sound of traffic from the street below. Her favorite lip gloss and some eyeliner did the trick. Amy knew what a terrible state she was in but wanted to pass off what had happened that day as nothing more than a bump in the road. This was a test, and she was determined to pass it.

The street outside was still bright and packed, with the usual mix of tourists and 9-to-5ers loosening their ties as they spilled out of office buildings and into bars and restaurants. The jarring loss of her job was fresh in her mind among thoughts of her life and family as she walked, and it only grew more acute as the bar her former colleagues were gathered in came into view. The notion of keeping on moving entered her mind, and if Sara wasn't inside, she might have followed it. Instead, she pushed open the wooden door to the Irish pub.

The group she was meeting was at the far end of the room, and Mike, the junior reporter, waved her down to where they were standing. The bar was crowded and about 40 feet long. The pub was paneled in dark mahogany with pictures of Irish revolutionary leaders on the wall, which made Amy contemplate her own Irish heritage. Sara emerged from the crowd to greet her. Her bright brown eyes betrayed her ignorance of what had happened. Amy wondered whether she should tell her at all. She seemed so happy. They all did. Just having a drink on a Friday evening. Why did she have to ruin it?

"I have to tell you something," Amy shouted above the music.

Her friend's face dropped as she digested the news. Tears rolled down Sara's reddened cheeks, and the others were soon gathered around.

"They fired her!" Sara said, her voice thick with vitriol before taking her aside again. "Why?"

"I wasn't given a reason. Nicole said they didn't have to. Maybe they thought I wasn't good enough." It didn't seem right to implicate Ryan when she had no idea whether he was involved. Amy rechecked her phone—still nothing.

"They didn't give you an official reason?" her friend responded. "That's ridiculous. You're the best reporter in the whole newsroom." Sara reached over and put her hand on hers. "It's insane. The whole paper will regret this."

The group gathered around, and she told them the story, still leaving out Ryan's name.

Various levels of shock and disgust reverberated through the group. Some were sad for Amy, and others were just scared for themselves, but the effect was apparent. The joyous mood was broken.

Mike stood next to her with concern in his blue eyes. He

asked her to go through what happened again, but Amy didn't want to and gave him an abbreviated version.

"I can't believe they did that," he said. "Your reporting was some of the best in the whole organization. That story you did from Mosul last year was incredible."

Amy smiled, remembering her time in the dusty chaos of Iraq the year before.

"Thanks," she said and accepted the martini Sara handed her. She took a generous swig before turning to Mike once more.

"Did they tell you why?"

"Didn't have to," she replied and drank more. "I was trying to get permission from the powers that be to release the copyright on the articles I published with Ryan Smith. He told me he'd arrange it, that I was this amazing writer, and my book would take over the world. I don't suppose the other senior editors liked the idea as much. I can't think of any other reason to fire me." For some reason it felt natural to tell Mike. It made no sense. She didn't know him that well. He'd only been with the organization a few weeks.

His face contorted in anger. "You *are* an amazing writer," he said. "And are you sure Smith didn't push you out to publish that book himself? I've heard he's not to be trusted. You wrote all those articles yourself, didn't you? The ones with the joint by-lines? Did you ever think he was just stealing your work for himself?"

Amy almost found herself defending Ryan, but the words died in her throat as the realization of what had happened set in. She'd been making excuses in her mind all this time—trying to excuse the man she loved, but the evidence was damning. She was finding it hard to breathe, and the walls seemed to be caving in on her. Sara walked over just in time. "Are you all right?" her friend said.

Mike repeated his theory as Amy sat on a barstool to listen.

"Makes sense to me," Sara said. "I wouldn't put anything past that snake." She shook her head before she spoke again. "I never told anyone this, but he came onto me a couple of years ago at the Christmas party—in a serious way. He was married at the time and knew I was too. I told him where to go. Someone told me last week his wife took him back too. What an idiot she must be."

Her friend's words tore apart the last threads holding her heart together. "No, I'm the idiot," Amy said under her breath.

She excused herself and went to the bathroom where she sat on the toilet for ten minutes, wondering how she'd ever let herself be played like a grand piano by Ryan Smith. He still hadn't texted back, and she sent another. *You're back with your wife! It's all clear now. You make me physically ill. I only hope she comes to her senses.* She pressed send and shut the phone, determined not to engage with him again. Nothing good could come of it. She took another few minutes to gather herself until she heard Sara's voice.

"Come back out," she said. "Everyone's looking for you. We love you."

Amy nodded and opened the stall. They left the bathroom together and rejoined the group.

"Ryan Smith pushed me out," she said when she returned to the bar. "My contract coming up for renewal made it easy for him."

Her words were met with concerned faces, sincere anger, and sorrow, but she couldn't say how she felt out loud. The truth was she still loved Ryan, and this was killing her. It was a private agony. Too embarrassing, too pitiful to share.

Mike put a warm hand on her shoulder when they were speaking alone again. "I'm so sorry. Have you any idea what's next? I'm sure anyone would want to take on someone as talented as you."

"Don't bother my girl with thoughts about what's next,"

Sara said, wrapping her arm around Amy's neck like she was about to get her in a headlock. Her friend dragged her to the bar just as Amy realized how little she knew about Mike. He faded into the background as Sara eclipsed the rest of the group. They spoke about the interview for a few minutes, reiterating the same points over and over before Sara asked the question Mike had.

"Have you thought about what you're going to do?"

"They're paying my salary for a few more months, but I don't know. I might try and do some writing, or some freelancing. I can't think past the next cocktail right now."

"Nor should you," her friend replied.

Mike appeared by Amy's side and offered to buy another round which the women accepted. He delivered the drinks and slipped away once more to talk to some of his fellow junior reporters, but Amy could feel his eyes on her.

"Almost time to go home?" she asked Sara as the clock above the bar struck eight.

"It's probably about that time," she said. "The babysitter's not going to be happy if I'm back too late."

"You're referring to your husband, I assume?"

"Yes—that babysitter. He'll be expecting me back." She finished her drink and took Amy in her arms. "Everything will be all right. It's just a job, and at least you won't have to see that smarmy look on Ryan's face every time you walk by to use the ladies' room anymore."

"Yeah, the heir to the throne expelled me from the kingdom. He's welcome to it." Amy finished the rest of her martini. Her head was spinning a little now, and she wondered if she should follow her friend out of the bar.

"You coming?" Sara asked.

Amy turned around and caught eyes with Mike, who was chatting with someone outside the group.

"Yeah, I'll share a cab with you."

The two ladies picked up their bags and said their goodbyes to Amy's former colleagues, who offered their condolences once more. Just as they were leaving, Mike took her by the arm.

"Is this it?" he asked with a smile.

"Looks like it."

"Can I get your number? I want to see where the great Amy Sullivan ends up next." His smile was convincing enough for her to give it to him. "I'll send you a text, and maybe we can discuss the state of journalism in America today."

"Please don't," she said.

His face dropped before he realized what she'd meant. "No, don't text me about journalism. Anything but that."

"Oh, all right," he said. "Just remember. You're one of the best writers I've ever met. Maybe this is the universe telling you what to do. Take time out, write a book."

"Writers need stories," Amy said, "and Ryan just stole mine."

"Find another. You're a reporter."

"Where?"

"Everyone has a story in them. It's just a matter of finding it."

"What about your life?" she asked.

He laughed. "You don't want to write about a boring nobody like me. Just be patient. I believe in you. Let Ryan Smith drown in his villainy. He'll get what's coming to him in the end. He wouldn't have done any of this if he was still able to produce good work. He's washed up."

"Maybe you're right."

"He knows that as well as I do. One thing I've learned over time, Amy, is that just when you think things can't get any worse, they sometimes do, but if you want to get out of a hole, you've gotta start climbing. No one's coming with a ladder."

"Thanks kid," she said. "You're not so bad."

"Stay safe," he said,

She kissed him on the cheek and walked out of the bar.

It felt like an ending. Sara was waiting in a taxi, and she climbed in as they were heading in the same direction.

At home, she turned on the light in the living room. She'd never experienced anything like this before, such desperation. Suicide wasn't something she'd ever thought about before, but she could see now why people resorted to it. She looked at a picture of her mother and then at all the other old photographs on the walls. The eyes of her relatives, dead and alive, stared down at her as she sat on the couch. Her phone buzzed and she picked up. Sara's voice came on.

"I spoke to the babysitter."

"—your husband, Sam," Amy answered.

"Yeah, that's the guy. I told him we're going out late tonight, and that I'll stay at your place. A friend of mine is opening a club uptown. You still dressed?"

"Yes. I just got home."

"I'll call you when I'm outside. Be ready in five minutes."

Amy hung up the phone with a relieved smile. She couldn't be alone with her thoughts tonight.

2

Saturday, April 29, 2006

The hammers inside Amy's head started as soon as she opened her eyes. The familiarity of her own bed was the sole comfort she felt. Her mouth was like someone had laid carpet in it while she slept, and she reached to her side table for an empty glass of water. It fell to the floor with a crack as she fumbled for it. Still in her makeup from the night before, her clothes were strewn on the ground where she'd thrown them. She reached into her mind for some memory of getting home last night, but it was like trying to grasp thin air. The last thing she remembered was being in the club the night before and staying on after Sara left. Remembering talking to several men, she checked the bed, thankful none of them were in it. Her phone might have offered some clues, but it was in the living room. Turning to more urgent matters, she got out of bed and picked up the unbroken glass from the floor.

It was almost noon, and she could hear the faint sound of the radio in the kitchen, and she remembered Sara had stayed the night last night. Perhaps suffering her friend's platitudes about her drinking would be the price she'd have to pay for quenching her thirst. Her robe hung over her closet door, and she put it on over her pajamas.

Sara was sitting on the couch reading in the bright light of the morning.

"Good morning," Amy said in a huskier voice than she wanted it to be.

Sara put down her magazine. The look of concern was impossible to miss. "That was some night."

"Yeah," Amy said as she opened the fridge and poured a glass of water from the jug inside. The precious liquid felt heavenly as it slid down her throat.

"You want to talk?" Sara asked.

"About what?"

"Your time in the club last night, whatever?"

Visions of throwing a glass across the bar appeared in her mind like a virus, and an almost debilitating shame followed in its wake.

"I've never seen you like that," Sara said. "That girl was out of line. You remember, don't you? The one whose boyfriend hit on you?

Screaming faces and crowds clearing to avoid flailing fists flooded her mind.

"Oh God," Amy said. "I'm so sorry. I was upset. I've never done anything like that before in my life."

Amy finished the water in her glass and poured herself another. The eyes of her relatives followed her from their place on the wall as she sat opposite Sara. Her friend was a couple of years younger than her and had a round face with blond hair. She took off her glasses and set them down on the couch. "You think you'll be okay?" Sara said and then cut Amy off before she could answer. "I'm not your keeper and certainly not judging you. But I have to go home soon, and I'm worried about you. Some of the things you said last night got me thinking."

Amy wanted to blame Ryan for all this and saw her phone on the coffee table.

"Yesterday must have dredged up a lot of bad memories, said Sara. "About your parents?"

Amy nodded.

"I understand, but the person I saw last night wasn't you. Please be careful."

Amy tried to rub the pain from her eyes, but it didn't work. "This time six months ago my biggest problem was convincing Ryan Smith to admit in public we were together. Seems like a big joke now."

"You were seeing each other without telling anyone? Oh, God, Amy. It makes even more sense now." Sara tilted her head and reached out with genuine concern. She took Amy's hand. Amy supposed she was only doing what her mother would have if she were still alive.

"You'll get through this."

"Thanks," Amy replied but doubted her words. Perhaps her cell would offer some clues to her behavior the previous night.

The message she'd been waiting for from Ryan was on her phone. Her heart skipped a beat as she flipped it to reveal the words she'd craved. She didn't know what she wanted him to say—just something. A confession, an expression of contrition, his sympathies. Even a final insult would have been preferable to nothing at all. *They laid you off?? I had no idea. That's awful. I got a call from my sister-in-law in Denver last night. My brother had a heart attack. I'm at the airport now. I'm so sorry I didn't get to respond to your text last night. I didn't see it with all the running around. I'm about to get on a plane. I'll call you in a few days when things settle down. In the meantime, don't forget what a great writer you are.* And that was it. No admission of guilt. No mention of his wife. It seemed like a cover story. He was a great writer too. Perhaps he should move into fiction.

It was hard to know how to process what he'd said. She was almost sure he wasn't lying about his brother, but why hadn't he mentioned his wife? Or the plan to release the copyright on Amy's stories? It didn't add up. He was lying about something, and curiosity was tearing her up inside.

"It's from Ryan," she said, passing her friend the phone.

"You believe him?" Sara said a few seconds later.

"It's possible. His brother's older."

"Don't call him back, Amy. Promise me you won't. This man is a leech. A disease. I'm sorry he dragged you in this far. I'm sure he's the reason you got fired. He has the power to do what he wants."

"How do you know so much about him?" Amy said. Sara didn't answer and just stared back with dull eyes. "Oh, my God. When?"

"A few years ago. Before I was married. It was short and he made me promise not to tell anyone. I'd never have kept quiet if I'd known about you two."

Amy stood up and walked over to her friend. Sara stood up, and the two women hugged one another.

"I have to go," Sara said. "Tell me you'll be all right. Forget about that rat. Move on with your life. You're talented and beautiful. You can do anything."

"I'll be okay. Thanks. I'll call you later."

"Please do."

They embraced again, and Sara left.

Amy fell back on the couch, haunted by visions of fighting in nightclubs and Ryan Smith laughing at her. Unable to endure any more, she stood up and retreated to the shower, where jets of almost scalding hot water brought her back to some semblance of life.

She resisted the temptation to call or text Ryan back and threw the phone onto the couch. She needed to forget about Ryan Smith. Apart from the fact that he was a philandering rat, 49 was too old for her. He had three kids in their teens who didn't know she existed. Perhaps Mike was wrong about him getting back together with his wife, but Sara hadn't been lying. Amy wasn't going to ask anyone else about the details of his marital situation. It was time to move on. If Ryan called, she'd talk to him, but summoning the self-discipline not to crawl back to him was vital now. Thankfully she had more on her mind than just him. Finding a reason to go on was ever more paramount. Going back to Ryan might have been the thing to drive her over the edge.

Her phone buzzed as she sat on the bed in her dressing gown with a towel wrapped around her head. The text message was from Mike. *So, you don't want to talk about the state of American journalism?*

Amy was surprised at how pleased she was to hear from him and smiled before she wrote back. *At this time on a Saturday? I'll forgive you for asking since you don't know the state I'm in right now.*

A better or worse state than American journalism—whoops, I wasn't meant to mention that, was I?

Amy's enjoyment of the conversation faded as paranoid anxiety forced images of Ryan into her subconsciousness like an oil spill. She tried to push them away, but they came too thick and fast. She didn't even know Mike, and he wasn't her usual type at all. This needed to end.

She put down the phone and finished getting dressed. The mirror above her dresser provided a stark insight into the week she was having. The lines in her forehead would have given the Grand Canyon a run for its money. The whites around her green eyes were webbed with scarlet, and black rings sat underneath like saddlebags on a horse.

A few minutes on the makeup chair worked wonders, but she knew what lay beneath.

After changing into sweats, Amy got up and had a light breakfast. Her laptop was on the table by the window, and she opened it up and navigated to the document that would one day become her bestselling book. It was still blank. Was this really the day to begin? Tomorrow seemed a better option. She'd have a clear head then and could plan her day around it. The cursor flashed on a white page.

Writing had always been a part of who she was. The trophy she won as a second grader for her story about the malfunctioning time machine was on her shelf—one of the things she'd taken from her parents' house. Her father was always so proud of it. It was the first trophy she ever won, but he always talked about it, even more than any basketball or field hockey championships. The tiny silver trophy, engraved at the bottom to show the year she won it—1980. But now, it seemed to mock her.

What's the point of it all? She'd had such big dreams, and she'd been so in love, and now she was unemployed and betrayed, and she'd been so stupid. Stupid! *God, I might as well be dead.*

She stood up from the desk and walked to the window, pressing her nose against the glass.

Her phone was on the couch beside the laptop, and she still hadn't texted Mike back. She had to push him away. She strode over and picked it up. Composing a reply wasn't easy when she had no idea what she wanted from the exchange. He wanted to ask her out. One word back from her, and his text would come back. How could she deflect him? Why was she determined to do what she didn't want to?

The landline phone ringing through the empty apartment rescued her from her quandary. The only people who called on the landline were telemarketers and old relatives. Amy picked up the phone, hoping for the latter. Silence greeted her as she picked up the headset.

"Hello?"

"Amy?" came the voice down the line after two long seconds. "It's your grandmother, in France."

She spluttered and smiled at the same time. "Great to hear from you, Grandma. How are you?"

"Oh, I'm fine, just checking in on my favorite grandchild, with her fabulous job. I read all your pieces you know, my dear. We get the *Times* over here. A few days late but still."

"I know, Grandma. You tell me every time we speak!" Amy laughed.

It had been months since they'd talked, and a year since they'd seen each other. Her grandmother Maureen had made the journey to America for her sister Hannah's funeral the year before and had dropped in to see Amy in New York before visiting Great Aunt Fiona in Los Angeles. Fiona was 85 but had been suffering from dementia for several years.

Amy had invited her grandmother to stay, but the old lady had returned to her home in France soon after. She and Amy's grandfather, Edward, a doctor from Philadelphia, had moved there in the 80s when he retired, and she'd stayed on after he died ten years later.

Amy glanced at a photo of her grandmother, which hung among several old black and white framed prints on the wall.

"And I just read another piece you wrote about the war." her grandmother said. "I hope they're paying you enough."

Amy's heart sank. "It's been a difficult couple of weeks at work," she said. "I don't know if journalism is for me, maybe I need to start something new."

"Really, dear?"

"It's not working out. In fact, they... I'm not working at the paper anymore."

"Okay." The strength in her voice didn't waiver. "I'm sure

you have your reasons. If you've got some time off, you should write a book. Maybe about your time abroad. You could bring together the stories about Iraq."

"You make it sound so simple."

"Isn't it? You need to be doing what you're best at. I always thought you were meant to be a writer of books. God knows I could never do it, but you've always had that spark in you, ever since you were a little girl."

Those words from her grandmother were like icy water on the fire inside her, and a surprising new sense of calm spread through her. Maybe she *could* find an idea for another book.

"How are you, Grandma? What's it like in the South of France at this time of year?"

"It's wonderful but I'm thinking about coming to America."

"Now? Oh…"

"I called Fiona's son the other day."

"You spoke to Charles in LA?"

"He told me his mother is fading fast, and when I hung up the phone I felt the most profound sense of time slipping through my fingers. I decided in that moment to visit her before it was too late."

"You're flying to the west coast?"

"To the east first, to see you. I hope you have room in the old apartment."

"That would be wonderful."

Amy felt mixed emotions at the prospect of her grandmother's visit. It was always good to have her around, but did she really want Maureen seeing her like this? She was a mess. Her life was a shambles. Her grandmother had always been proud of her. She didn't want to jeopardize that.

"I was thinking about things I've never done," the older woman continued. "When you get to my age the dreams you never acted upon can turn into nightmares. I don't intend to leave this life with any regrets."

Amy tried to imagine what regrets her grandmother might have had, but realized she didn't know her well enough to even guess.

"In fact, Amy, I believe I've just had one of my better ideas."

"Right now? And what's that?"

"I've never driven cross country in the land of my birth. I've been all over Europe, lived in Germany and France, but there are still so many places in America I haven't seen. My father worked all over during the depression. I think about where he was during those times still, and I think I'm ready to see them now."

Amy didn't know what to say. The woman was 90 years old and wanted to drive around the heartland of America! Did they even let people her age drive?

"That sounds wonderful, but it could be a lot," she responded with as much diplomacy as she could muster.

"Oh, I couldn't drive myself. It pays to know one's limitations," she said with discernible mirth. "I thought, since you're at a loose end right now, you could do the honors. I'd pay for the car and any costs we might incur, of course."

Images of being with her grandmother for days on end flashed into her mind, but she greeted them with the same calm the old woman had lent her.

"Are you serious about this?"

"Do you really think I'd call to ask you this as a joke?"

Amy smiled at the notion. "No, I don't. When were you thinking of coming?"

"I could travel to town tomorrow and book a flight to arrive in a few days. I'm beholden to no one these days, much like yourself."

"So, you'd want to leave next week?"

"Not right away, but I thought we could figure out that much when I arrived. I'm thinking you and I can fly from New York to LA, spend a few days with Fiona, then rent a car and drive back east. There are so many places I still want to see. I'm 90, but I'm not dead."

Amy was finding it difficult to find words, but perhaps a week with her grandmother was what she needed, and this seemed like the last chance she'd ever get to see Aunt Fiona.

"Let me know when you book your flight. I'll pick you up from the airport."

"I'll call back tomorrow evening with all the details."

"I look forward to it," Amy said, unsure if she would follow through.

Maureen hung up the phone, and Amy burst out laughing, trying to comprehend the conversation she'd just had.

Family history had it that Maureen was wild and impulsive in her youth, but to decide on the spur of the moment to drive across America at the age of 90...well, she definitely put Amy to shame.

Amy returned to the photos on the wall, picking out one of her grandmother posing with the rest of her family in Paris in 1937. It was remarkable how much she looked like Amy's mother. It was almost as if the impulsive unflappable woman from the South of France was her mother at a later stage. It was like seeing what she would have looked like if she'd lived on.

3

Friday, May 5, 2006

Her grandmother emerged through the security gate in a wheelchair, chatting to the young man pushing her through. She asked him to stop short, so she could walk the last few steps to where Amy was standing, professing that she "didn't need that contraption." Her hair was longer than most women her age and fell in straight, gray lines below her shoulders. Her green eyes ignited as she saw Amy. The skin on her face felt like paper as Amy kissed her cheek, but her grip was strong. The older woman pulled back, beholding her granddaughter.

"You were right," the airport employee said. "She does look like you."

Maureen introduced the man as Omar and then bid him goodbye. He shook her hand and wished her a pleasurable stay. Amy took her by the arm, and once they'd collected her grandmother's bags, they walked into the warm spring air together.

"How was the flight?" Amy asked.

"First class makes a difference, particularly at my age."

Amy took her grandmother's bags.

"Coming back seems like returning home, even though I haven't lived here for 30 years," Maureen said. "I still enjoy the way the city makes me feel."

Amy hailed a cab. "Sorry, I feel bad I don't own a car."

"That's all right. It's good you can drive one as we can't get taxis all the way back from Los Angeles."

The driver, an African man in his forties, smiled at the two women and lifted Maureen's suitcase into the trunk. They took seats in the back, and the car set off toward the city.

"You must be exhausted," Amy said.

"I've never been afraid of travelling. Fears are something that can hold you back in life. With every pleasure comes the pain required to experience it—and sitting in first class on that flight wasn't what I'd call excruciating."

"Well, you can get some rest when we arrive at the apartment before dinner."

"That apartment has a lot of memories for me. My entire family lived there when they returned from Berlin in 1939—seven of them all squeezed in. Waking up there is going to take me back."

"So you didn't get on the ship back to America with them, did you? You stayed in France alone when they all left in '39?"

"They had reasons for leaving, just as I had to stay." The older woman stared out the window as the buildings on Queens Boulevard flashed past. A few seconds passed before she spoke again. "I can't remember. Have you ever been to Paris?"

"In 2001 with my ex-boyfriend and in the 80s with my family. We spent a few days there when we visited you back in the 80s, remember? I still have a photo of us all outside Notre Dame on my wall...your wall, I mean, really."

"Your wall, darling. And I'm sorry I forgot your visit. Sometimes it takes me a little longer to remember these days."

The car crossed the 59th Street Bridge into Manhattan, with Maureen still peering out the window in wonder.

"You know Edward and I lived in the apartment for a year after the war?" she said.

"No, I didn't know that."

"Yes, we moved in with my brother Michael and his wife Monika for a few months while we found our feet. It was a tumultuous time. So much confusion. But joy too. It was everywhere you looked. Europe was a mess."

"But you went back 40 years later."

"The South of France still had my heart."

The taxi pulled up outside Amy's apartment building, and the smiling driver helped them with Maureen's luggage again. Her grandmother's strength and dexterity were impressive. She was 90 years old yet didn't require a cane or any other aid to walk. She moved and looked like someone 20 years her junior, or so Amy thought. The truth was she didn't interact with many people her grandmother's age and had little idea what they could or couldn't do. Interactions with anyone over the age of 60 were rare in her life. Her grandfather was dead, and her father's parents were also gone.

It was just after three o'clock in the afternoon, and they had no plans until dinner. Amy brought her grandmother's bag to her bedroom and returned to find her gazing at a photo of Amy's family when Amy was 16, her brother 13. Her parents were vibrant and happy in their early forties. They looked untouchable by death, yet eight years later, they were gone.

Maureen took several seconds to examine the old picture, the smile on her face transforming over that time to where her eyes were dewy and wet as she handed it back.

"I think about your mother every day—my only child."

"I think about her too, and Dad. Sometimes I still can't believe they're gone."

"I'm the same, darling," Maureen said, putting her hand on Amy's.

"I thought I'd learned to live without them. I thought I had, until everything with my job. The house of cards collapsed."

"We all need to learn to rebuild. I've felt like you do now in the past more times than I care to remember, but it's how we react in these times that defines us, and sets the tone for our future."

Amy looked into her grandmother's green eyes. The notion that she'd wasted so much time not knowing her was impossible to avoid. She had an overwhelming urge to hug her but held back for a reason she couldn't understand or explain.

"Thank you. I'm glad you're here," was the best she could muster.

Maureen smiled and pointed to another of the black and white photos, in which The Brooklyn Bridge loomed large in the background.

"That's your great-grandfather, Seamus Ritter, and that's his German second wife, Lisa." Both wore broad smiles. The writing in the corner said September 1939.

"And there we are, his children from his first marriage in the photograph beside it. Michael, Fiona, Conor, and myself. And there's Lisa's little girl, Hannah."

This one was dated June of 1938, and the Eiffel Tower behind them left little doubt about where they'd been when it was taken.

"You're tired. You want to take a nap, Grandma?

"Thank you," Maureen said. "I enjoy a good siesta. But don't let me sleep too long. I don't want to miss dinner.

Amy smiled. "I have a reservation in an Italian place. You'll think you're in Tuscany."

"Bellissimo. I look forward to it," she said and shut the door.

Amy took a breath and sat on the couch. Her phone buzzed just as she sat down. It was Mike. She greeted the text with an excitement she hadn't expected. *You want to grab a bit to eat this week?* Not in the mood to play games, she replied in seconds. *That'll be tough, my grandmother is visiting from the South of France, and we're driving cross country.* She sent the message and received a reply a few seconds later. *I have to admit, that's an original excuse. How about a rain check?*

Amy let the phone drop to the fabric of the couch. Now wasn't the time to make plans with a man she didn't know.

Mike didn't know about her and Ryan. He had no clue as to how she was feeling. The kindest thing she could do in this situation was not to lead him on. And since she couldn't find the right words, she didn't respond.

The clock on the wall struck six o'clock. Dinner was in an hour. Amy rapped on the bedroom door with one knuckle. A faint voice greeted her from inside.

"I'm getting up now, dear."

"Shall I keep the reservation? I could cancel if you're not up to it."

"Nonsense," Maureen said as she opened the door in her nightdress. "I'm not passing up the chance to taste a piece of Tuscany in New York. I might be old but I'm not crazy."

Amy nodded with a smile. Maureen disappeared into the room and emerged with a leather washbag, answering the question her granddaughter hadn't asked by shutting the bathroom door behind her.

Amy had her own outfit ready when Maureen emerged ten minutes later, and the older woman changed while Amy took a shower. Maureen wore a chic white dress with a matching blazer. Amy went with a belted dress with a blush, neutral tone.

A taxi was waiting outside her apartment block, and Amy helped her grandmother in. During the cab ride, they spoke about her home, just outside a small town called Salon de Provence, about 40 minutes north of Marseilles. Her grandmother was proud of her garden and spoke at length about the flowers and the work she'd had done on the porch the year before.

"What do you remember of your grandfather?" Maureen asked.

"Not as much as I'd like. Trying to hold onto the memories of him is hard. Sometimes it's like trying to hold water in your hands, you know?"

"I feel the same way. Edward's gone years now and I feel like I lose another tiny piece of him every day. My mind is more like a sieve than the bowl I wish it was."

"What's life like without him?"

"It varies. Sometimes, I don't feel like he's gone. It's as if he's with me but just in the next room. But other times it's not like that at all."

"I know you have your friends you play cards with every day, and you keep busy, but do you ever get lonely?"

"I'm a human being," her grandmother replied. "We all do. That's one of the prerequisites of being alive. I wish your grandfather was still with me, and that I could sit with him in the evening sun and enjoy a glass of wine, but that was his time. I miss him and your mother like lost limbs. And your father also. I learned a long time ago that those who die would wish us nothing but all the happiness they never lived to experience, and that's it our duty to them to fulfill those wishes."

The taxi pulled up at the restaurant. "Here we are," the driver said. Amy handed him the fare with a generous tip, and the two women climbed out.

The interior was lined with carved mahogany and decorated with beautiful paintings of the Italian countryside from Sicily to Lake Como. The smell of freshly made pasta filled their nostrils. They both ordered the bruschetta to start. Amy ate gnocchi for her main course, which melted in her mouth. Her grandmother ordered scallops that she shared with Amy. They tasted like they had been plucked from the ocean that morning. They washed it down with a bottle of Barolo, which the waiter recommended.

The conversation from the taxi didn't continue into the restaurant. They talked about practical things instead, like what Amy needed to do to lock up the apartment – very little – and whether it would be best to hire a car in L.A. or just buy one cheap and sell it again in New York.

The waiter returned, and they both turned down dessert.

Her grandmother fixed her eyes on her. "Tell me about yourself, Amy. Why did you lose that job? It wasn't for lack of talent or hard work."

"It turned out I wasn't a good fit for the newsroom," Amy said, hoping her grandmother would accept her answer. She didn't, and just stared back, waiting for Amy to speak again. It seemed the older woman could see through her. "I grew close to the head of the foreign desk."

"A man?"

Amy nodded. "He wasn't married but had children. He was separated. It was complicated."

"What happened?"

Amy explained the situation with the bylines and the book. She told her everything.

"So, I had a book, and now I don't. I also had a job and a boyfriend. Now I have neither."

Her grandmother sipped her wine.

"It's natural to feel down at times like this, but you might be surprised at the resilience you'll find in yourself. You're my granddaughter. We were never ones to lie down in difficult times." She reached across and took Amy's hand. It felt wonderful.

It seemed like she and Maureen had only just discovered each other. Amy had been so wrapped up in herself for so long that she'd ignored her. But then, how was she supposed to be close to someone who lived 3,000 miles away?

Amy had taken a trip to Europe in 2001 with her then boyfriend Adam. They were in love and couldn't see far past each other. They spent an afternoon with Maureen, drinking coffee on the porch of her house, facing her manicured gardens. Despite her grandmother's protestations, they left after only a few hours with the promise to return after visiting St. Tropez. But an impromptu trip to Monaco and Northern Italy rendered her a liar. It was hard to forget the look on her grandmother's face as she left that day. That mix of sadness and acceptance had stayed with her. Now Amy was the sad and lonely one, desperate for this old woman's company.

"Perhaps I can help you," her grandmother said. "Maybe I could tell you my story."

Amy smiled. "Your story, Grandma? I'm trying to build my profile as a war reporter."

"You want to write about the war? A noble subject, and one you're an expert on," Maureen said. "I was in France during the war.'

"And you were working as a waitress, I think. Weren't you living in Paris?"

Her grandmother's eyes twinkled. "Does that sound boring and safe to you? I was captured by the Gestapo, more than once!"

"What?"

"The first time was in Paris in '37. Yes. My father and brother came for me."

"Seamus and Michael?"

Amy tried to imagine her father and brother rescuing her from the Nazis. It was almost impossible to comprehend. Amy couldn't believe she didn't know this.

"Many people went through similar things. I know it seems unimaginable in today's world but those were the times we lived in. We were a normal family who wanted nothing more than to survive."

"I suppose I knew you were all in the war, one way or another. I know nothing about you back then, except people said you were impulsive. What did you do to rile the Gestapo?"

Maureen smiled and took a sip of wine from the extravagant high-stemmed glass. "Plenty."

"Why did I never hear about it?"

"Because I never told my father or anyone else in my family much of what happened to me in those years. Some things are best left unsaid. Lots of people never ever spoke of their experiences in the war. I told your grandfather, of course, much of it, anyway."

"You didn't speak to Great-Aunt Fiona, or Michael or your other siblings? "

"I didn't want to shock them. But it was more for me. I didn't want to relive a lot of those awful times. I wanted the past to be just that—past."

Maureen fiddled with the stem of her wineglass and peered into the swirling red liquid as if into her own history. "There's still so much pain. Sometimes it doesn't pay to dredge up bygone days."

"You never told anyone other than Grandfather about your experiences?"

"I didn't want to burden them, or myself. Life isn't easy at the best of times. I left what I did during the war behind and moved on. In many ways it was the worst time of my life, but perhaps I'm ready now."

"To talk about it for the first time?"

"Some of it I never even shared with Edward."

"I understand you don't want to relive the painful memories of your past, and I promise I won't push you, but could you tell me the story of what you did, even in a few sentences?"

"I'll tell you what my family did in the 30s. That should be more than enough."

"Okay," Amy said, regretting she didn't have a tape recorder.

"My mother died in '29 and your great-grandfather, Seamus Ritter left us with his sister in Newark about a year later to find work. He was digging ditches in Ohio during the depression before he returned home to us in '32. Soon after, he received a job offer from his uncle in Berlin and moved us all to the city just before the Nazis rose to power in 1933."

Time faded into oblivion as Amy listened to the family history. The hurdles they faced were monumental compared to her pitiful life. They had to fight every day just to survive.

"Your great-aunt, Fiona was indoctrinated by the League of German Girls," Maureen said.

"Who?"

"The female equivalent of the Hitler Youth," she replied.

Amy's blood was racing, just as it used to in the newsroom. The story was calling her.

"My great-aunt was a Nazi?"

"Many of the rioters on Kristallnacht were the same children the Nazis had been brainwashing since they attained power back in '33. That night was the culmination of years of conditioning. It's easy to think of the people who commit heinous crimes like those as insane, but they're just ordinary citizens like you and me. Hundreds of thousands of young people were exposed to propaganda in Germany. It turned them into the saluting fanatics in those old newsreels. Can you imagine dealing with that as a teenager, and all your teachers preaching about how wonderful the government is every day? And there's much more. Your great-grandfather was an armaments maker. My father sold bombs and bullets to the German army."

"He was a Nazi too?"

"Not at all. He got into it by accident and helped his Jewish workers escape the country when the vise began to close on them."

"Sounds like quite a story."

Her grandmother told her about meetings with a secret group plotting the downfall of the Nazi state. Amy marveled at her bravery to do that in a society that would have executed her if she'd been caught. Great-Aunt Fiona worshipped Hitler and was determined to marry a dashing member of the Hitler Youth. Great-Uncle Michael was only concerned with running and qualified for the 1936 Olympics. Amy knew some of his story but not in the detail her grandmother went into. He ran the 100 meters. Amy wasn't a sports fan but knew the man who won the race. Jesse Owens was one of the most famous athletes ever. Michael got injured and didn't finish the final, but he found his real reward when he met his wife. Maureen fled Berlin with her brother soon after, splitting the family up.

Maureen had studied to be a doctor in Berlin in the 30s. That dream must have been destroyed by the coming of the war, though Amy knew how hard it was for women to advance in any profession in those days.

Her grandmother seemed happy as she finished up the story.

"Have you traveled to Germany many times since the war?"

"Oh, yes," Maureen answered. "The last time I was in Berlin was in '93. It's a city I still love, even after everything that happened there. I suppose our love for certain places is like family—we still love them for the good times no matter how they treat us during the bad." Amy smiled at the allusion. "But Germany is such a different place now. It just goes to show the sickness that infected it in the 30s and 40s was down to the regime, not the people."

"And your sister fell prey to it."

"For a few years, yes. Thankfully she woke up from the

nightmare of following Hitler, but so many followed him all the way to the grave."

Amy was amazed to learn that Maureen continued her rebellious behavior even after moving to Paris and being captured by the Gestapo in France. Amy listened with bated breath as her grandmother told how her father came to rescue her with a hand-picked group of freedom fighters, including her brother.

She had to force herself to get up to walk to the bathroom and then returned to dive into the conversation again. It was hard to believe the life her grandmother had led. It made her own seem so.... inconsequential.

Her grandmother's enthusiasm didn't wane as she explained how the Ritter family escaped Germany to join Maureen in France. Then they left without her. She remained in a small town in southeastern France to focus on helping the Jewish refugees from her father's factory in Berlin escape to safer countries like Brazil, Cuba, or America. The tale ended with Seamus's return to New York with his children and German wife.

"Is that enough of a story for you?" her grandmother said with a smile. The restaurant was almost empty and would close soon.

"You stayed on alone?"

"I wasn't alone. Far from it," the older woman said.

"I want to hear what happened next, once your family left. That's the most interesting part to me."

Her grandmother held a hand up to grab the waiter's attention and asked for the check. "That's not enough for you?" she said. Her lips tightened as she spoke, and the fire in her eyes when telling her family story was extinguished now. "Nothing else interesting to tell," the older woman said with an awkward smile.

"You were alone in France in a house full of Jewish refugees. Of course there was!"

"Haven't I already given you enough for several books?" her grandmother snapped. "Without trying to turn me inside out?"

Amy's heart fell. "I'm so sorry, Grandma. I didn't mean to push."

Her grandmother reached into her bag and drew a credit card from her wallet. After a short fight over the check, Maureen got her way and paid. They left clouded in awkward silence a few minutes later.

Amy threw out a hand and flagged down a taxi. She apologized again. Her grandmother didn't speak, just nodded as Amy helped her into the car.

"I hope I didn't ruin dinner," Amy began as the cab sped along Broadway.

"No. It was wonderful. I think I just need to rest now."

They spent the rest of the ride in silence. Amy paid the driver outside her apartment block and helped Maureen from the car.

Amy had to flick on the lights as they walked inside.

"I think I'll go straight to bed," Maureen said.

"Of course."

Ten minutes later, the bedroom door was closed, and her grandmother was in bed. Amy sat alone in the living room, wallowing in the guilt of pushing a 90-year-old to discuss the most painful moments of her life. It wouldn't do any good to apologize again. Apologies tended to lose their power after multiple uses. The TV off, Amy heard the low sound of sobbing from the bedroom and the gentle creaking of the springs in her bed. She wondered whether she'd destroyed her relationship with her grandmother.

"Everything all right in there, Grandma?" she asked after tapping on the door.

The answer bled through the door a few seconds later. "Just fine, my darling."

"Let me know if you need something," was all she could say.

After retreating to the couch, Amy sat up straight, worrying about her grandmother and what she'd done to her.

Two agonizing minutes passed until the bedroom door opened. Amy leaped up from the couch. Maureen's eyes were red, but her cheeks were dry.

"I so want to tell you the rest of the story, but I'm not sure I can."

"I don't want to upset you, Grandma."

"But you need this, don't you, my dear?"

"What I need isn't important," Amy said.

"You need it for your career. And I was ready to do that, to tell you the whole story, until the memories flooded my head again. I've been silent for 60 years. It's a hard habit to break. But perhaps all those painful moments I suffered will be wasted if no one learns from them. I see the same madness today that set the entire world on fire when I was in my twenties. Perhaps I'll be able to shed some of this weight I've been carrying all these years." She reached out and embraced Amy.

"Are you sure?" she said, and her grandmother nodded. "We'll go at your pace and only talk about the things you want to."

"No," Maureen answered. "It has to be the whole story or nothing."

"It seems like you did so much good. I'd love to write this. I thought everything was pointless, and then you called me. I'm not sure if fate exists, but if it does—"

"I learned during the war there is no such thing as fate. We're the ones who chart our course through life. If fate ends in a child dying in a concentration camp, I have no use for it. And for what end? To teach me a lesson about death, or letting go?

What of their wants and dreams? Why did they have to be the ones to die while I survived? I was luckier, that's all."

Amy was invested now and could see her grandmother wanted to tell her story. "I'm a writer, Grandma. You mention children dying. If I write your story that lesson is passed on. It's the very least to be gained from their deaths. It's something. Otherwise—"

"Their stories are lost forever." Maureen said. "It wasn't all death and defeat. We had many triumphs too."

"And I can write about each one of them," Amy said with a surge of excitement.

Maureen raised a handkerchief from her handbag to catch a tear, and in seconds her grandmother was sobbing. Amy's heart split in two. She reached forward and embraced the older woman.

"I need to rest now," her grandmother said, pushing out a breath.

"I'll be here on the couch if you need anything."

"Thank you my dear. This is the bedroom my father slept in when he returned from Berlin, you know. It feels like a homecoming."

"That's because it is," Amy answered with a smile.

~

The next morning arrived with a blanket of golden sunshine over the city. Amy heard the sound of her grandmother wandering around the living room and got out of bed. Her grandmother was in the kitchen. The smell of bacon and eggs wafted through the air.

"Have you been up long?" Amy asked. It was almost nine o'clock.

"About an hour. I called the airline and changed our flights to this afternoon. We're off!"

"But I thought...?"

"I don't want to waste any more time. The conversation we had last night brought home to me how precious every moment is. I want to see my sister as soon as I can."

"Okay, then," Amy said with a smile. The old woman's vitality was stunning. Amy didn't mention what they'd spoken about the night before. She needed to let her grandmother open up in her own time.

They were in the taxi to the airport when Amy's grandmother turned to her. "We'll start with my story after we see Fiona."

The older woman reached over and took her hand before settling down to look out the window.

4

Saturday, May 6, 2006

Los Angeles wasn't a city Amy knew. Her ex-boyfriend Adam had often spoken of it as if it was some kind of Xanadu on the west coast. For him, it was the culmination of a dream—where the most successful entertainers dominated not just the American market but the whole world. No matter how often she reminded him that he was an investment banker, he never stopped harping on about his dreams of movie stardom.

Maureen's eyelids flitted open like a butterfly's wings, and she turned to Amy. "Are we almost in Pasadena?" she asked. The older woman was asleep in the passenger seat of the rental car they'd hired at the airport.

Amy was just about to confess she wasn't sure when a sign for Pasadena flashed over their heads. "We're close. All right, Grandma, what's that address?"

Maureen extracted a piece of paper from her bag and called out the street name and number. Amy followed the directions on the map but got turned around, only finding the old folks' home after stopping to ask someone on the street.

"We're here!" Maureen said as they pulled up outside the sprawling two-story building.

"Let's go in and see your sister," Amy said. She held the door open for Maureen before helping her out of the car. Her grandmother locked arms with her, and they strolled up to the nursing home together.

"I hope she's having a good day," Maureen said. "Sometimes she doesn't recognize her own children."

Amy looked at her watch. They were just on time to meet Fiona's son, Charles, whom she'd called the day before. He was at the door, dressed in slacks and a golf shirt. He was in his late fifties but still had an impressive thick head of hair. He greeted each of them with embraces. Amy hadn't seen him since her great uncle Michael's funeral in 1998. She wondered if he knew of his mother's flirtations with Nazism in Berlin in the 1930s. He caught up with them for a few minutes before he addressed the situation with his mother.

"Mom's doing well today," he said. "She pretty much recognized me. I told her you were coming. I think she's ready." Charles motioned for them to come to one side and lowered his voice. "One thing I would warn you about is her Nazi references. She sometimes talks about Hitler as if he's still alive, singing songs in German about him."

"Reverting back to her youth," Maureen said. "How is her health apart from that?"

"Fading. My sisters and I have been in and out every day for the past few weeks. The doctors and nurses are doing their best. Your brother Conor is traveling from Florida to see her in a couple of days."

"We spoke to him," Maureen said.

Charles took his great aunt's hand and led her past reception, where a pretty young nurse waved to them. Amy followed behind. They stopped at a door, and Charles knocked. He motioned for Maureen to enter ahead of him. The room was simple but well-furnished and bathed in sunlight. The large windows offered views of the well-kept gardens outside. Fiona looked over with a curious look as they walked to the bed.

"It's me, Maureen."

Fiona seemed to accept that and held her arms out to hug her sister. They held the embrace for several seconds before drawing back.

"You remember my granddaughter, Amy?"

"Is that Hannah?" Fiona said.

"No, this is Amy, the reporter."

"Oh," Fiona said, looking disappointed.

Amy didn't have the heart to tell her she was an ex-reporter now and stepped forward to embrace the older woman. Her skin looked almost see-through in the white light. Her hair was cut short and tight. Her hands were cold as marble.

Amy pulled up a chair for her grandmother. Charles made his excuses and told his mother he'd be outside.

"He's a good boy," Fiona said. "But I'm not sure what his name is."

"It's Charles, your son," Maureen said. "I missed you." She took her sister's hand. "I should have come sooner. I'm sorry. It's been too long."

"What about Michael and Hannah?"

"They're dead, my love," Maureen said, rubbing her sister's shoulder. "But we're all excited to see Conor tomorrow."

"No. Hannah's just a little girl," Fiona said. "She'll be ready to join the League of German Girls next year. Someday she might even perform for the Führer as I did."

"You were conditioned to think the way you did," Maureen said. "There's no one to blame but Adolf Hitler himself."

Fiona looked confused. "Performing with my troop at the Olympic games was the greatest honor of my life."

"No. You forged a wonderful life for yourself in America," Maureen said. "You had three beautiful children. Father was so proud of you."

"You always did have a way of making his blood boil!" Fiona said, and they all laughed. "We never did see eye to eye about my loyalty to the Führer." The laughter faded. A tear slid down her face.

They sat with Fiona for another hour before it all became too much for her, and she fell asleep on the pillow in front of them. Charles and his wife ushered them out with a promise to call Amy's cell phone to arrange a time to come and visit the next day.

Maureen seemed deflated on the ride to the hotel. "Are you upset?" Amy asked her. "Fiona wasn't herself. All that talk about Hitler."

"She's returned to who she was when she was 15." She said and pushed out a breath. "I might be 90, but I'm still learning every day. I suppose that's how we know when we're finally gone—we stop finding out about ourselves and others. I see now how I was selfish all these years, staying in France."

"You had your own life to lead. Fiona has a family. You're not her keeper."

"I should have been there for her, just like I should have been for you."

"You're here now. I'll come over and visit as soon as possible after you leave." Amy already felt the lack of her grandmother in her life, as if she'd gone back to France already. It wasn't something she wanted to contemplate.

"I'd like that," Maureen said. "But I'm not going home yet."

The call from Charles came the next morning, but it wasn't to make arrangements to meet as they expected. He was crying as he spoke. Amy passed the phone to her grandmother and let him tell her himself. She nodded into the phone, stoic and calm, and then handed it back to Amy when he'd finished. She walked over to the hotel room window, stared out at the garden, raised a hand to her eyes, and began sobbing. Amy walked over to her grandmother and put her arms around her slender frame. The older woman rested her head on her shoulder. Amy felt a surge of love and privilege at being here to support her in a time of need.

They stayed another week. Conor, Maureen's only surviving sibling, arrived from Tampa with his wife, Dora. Maureen was comforted by his presence, and they spent their days with each other, but every night it was still she and Amy alone in the hotel room. Her Grandma didn't speak any more of her experiences during the war—she promised that for the drive back.

The day after her sister's burial, when everyone else who'd attended had returned home, Maureen asked to visit Fiona's grave one last time, just the two of them. It was a warm California afternoon. The graveyard was pristine, rolling over several acres of green grass dotted with white stones, each marking the end of a life. The grave was covered in fresh flowers, and one of Fiona's great-grandsons had left a drawing among them. Maureen asked Amy to reach down for it and then examined the picture of her sister smiling in the nursing home as a stick figure.

"It's a bizarre feeling," Maureen said.

"What is, Grandma?"

"Seeing those you love die. It reminds me of the war. Death was all around us in those days. It seems like it's hovering over me again."

Amy reached over and took her grandmother's hand. A

smile blossomed on the older woman's face. "Listen to me," Maureen said. "I never used to be so gloomy."

"It's understandable. Fiona went out surrounded by family, bathed in love. Any of us would be lucky to experience the same."

Maureen turned to her granddaughter. "You're right, my dear. I should be grateful. Nothing more. Now, let's go to lunch and plan our route back to New York. I want to visit Las Vegas first."

"Sounds like a great idea."

Maureen must have read Amy's mind before speaking again. "And don't worry about money. I appreciate you must be short after losing your job. I'll take care of any expenses."

Amy protested, but her grandmother wouldn't hear it. After a bit of back and forth, Amy suggested they return to the car.

"Can you give me a minute alone with Fiona before we leave?" Maureen said.

"Of course."

Amy stood out of earshot and watched her grandmother say goodbye. A few minutes passed before Maureen turned around and walked over to interlock her arm with Amy's. They walked together.

"Did I ever mention what my nickname was during the war?"

"No. I didn't know you had one."

Maureen smiled. "My father coined it. I don't think I've mentioned it in years."

"He called me 'The Lioness.' But most of the French called me 'The American Girl.' Most of them underestimated me, until they saw me in action—just as people do to you today. You have the same strength I had."

"That you still have," Amy said.

Her grandmother laughed. "I hope so. We'll talk on the

drive. I'll be more comfortable speaking while we're on the road. Do you have a tape recorder of some kind?

"In my bag. I've carried it with me almost everywhere for the last five years. I didn't have it when we were at dinner in New York, but the truth is it's your story I'm interested in. I want to hear what it was like from someone who saw it all firsthand. You sure you want to leave today?"

"I just have one request before we leave."

"Whatever you want."

"Let's have lunch first."

Amy agreed. Like all interviewees, her grandmother needed to be relaxed, and a long car drive would be perfect. She had no idea what she'd do with the story once she'd heard it. Perhaps it would end up as a family history, something to pass down to future generations. Maybe for her kids, if she ever had any. An errant thought of Ryan and how she'd never have his children crept into her mind and wallowed there for a few seconds before she threw it out.

They drove back to the hotel and left after a hearty lunch. The man behind the desk couldn't believe Maureen was driving cross country.

"It's something I've always wanted to do," she replied with a quiet smile. "At my stage in life, the phrase 'now or never' becomes all the more relevant.

Amy loaded the car and took her tape recorder from her bag, laying it on the gap between the two front seats in front of the handbrake.

The man wished them luck and handed over the keys with a beaming grin.

Amy drove out of the city with her grandmother in the front seat. She leaned against a cushion they'd bought and proclaimed that she was comfortable.

"It's a long way to New York," Amy said with an excited laugh.

"I'm ready!" her grandmother replied.

Amy helped Maureen into the car. The tape recorder was between them.

"Can I turn this on now?" Amy said as she picked it up.

Her grandmother nodded. "Too late to back out now, I suppose."

"You don't have to tell me anything you don't want to."

"No, it's time," she said and began to speak.

5

The village of Izieu in southeastern France, April 24, 1940

The houses, which had sheltered more than 100 people a year before, now only held 18, and Maureen knew all of them well. They were the last of the Jews from Ritter Metalworks—the company her father had run in Berlin until he escaped to America in 1939. Maureen had been born in New York and had never been to Germany until her father brought her to Berlin as a 16-year-old with the rest of her family just weeks before Hitler rose to power in 1932. She had been in France since '36. The Jewish workers came here early in '39, when she and her father had helped them escape persecution in the land of their birth.

The men had picked up work as laborers for local farmers, the women as seamstresses and cleaners, and their children went to the local school. But all of them considered themselves temporary here. These houses were to be little more than holding stations for those waiting for visas to arrive so they could depart for the new world. Some others had passed through too, using the residences as a safe house on their way to the port at Marseille or to Spain. Maureen had seen several refugees for just a day or two before they left.

Most of the Jews she had brought here had left in April and May of the previous year, but when Cuba and other countries cut off the lifeline of visas, those who hadn't yet left had no other choice than to stay and wait for their turn. The last 18 refugees from her father's factory in Berlin were still here and had been for over a year. All were in the process of applying for US visas. Maureen was in regular touch with the American Embassy in Paris along with her father and others in New York on their behalf. But the tide in the States was against any involvement in the war in Europe, and Congress had cut the number of visas available to Jewish immigrants when they needed them the most.

As an American citizen, Maureen could have left whenever she wanted, but she had no intention of doing so until everyone under her care was safe. It was the children who worried her most. Just before the war began, she'd agreed to take in some Jewish kids from Berlin. The parents were meant to follow a few weeks later but had never arrived. Hence, little Rudi Bautner, eight, and his brothers Adam, five, and Abel, who was just three, were alone in the house with the others. Nothing was heard from their parents again. Maureen assumed the worst but kept the boys' hopes alive as much as she dared. Over time she'd taken them under her wing. The other parents had so much to deal with, and she was happy to be their surrogate parent until their real mother and father arrived.

The other families had their own rooms now and many other comforts they didn't enjoy when the buildings were packed the year before, but they still remained in limbo, waiting for visas that seemed like they might never come.

In the days after the declaration of war some spoke of escaping to Africa or stealing into Palestine, where the British had also slashed the number of visas to join the half a million

Jews already there. Anywhere the Nazis couldn't reach would do.

But as time passed and the village accepted them, it became harder to envisage risking their children's lives by moving on without visas.

This was still a free country, and though the refugees were illegal here, the authorities showed no desire to hunt them down. Not that the threat the Germans posed had been extinguished. The declaration of war after the invasion of Poland in September of '39 had raised temperatures in France to a boiling point. Everyone old enough to drink had some memory of the last war or at least the immediate aftermath. The crippled soldiers from the Great War were only middle-aged now, and the loss of much of an entire generation was still felt in every town and village throughout the country.

At first, the already battered population of France had braced for the worst. No one believed Hitler's claim about wanting peace after all the suffering and violence he'd already caused.

But then nothing happened. The rumors of an invasion were everywhere, but the French relaxed again, feeling smug behind the Maginot Line—a vast array of bunkers and gun emplacements along the Franco-German border built to hurl the Teutonic invaders back to where they came from. President Lebrun expressed his confidence in his country's army and its defenses. It seemed the Nazis had nowhere to go and that if anything, a brutal protracted war along the border would be the most likely result of any attack.

The Jews with Maureen in Izieu had panicked more than most at first. If the country they fled to was overrun by Germans, they'd be as much at risk as ever. But as the months wore on, the families settled into the same pattern of complacency as their French neighbors. They sat and waited for their visas. No one knew when the all-important stamps on their passports might come through, so it was too easy to wait one more week or another month.

It seemed they were safe here in the mountains by the River Rhône. The closest part of Germany was over four hours away, and few thought the Nazi hordes would maraud across from Switzerland. Even that border was over 90 minutes from the tiny hamlet. They were close enough to allow access to refugees coming across and just far enough to give them time to evacuate should the worst happen. It was the main reason Maureen had chosen these houses back in '39. Paid for by her father, they were lined with bunkbeds, now almost all empty.

Today, the sun was shining through the classroom window as Maureen sat with Rudi Bautner and his two brothers, as they smiled at their teacher and hoped for praise that might earn them extra treats. In the absence of the boys' parents, she had taken to attending their parent-teacher meetings. She was the only single person. It made sense.

The previous September, when it became clear that many refugees would be stuck for some time, Maureen had persuaded the local school to help. Between the three Bautner boys, the four Nusbaum children, and the four Ohlmanns, Maureen had placed 11 children with the local schoolmistress, Madame Dupont, who taught every village child from the age of three all the way up to ten. The number of students in her classroom had ballooned from 26 to 37 as a result.

"I hope you don't find me rude," Madame Dupont, the teacher, began. She was a large woman in her fifties with hair turned white before her time, no doubt from a lifetime of chasing after other people's kids. "I love your boys. But I have 37 children in my class, it's too much for one teacher, and my other parents are starting to complain. I told them these pupils would only be in my classroom for a few weeks. That was back in September, over seven months ago. What are your plans? I'm asking this of all the mothers of course, and they say their visas will be here soon. But what about these three? Are their parents planning to just leave them here indefinitely?"

Madame Dupont had been fantastic with all the boys, who hadn't spoken a word of French when they first arrived, and so had taken up much of her time, but Maureen didn't blame her for pointing out her other students were suffering.

Maureen shifted in her seat. "I was expecting their mother and father here months ago. What I said to you in September was what I believed at the time."

"Where exactly are they?"

Maureen turned to Rudi. "Can you take your brothers outside to play?" she said in German and waited until the boys walked out of the schoolroom before she answered the teacher's question.

"Their parents are most likely never coming. I'm working on connecting them with relatives but the visa process has been torturous. It wasn't until the new year turned that I gave up on their parents and began applying for them myself."

As Maureen spoke, the boys were chasing each other around a tree outside the window. As she looked out, a terrible fear gripped her that she couldn't explain. The thought that the Nazis would come for them and take them away overcame her like a tsunami. She'd been as complacent as the others for too long. This beautiful place had drawn her in. It seemed safe and welcoming, and they were happy here, but the fact was the country they were in was at war with Germany, and the Nazis were coming. Who knew if they'd make it down this far south or to somewhere this rural, but was that something they wanted to find out?

The sudden panic that overtook her caused her to lose the run of their conversation, and she realized the schoolteacher staring at her.

"I'm sorry. What was that?"

"I said, are you saying they might be in my class for years?"

"That's not my intention." Maureen pushed her hand back through her hair. "I appreciate the pressure you're under, Madame, and I'm grateful for what you do for the boys, but there's not a lot I can tell you at this point."

"What is that place you run anyway? Some kind of halfway home for people escaping from Germany?"

"You could call it that," she answered. She never would have said that much if she hadn't known how much the teacher hated Hitler and his rabble. "And I'm sorry it's taking so long to find a place for them elsewhere. Do the boys have a place in your classroom while they're still in Izieu?"

Madame Dupont sighed, looking put upon, but she said, "Of course. They're wonderful children."

Maureen glanced out of the window again just as Abel jumped out from behind the tree to scare his brother, who fell down in faux shock. "Yes, they are," she smiled.

"What about the other children? I saw their mothers earlier but I wondered if you had more information than them."

"I don't, but when I know, rest assured, you'll be the first person I'll tell. The people of Izieu have been so kind to us, but no one more than you."

The teacher smiled as she looked out at the boys, now rolling in the dirt. "They're all sweet children. The people around here know that what you're doing in those houses is a good thing."

"Thank you." Maureen said and stood up. She shook the schoolteacher's hand and stepped out into the bright sunlight.

"Come on, boys, let's go," she called out. They didn't come at first, but after the third or fourth time calling their names, ran over to her.

"Your teacher had nothing but excellent things to say about you," she said.

"School's boring," five-year-old Adam said.

"Don't say that in front of Maureen," his brother Rudi responded and clipped him on the ear.

This led to them running ahead. Abel, the youngest, stayed behind, took her hand, and looked up at her with massive brown eyes. They spent the next few minutes discussing their favorite colors, animals, and books.

It was a 30-minute walk to the houses from the small wooden school building. It was pleasant on a warm spring day like this one, but in winter, when the winds howled over the mountains and the snow swarmed down from above, just getting to school was a Herculean task.

They turned a corner onto the final stretch toward the houses when Maureen heard a familiar voice calling out from behind them. Hans Ohlmann, father to four of the children they'd burdened Madame Dupont with, was twenty paces behind them as he returned from a day's laboring in the fields. He'd been a metal worker in her father's factory in Berlin, producing ammunition for the Wehrmacht, and had never even visited a farm until he arrived in France. Now, he worked on local farms every day and could swing a scythe and drive a plow better than almost any local.

Maureen was still holding Abel's hand as the tall man with a dark beard and massive shoulders caught up to them. He greeted Maureen and the young boy, slowing to walk beside them.

"Were you good in school today?" he asked Abel.

"I'm always good," the little boy replied.

"We were at a meeting with the teacher. Martha was too, earlier" Maureen said. Martha was Hans's wife of more than fifteen years.

"Did you see her?"

"No, but I know she got the same question I did—when is this temporary arrangement going to end?"

"I wish I knew," he answered.

"I said the same thing to Madame Dupont, but hearing her even ask that question shook me out of my complacency."

"What do you mean?" he asked, removing his cap to scratch his head.

"I'm worried that the Germans will be here soon." She shivered, despite the warmth of the day.

He laughed in surprise. "All the way down here? You're not serious?" he said. "We're so far south of where any fighting would be, protected by the Maginot Line. Hitler's no fool. He's not about to send his best armies crashing up against it. If the Wehrmacht does come, it'll be far to the north, and the French will be ready for them. Even the fighting in the Great War never made it to this region."

They were approaching the houses now and could see Hans's wife with another mother, Ella Salzmann, sitting outside in the warm evening sun, watching the children play.

The pleasant, peaceful scene made Maureen feel even worse. A disaster was coming to engulf them all. She knew it. "You worked in my father's factory for how many years churning out bullets and bombs for the Nazi war machine?" she asked him. "They've been preparing for this moment since 1933. People said the invasion of Poland would take months, but they swept all opposition aside in weeks. Do you really think we're safe here?"

Hans didn't answer, just reached into his pocket for a pack of cigarettes. He offered Maureen one, but she refused. The three Bautner brothers ran on to join their friends playing outside the houses. He drew on his cigarette. "So, what can we do, even if you're right? We're waiting for the visas to come through. Our options seem to narrow by the day. Most of South America is cut off to us now, and it's obvious we're not welcome in your home country either. The American public have shown their indifference to our plight, and the politicians are happy to follow their lead. But you could leave if you wanted to."

"I could never leave those boys here. They're like my own now."

"We all know that. Can you speak to your father about sponsoring your three boys?"

That's what they were now, Abel, Rudi, and Adam—her boys.

"Each visa requires a bond of $5,000—four years wages for a working man. My father doesn't have that kind of money anymore. He can barely afford his mortgage these days let alone $15,000 for the boys. Believe me, if he had the money he'd give it, not just for them, for all of you."

"I believe that," Hans replied. "He got us this far."

"I'm going to take a trip to Paris, see if I can move things along, or maybe just to raise some money for the emergency travel fund in case we all have to run for the port in Marseille or the Spanish border soon."

"You think it'll come to that?"

"I don't know, Hans, but a dark cloud came over me today. It felt like a premonition of disaster."

The women stood up to greet them as they reached the house.

"Maureen's off to Paris to rattle some cages," said Hans to his wife. "She thinks Hitler's about to invade Izieu personally."

"What makes you so sure that despot is going to invade France at all?" Ella asked. She was a slight woman with a pretty face and was only three years older than Maureen at age 27.

"It's who he is. Conquest is the Nazis' entire reason for being," Maureen answered.

"But they want the Soviet Union. He's always professed that France and Britain are civilized nations. He says he wants peace with them," Martha Ohlmann said. She was a tall woman with long brown hair and sallow skin.

"Yes, Hitler wants the Soviet Union," Maureen agreed. "He wants it more than anything else in this world. The lebensraum in the east for the German people the Nazis have been talking about for 20 years is his obsession. But what do you think will happen when he invades?"

"She's right," Hans said. "As soon as he invades, the British and French will mass their troops against Germany in the west. He'll be caught in a war on two fronts, just like my father fought in 25 years ago. You saw how that turned out for Germany."

"He'll invade France as sure as the sun rises in the morning, and he'll do it to eliminate opposition in the west, so he'll have a free hand to fulfill his primary ambition in the east," Maureen said.

"Why are you suddenly so worried, Maureen?" Otto asked. "It's been almost eight months since France and Britain declared war on Germany. We've been sitting here this whole time, just waiting and getting on with life, and now you're talking like there isn't a second to lose."

"Because today I woke up, Otto. I saw things as they are. We've gotten too comfortable. This village is so charming and remote. I'd forgotten it's part of the real world."

She walked inside. Abigail Nusbaum was in the kitchen chopping carrots. A mountain of orange peel eight inches high stood beside her. Maureen greeted her before putting on an apron. Abigail had also been talking to Madame Dupont about her four children. All were doing well in school and seemed happy here.

"Sometimes I wish we could stay right here forever," Abigail said. "It's so peaceful and beautiful."

The houses they all lived in were huge and always clean. The children knew better than to wear dirty boots inside and always tidied up after themselves. Each was instilled with the idea that they were only guests. It wasn't easy to reinforce that after living in the house so long. The children saw this place as home now.

"It is those things for sure," Maureen replied. "But I have a feeling everything's about to change."

"What do you mean?"

Maureen picked up a sack of potatoes and reached in to pull a dozen out. "We have to be ready for any eventuality. Maybe the US visas aren't going to arrive in time."

"The thought of leaving this beautiful place for some Godforsaken desert in North Africa isn't an appealing one," Abigail said, shaking her head.

"The choice might not be between here and North Africa. It might be between North Africa and a concentration camp in Germany."

"I hope you're wrong, Maureen."

"Me too," Maureen said. She was beginning to feel like a modern-day Cassandra, cursed by the ability to see the future but have no one believe her warnings. "I hope I'm wrong. But it feels like a vise is closing around us, and we're just sitting here."

"Where is all this coming from?" her friend asked, putting down the peeler and turning to her. "Did something happen?"

"No. I just had a sudden feeling when I was talking to Madame Dupont."

"So, you haven't heard anything we haven't?"

"Other than the fact that we're at war with Germany?"

"We're quite safe this far south. What would the Germans want with Izieu?" Abigail threw down her knife and put a hand on Maureen's shoulder. "I know you feel responsible for all of us, but you don't have to. We're adults with our own children. We don't need you to look after us. If you feel you need to go back to America—"

"The boys need me."

"We can look after them, and unless the visas come through soon, I can't think of a better place to be than where we are."

"Everyone else who came here from Berlin is gone. They're safe in America or Brazil or Cuba. These houses were only meant to be somewhere to pass through on the way out of France. And we find ourselves stuck here."

Abigail picked a potato from in front of Maureen. She peeled it with a dexterity Maureen didn't possess. It was clean in a second, and she moved on to the next. "This house, this place, with the mountains and the river and the beautiful countryside—it's so much better than where we lived in Berlin. I don't want to give this up to take a steamer to Algeria."

"We have to be open to whatever eventuality occurs," Maureen said.

"And we will be," her friend said in a calm voice. "But let's not throw all this away because of some irrational feelings."

Maureen didn't answer and stayed to help for a few more minutes before excusing herself. She paced through the hallway and upstairs to her room. Once inside, she took a pen and paper to write a letter to the one person she knew she could rely on. Someone who'd do anything for her and vice versa.

GERHARD,

I'VE BEEN DOWN HERE TOO LONG AND HAVE LOST THE URGENCY I NEED TO AVOID DISASTER. THE GERMANS ARE COMING. WE BOTH KNOW THAT. I'M SURE THE PEOPLE IN PARIS DO TOO. PERHAPS NOT BEING IN THE DIRECT PATH OF THE STORM HAS INSULATED US AGAINST THE TRUTH. I HAVE TO COME UP TO THE AMERICAN EMBASSY AND GRAB THEM BY THE LAPELS. THEY NEED TO REALIZE THAT PEOPLE ARE GOING TO DIE WITHOUT THEIR HELP. IS THERE AN INFORMAL WAY TO MEET WITH THE US AMBASSADOR OR SOMEONE ELSE WHO CAN HELP US? LET ME KNOW.

. . .

Y*OUR FRIEND,*

M*AUREEN*

She and Gerhard had been through more than most people experienced in a lifetime together. Having met through mutual friends, they joined forces to try to organize a coup against the Nazis in Germany with Gerhard's father, who was a general in the Luftwaffe and more loyal to his country than the regime that ran it. But it failed, and Gerhard's hatred of the Nazis grew even more intense after his father was executed. Soon after, the Gestapo came for her and Gerhard and smuggled them to a château south of Paris, where an SS man tortured them both for a day. Maureen never allowed herself to remember but couldn't forget. But justice was served when she and Gerhard assassinated the SS torturer in a café along with the traitor who'd betrayed them. They'd killed together, and neither felt an ounce of regret. They both knew the real war had begun several years ago, and they were merely soldiers fighting in it.

6

Thursday, May 2, 1940

I t was all too easy to doubt her own choices. A year before, her father had fled to New York with the rest of her family and had begged her to come. But she had refused. Now, in the middle of sleepless nights alone in Izieu, Maureen questioned that decision. The choice she'd made to remain in the path of the coming storm while she could have been lounging in safety in New York with her family seemed insane, but it was the only one for her. Maureen's mission in Europe hadn't finished when war was declared or when her own family was forced to flee. Her duty was to the refugees in Izieu. Leaving them behind now would be like abandoning family. Especially her boys. Brushing off doubt wasn't easy, but the sheer scale of what she had in front of her left little time for second thoughts. She got dressed. The morning was still ahead of her, and she had much to achieve. The sun was already up, but the boys weren't. She roused them from their slumber and brought them downstairs for breakfast before dressing them for school.

The letter from Gerhard was on the kitchen table as she went downstairs as she'd hoped. Abigail handed it to her with a smile. Maureen opened it with a knife and read it alone in the corner.

MAUREEN,

I UNDERSTAND YOUR SENTIMENT. PEOPLE DON'T BELIEVE THE BAD THINGS IN LIFE WILL EVER HAPPEN TO THEM UNTIL THEY DO. A FRIEND FROM MARSEILLES HAS GOTTEN US ON THE GUEST LIST FOR A RECEPTION THE US EMBASSY IS HOLDING IN THE CITY ON FRIDAY NIGHT. PACK YOUR BEST EVENING DRESS, AND I'LL SEE YOU WHEN YOU ARRIVE.

I'LL SEE YOU SOON,

GERHARD

My friend must be going up in the world, she thought to herself. The ragged anti-Nazi with whom she'd tried to organize a coup against the regime in Germany wasn't usually the type to attend high-class events. Neither was she, but not necessarily through choice.

After readying the boys for school, she returned to her room to pack her bag. Rudi carried her suitcase. It was hard saying goodbye to them. They followed her to the gate with anxious faces.

Adam clung to her. "When are you going to be back?" the five-year-old asked.

"Soon, darling. I have to go to Paris for a few days to see about some things."

"Are you sure you're coming back?"

"Of course,"

"Frau Nusbaum and Frau Ohlmann will look after us," Rudi said. "Maureen's not our mother."

"They'll take good care of you and I'll be with you again before you know it," she said to the two younger boys.

The earnest look in Adam's brown eyes almost brought Maureen to tears in front of him. She took a few seconds, hugged him again, and then spoke. "Perhaps when I get back, we could take a trip to the river and I could teach you all how to swim. Would you like that?"

"Like it? I'd love it," Rudi said.

"Please don't get captured by Hitler," Adam said.

"He's not in Paris," Maureen replied. "I'll be safe." She wondered how much longer those words would be true. "Run on back now and be good boys while I'm gone."

Sad about the boys, she set off on foot down the road, carrying her bag. She kept turning around to look at the houses and the backdrop of the snow-peaked mountains rising up behind them, even after the boys were gone. It was a sight she'd never grow tired of.

Leaving her boys was tough, but it was good to do it every so often. One day she'd have to do so forever. Not getting too attached was vital when running a safe house for refugees. Talking to them too much, getting to know them, was dangerous, but it was a trap she'd fallen into head-first. Parting from Rudi, Adam and Abel would feel like a death.

It was about ten minutes to Monsieur Corbin's farm, where she kept her car to protect it from the snow and ice of winter. She knocked on the farmer's door, and Madame Corbin answered the door in an apron. The smell of fresh bread wafted from the kitchen behind her.

"Come in," she said. Her husband was in the fields, and the older woman offered Maureen some breakfast.

"No, I've eaten, thank you."

Realizing she wanted to leave, Madame Corbin led her to

the barn where the old Mercedes was covered with a tarpaulin. It started the first time, and Maureen was on the road to Paris moments later.

The journey offered a rare opportunity to contemplate the four years she'd spent in Berlin, and she wondered if she'd ever visit that magnificent, lively, exciting city again. Hitler had professed that his Reich would last a thousand years. Would France be a part of it soon? The sense of claustrophobia she felt increased with each mile she drove.

Germany loomed to the northeast like a wraith. Every day the newspapers were filled with stories of German atrocities in the east. Poland had been divided in two in an uneasy alliance between the previously sworn enemies, Hitler and Stalin. At first, Maureen struggled to understand why until she realized the Soviets felt they had little choice. At the debacle of the Munich conference in 1938, the French right wing and the British Tories had sold Czechoslovakia down the river and made many in Eastern Europe nervous.

The Poles, understandably enough, wouldn't let Soviet troops enter their sovereign country, even if their intention was to defend Poland as they'd stated. So Stalin entered into an agreement with the leader who'd sworn to destroy him and made conquering his country and subjugating his people a manifesto. It was impossible to tell exactly what the Soviet Premier was thinking, but perhaps he felt a buffer zone in Poland would afford him the time he needed to rebuild his army, which like every other fighting force in the world, was light years behind the Wehrmacht.

The Soviets were always an ill-fitting alliance with the western powers. The ruling classes of Britain and France were far more in tune with Hitler's ideas of promoting big business than with Stalin's outward obsession with advancing the working man. Prior to war being declared, it would have been far more common for the more monied members of London and Parisian society to have expressed support for the Führer than his counterpart in Moscow. The situation was ripe for a ruthless despot with a powerful army to take advantage of. As much as she wanted the opposite to be true, Maureen knew the situation in Europe would grow far worse before it got better.

Paris was a city she knew well, having lived there for the three years she'd spent in France before moving to the houses they'd acquired in Izieu. She drove across the river and toward the 3rd Arrondissement, where the apartment her father had bought when he was an armaments king in Berlin still stood unoccupied. He'd held onto it for her, even when he could have put the money for it to good use in New York. Parking the car as close as she could, she grabbed her suitcase and sprinted through the rain to the wooden door to the apartment building. She turned the key and stepped through.

Entering the old place was so familiar that it was like she'd never left. All that was missing was her brother Michael, and his wife, Monika, who'd lived here with her for the time she'd been in the city.

The bedroom she'd slept in was still tidy, the bed made from the last time she'd been here two months before, and she threw down her suitcase before opening the curtains. The rain had cleared, and the sun was peeking out from behind a blanket of gray clouds. The city seemed so perfect, but then she looked out toward the horizon as if she'd be able to see the Nazi hordes approaching.

After popping out to a boulangerie around the corner for some fresh croissants and a baguette, she had a late lunch alone at the table on the terrace of her apartment, watching as the streets came back to life.

After finishing her food, she returned to her suitcase and laid her black sequined dress on the bed along with her makeup. A ripple of excitement spread through her at the prospect of getting dressed up, but that wasn't until the next night, and she hung the dress in her closet alongside some other clothes she'd left here for emergencies.

She gathered up the keys and strolled out the door. It was almost five o'clock, and though she was tired from her journey, she was eager to see her friend. Paris seemed born from a different world than the tiny hamlet she'd come from. The excitement of the big city was something she missed, but she'd grown to appreciate the quiet of the countryside, the slower pace of life, and the different type of stunning scenery she enjoyed in Izieu.

On the way to her friend's apartment, she heard the sound of a demonstration and saw thousands of people gathered, with hand-written signs, shaking fists in the air as they sang anti-government chants.

This was an undeniably gorgeous place, but France had suffered turmoil in the run-up to the declaration of war that was still raging nationwide.

She knew from the newspapers that the mobilization of the army had cost France billions of francs and left a gaping hole in the nation's finances which had to be made up.

Maureen passed the protest and kept on toward her meeting with her friend. She reached his place a few minutes later and knocked on the basement door, and seconds later, it flew open to reveal Gerhard standing there. The German dissident had been handsome once, but the scars the SS torturers left across his face had disfigured him. He'd grown a beard to hide them, but the deep red gashes on his jawline still showed through. The ones they'd left on her were invisible, at least when she was fully clothed.

"Maureen Ritter!" He threw his arms around her.

"I like the beard," she replied.

"It's all I could do to try to cover the damage those Nazis did to my face."

"It works."

"You're a good liar. I appreciate that on several different levels."

The basement was plastered with anti-Nazi posters, and a man Maureen didn't recognize was working at a printing press by the wall. He looked up with bespectacled eyes before returning to his work.

"That's Michel," Gerhard said. "He's not the outgoing type. One heck of a copywriter and printer, though."

"You're still churning out the pamphlets, I see. How are you smuggling them into Germany?"

"We can't anymore. All the borders are closed. We're focusing on the population here—trying to wake them up."

He handed her a piece of paper with a caricature of Hitler setting the globe alight on it.

"Too dramatic?" he asked.

"Not dramatic enough."

"You ready to leave?" he asked.

She nodded, and a few seconds later, they were on the street together.

"So, I take it there's no movement with getting those American visas for the last of the Berlin Jews in Izieu?"

"None," she answered. "The Americans have puckered up tighter than an oyster shell protecting a pearl inside."

"Well, that's what you're here for—to pry that shell open."

They arrived at the restaurant. It was a simple place with a thin layer of sawdust on the floor. A phonograph in the corner was playing Edith Piaf.

He led her to a simple wooden table and chairs in the corner, where a bottle of Chablis was waiting for them. He poured them both a glass as they sat down.

"The problem is we've all grown too comfortable in Izieu," Maureen said once they'd ordered. "The illusion of safety is strong with the river and the mountains in the background."

"Sounds beautiful, I'll have to come visit sometime."

"You should," she answered. The wine was delicious, and she took the liberty of pouring herself some more.

"What about you?"

"What about me?"

"Are you getting on the last steamer to New York when the refugees get out?"

"I suppose so."

He seemed to catch the reluctance in her tone.

"You can't save the world, Maureen. You should get your people out and follow them. A new life awaits in America."

"What about you? You're staying."

"I don't have a new world to escape to. This is my fight, and I intend to finish it. The Nazis killed my father. Whatever war comes is personal to me. I won't stop until it's over."

"That's how I feel."

"You're American. You've already done more than anyone would have expected."

"More than anyone would have expected," she said under her breath and took a sip of wine. His point was clear, and few would argue with it, but the thought of leaving, even if it meant reuniting with her beloved family, made her feel like a traitor. She didn't know what to say next, so she changed the subject. "What's the Nazi presence in Paris now?"

"Even less visible than it was last time you were here two months ago but, make no mistake, they're still here. Gestapo agents have been embedded in French society for years now, they're not about to pack up and leave now that their piece de resistance is so close, are they? This invasion, whenever it happens, has been a long time coming."

"You don't think they'll founder against the rocks of the Maginot line?" Maureen said, hoping he'd provide her with some hope.

"With their tanks and airplanes? I don't think so. The line of bunkers along the border is the main source of derangement in

France today. It might have bought us some more time, but Hitler and his generals will find a way around it."

"I wish I disagreed with you," Maureen said. "So, why don't you join the army and fight against the Nazi forces?"

"I can be more useful in other ways. Besides, I don't think the French army would roll out the red carpet to welcome a German into their ranks."

"You could be right about that. What if the Nazis come to Paris?"

"Then I'll disappear underground and snipe at them in whatever way I can. What about you?"

The thought of SS and Wehrmacht soldiers marching down the Champs-Élysées wasn't pleasant.

"You know what, Gerhard?" she said. "In all honesty, I have no idea what I'll do. I want to get the Jews in Izieu out of France but to where? Maybe they are right, and we can all hide out in those houses until the war sputters out. I know I can't leave until they're safe. That's about all I can be certain of." She thought of the brownshirts on the streets of Berlin and beautiful old buildings stained by the Nazi flags that adorned them.

"We'll meet some interesting people at this event tomorrow night. Several diplomats from the American Embassy are going."

"That's why I'm here," she answered. "Thank you for setting this up."

"My pleasure. I'll introduce you to the man who arranged the invites for us too."

"I look forward to it."

The meal arrived a few minutes later. They both dined on steak frites with a delicious béarnaise sauce.

"I passed a demonstration on the way here," Maureen said. "Have you seen much unrest in the city lately?"

"Plenty," he answered. "The government raised taxes on the entire population, but as always, the working classes were hardest hit. The labor forces revolted against the increase in the cost of living and the abolition of the forty-hour work week. But the most worrying are the strikes in the armaments industry when France needs to defend herself the most."

"The armaments makers are on strike?" she asked.

"Some of them."

"The French army is already miles behind the Nazis. That's the last thing they need."

"It's the same old story. The ruling upper classes and organized labor live in a constant state of open warfare."

They finished their meal with a delicate crème brûlée that melted in her mouth and promised to meet the following night for the main event.

She collapsed in bed after midnight. Her last thought was of the boys in Izieu.

∼

Outside Las Vegas, Nevada, Thursday, May 18, 2006

Amy's grandmother was asleep in the passenger seat. The tapes of her story were in the glove compartment of their rental car, and they had only just begun. Amy had no idea what to expect next, but she'd never heard of Gerhard in Paris or any of the other people Maureen had mentioned so far. The trip itself had been a blast since they left Los Angeles. Amy laughed as she remembered Maureen's insistence that they stay in Las Vegas. Amy had been to casinos plenty of times, but the previous night had been the first time with a 90-year-old. But, as with everything, Maureen relished her time in Sin City and wasn't out of place among the other retirees who poured money into the slot machines. Her grandmother was a conservative gambler, mainly there to people watch, and she and Amy had a wonderful time doing precisely that.

The next place the older woman had picked out was the Grand Canyon, somewhere Amy hadn't been since she was a child. But she looked forward to hearing the rest of her grandmother's story the most. Amy had more questions than Maureen could handle and had promised she would just listen from now on.

Her grandmother opened her eyes, waking from her afternoon nap. She stretched out a little, asked where they were, and began to speak again.

7

Friday, May 3, 1940

Paris was an endless parade of wonders, and Maureen took the opportunity to spend her day being a tourist in the city. Beginning with an early lunch in the Le Marais area, she walked the narrow streets alone, heading southeast until she reached Notre Dame, where she strolled inside. Looking around the magnificent cathedral, she tried to imagine what the people who'd built it were thinking. Was this their ultimate tribute to God and their personal ticket into heaven? She tried to guess who God might be and what form such an entity would take. She wondered how much such a being would care about this beautiful building constructed in His honor on the banks of the Seine.

The sun was high in the blue sky as she walked to the Louvre. She didn't venture inside the famed museum, just sat outside and dipped her feet in the fountains. The tricolored French flag flew above the magnificent building, strong and noble in the gentle breeze. Visions of the Nazi flag in its place and then draped all over the city drove bile to the top of her throat. She stood up and walked through the Jardin des Tuileries and past the Place de Concorde. She no longer had the means to shop in the chic stores on the Champs-Élysées, so she peered in the windows instead, marveling at the beautiful dresses on display.

After making it down to the Eiffel Tower, she treated herself to a glass of wine at a bar overlooking the Seine. And though thoughts of the impending war and questions about what she would do were never far from her mind, she enjoyed her over-priced Beaujolais and the flickering gold of the sun on the river.

She was back at the apartment at six o'clock and set about getting ready for the night ahead. Her dress was still hanging up in the closet, and she laid it on the bed before proceeding to the shower. Her fine dark blonde hair dried in a few minutes, and she slipped on her undergarments and then her dress. Unwilling to pass judgment on how she looked just yet, she sat at her makeup table and applied some subtle eyeliner, a little blusher, and then a fiery red lipstick to finish. She stood up and turned one way and then the other.

Satisfied, she went to the balcony to wait for Gerhard, her platonic partner, for the evening.

She didn't have to wait long. Gerhard appeared around the corner in less than five minutes and called up to her from the street. After promising to come straight down, she went back inside to collect her purse and lock up.

"You look handsome," she said as she met him on the street. The sentiment was true, but more in the way she might say to her brother.

"I could say the same of you." He smiled and then hailed a taxi.

Gerhard had never been someone she'd thought of roman-tically. He was a colleague, a confidant who'd become a close friend. He'd never spoken of any amorous connection with anyone to the point where she wondered if he was interested in any matters of the heart at all. For her part, she didn't feel any spark with him and knew she never would. Their relationship was focused on something other than fleeting romance. Everything they'd ever done together had been directed toward the end of defeating Nazism in Europe.

It wouldn't do to show up at an event like this from the Metro. Most of the attendees would arrive in limousines. The event was a fundraiser for the war orphans of Poland, organized by the US embassy. Perhaps it was the Americans' way of doing something when the overwhelming public opinion back home was to stay out of Hitler's war. Rumor had it that Roosevelt was growing more frustrated by the day of the prevailing attitudes in his country, but he could do little to change them and had to send his support in clandestine ways. The President's greatest triumph in helping the European nations—despite what Congress and the American people desired—was his Neutrality Act, passed in '39. It allowed the British and French to purchase American armaments and then transport them back on their ships.

The taxi pulled up outside the Hotel Lutetia, an enormous palace of luxury in Saint-Germain, which, even at the height of his wealth, her father would never have dreamed of spending so much to stay in. Gerhard took Maureen's hand as they ascended the steps into the lobby, where a doorman tipped his hat to them. They joined a line of dignitaries dressed in tuxedoes and evening gowns and shuffled into a magnificent ballroom hung with chandeliers from a ceiling fifty feet above their heads. The sound of Mozart's "Jupiter Symphony" lilted from the orchestra set up on a stage at the end of the massive room. Dozens of round tables sat in front of it, draped with pristine white tablecloths and fine silverware which glistened in the light.

Maureen wondered at how she'd been peeling potatoes in

the house in Izieu last night and was now here among the cream of Parisian society.

"It's time to haul ourselves out of the gutter, and rejoin the elite," Gerhard whispered to her.

She suspected his words were only partly in jest. Their resistance operations had been on a shoestring for the past few months.

They found their table within a few minutes and sat down as the waiters, dressed in black with white bowties, began to pour the wine. The room was filling up, and most seats were now occupied. Gerhard didn't know the old men and their wives at their table, but he and Maureen made polite conversation. All three men were industrialists with little time for the two younger people who seemed out of place here, but their wives chatted to them as the food was served. The first course was a consommé, followed by escargot. The main course was a sumptuous steak, served at the diner's pleasure. Gerhard ordered his tartare. Maureen didn't quite dare to eat hers raw but instead had it seared. The music and conversation continued throughout the meal before they finished with a splendid pear tart tatin.

Their table was at the back of the room, so they didn't have to move when those at the front were cleared. The patrons seemed happy to stand up after dinner as the way was cleared for a dancefloor in front of the band.

"Time to get to work," Maureen said as couples flooded the dance floor.

"Come with me," Gerhard said.

She followed him through the crowd of mainly older monied types until Gerhard stopped at a group of younger men. He shook hands with several as Maureen waited.

"This is Ernest Green of the US diplomatic corps here in Paris," Gerhard said, and Maureen took his hand. He wasn't much older than her. He was slim with thick-rimmed spectacles and slicked-back hair.

"You're American?" he said in English.

"Was it that obvious?"

"I heard your accent poking out from under there," he said in a Texas drawl. "What brings you to this place?"

"I got an invite—wasn't doing anything better," she said with a smile. Starting off with some charming small talk couldn't harm their cause. They spoke about how long he'd been in Paris and what he thought of the city. Ernest smiled as he told her he'd been here for three years and how much he loved the place.

"Could all be about to change," he said.

"Have you heard anything?"

"No more than you probably. The same rumors everyone talks about. I'm not privy to any special information in the embassy."

They talked about their families, especially his back in Austin. He was single, so she knew what he wanted but wasn't interested. Her only thought in speaking to this man was what he could do for the 18 refugees down in Izieu. But she let twenty minutes pass before mentioning what she wanted to talk about.

"I have some friends who could use a little help with the visa process."

His face dropped, and he dragged on the cigarette in his hand without responding.

"These people have nowhere to go. Whole families, and some children without their parents."

"How many?"

"18"

From his reaction, she might as well have said 18,000.

"You know how often I have this conversation?" he asked.

"Can you help these innocent people escape?"

"They're in France?"

"Yes, in the south."

"They should be okay for the time being."

"Every dog on the street knows the Nazis are coming any day now. How much longer are they going to be safe for?"

"My advice would be to keep out of the city. Stay in the countryside. Better chance of riding the war out there."

"What about the visas?"

"It was bad enough before the war started," he said and stubbed out his cigarette in an ashtray on the table beside them. "But now it's a nightmare. We received instructions from the State Department to slow down the visa process and exercise even more care in the screening process."

"Why?"

"They're terrified of Soviet and German spies coming over among the Jews fleeing Hitler. And the will just isn't there in Congress or on Main Street America. Most people would shut the entire immigration system down if they could."

Maureen tasted bitter disappointment but wasn't about to give up without a fight. She asked him again and received the same answer. He suggested sponsorship for the money required for the affidavit, but she explained how many times she'd already tried that.

"What these people need is someone in a position of power who can help them."

"I'm sorry, Miss, but that isn't me."

"Is there anyone here who can?"

Ernest seemed happy to pawn her off to one of his colleagues, whose smile faded as he realized what she was here to talk about. He gave her the same answer as Ernest but in a ruder manner, but then changed tack.

"Why is a pretty girl like you wondering about that, anyway?"

Maureen realized she was wasting her time. Only luck or good fortune or both would get her people into America. But she stayed with the lecherous diplomat just in case she could gain something from the inane conversation she was having with him.

"What are the most romantic places in Paris?" he asked. She answered, but her mind was elsewhere. Two men beside them, seemingly a British and French diplomat, were having a heated conversation.

"You're completely delusional," the Englishman said. "The storm brewing since 1933 is about to break, and the Wehrmacht will soon be unleashed on France. Hitler's hordes aren't going to be stopped by your feted Maginot Line or anything else the French could throw at them. Poland fell in weeks. The Nazis will soon infect all of France like a virus, not just the north but the south as well. And then Britain is next."

It was like the scales had fallen from her eyes. After witnessing the militarization of German culture during her time in Berlin and hearing from her father about the regime's lust for the most modern weaponry in the world, she knew it was true. The Nazis were going to conquer all of mainland Europe, probably Britain as well. And it was only a matter of time before their sickness reached the houses in Izieu. Images of Rudi, Adam, and Abel formed in her mind. They were her primary concern. She was sure now their parents weren't coming. The others could decide for themselves, but the boys needed to leave France now.

"Excuse me," she said to the man and walked past him. He looked disgruntled but didn't try to stop her as she weaved through the tables to where Gerhard was in conversation with another man. The German whirled around in surprise as she grabbed his shoulder.

Maureen looked around to ensure no one was listening in before she began. "I need to get my boys out of the country. The Nazis will roll through the French defenses and be here in weeks. What would it take to forge the documents they need to get them out of France?"

"Passports?" Gerhard opened his eyes wide and shook his head. "That's a tough one. My printer, Michel, has some contacts, but that could take a while."

"What about more basic documents. Just the ones required to travel across the country and get them to the Pyrenees?"

"That could be doable."

"How long?"

"Those IDs require photographs and details the children will have to learn.

"There's so little time."

"I think we have a little more than you might imagine—to get the refugees in Izieu out anyway."

Maureen was cooling off. The panic that had gripped her was subsiding. Gerhard was always the voice of reason—the ice to her fire.

"You might be right, but I'm not taking any chances with the boys. I still want them out of France as soon as possible."

"Whatever you say, my friend," Gerhard said.

He returned to his conversation, so Maureen let him be and slalomed through the thick crowd of fat cats. Plumes of cigar smoke filled the air between her and the bar. The young man serving seemed surprised when she ordered a beer.

"I didn't expect that either," a man said beside her.

Not bothering to look up, she didn't respond.

"You're not enjoying the night?" the voice said again.

Her heart jumped as she turned to him. He was tall, over six feet, with short brown hair in a cow's lick at the front. His deep mahogany eyes were set above high cheekbones and sallow skin, which stretched tightly over his lightly stubbled face.

"Pleased to meet you," the Frenchman said before she could speak. "Christophe Canet." He held out a hand. His skin was warm against hers.

"Maureen Ritter," she said. She found herself slightly breathless and hoped she wasn't blushing.

"You're American?" he said.

"I can't ditch that accent," she replied with a smile.

"Nor should you. I'd offer to get you a drink, but I see you already have one."

"And the drinks are free here."

"Yes," he said with a laugh. "I'm quite the gentleman, aren't I? Offering you a drink from a free bar? Perhaps next I'll offer to pay for your complimentary food."

"What a treat that would be."

He ordered a beer and rested his hand on the bar while waiting for it. He wasn't wearing a wedding ring. She guessed he was about 28.

"Are you with the embassy?"

"No," she said. "I'm just here for the party."

She had to be careful how she answered questions like this. Revealing too much to the wrong person could be fatal.

Nazi agents had infiltrated every part of French society since the mid-30s in preparation for what was soon to come. They had assumed countless disguises and made the acquaintance of clerks in military establishments, workers in munitions plants, and anyone who had access to secrets that might be helpful to a nation preparing an attack upon its neighbors. The fact that the Nazis were getting ready and that their businessmen, traveling salesmen, scientists, students, artists, and tourists were working for government agencies was known to everybody who cared to investigate. But the accusations were drowned out in the general clamor of French journalism, politics, and intellectual life.

"And you live in Paris? I can't imagine anyone coming as a tourist right now."

"Just outside Lyon. I'm here visiting," she said.

"Do you live there with your husband?"

"No. Just some friends," she responded, doing her best to act coy. It wasn't her natural state. The man was probing, and her suspicions were flaring. Christophe had a handsome, refined face—perfect for a Nazi spy.

"And what do you do outside Lyon?"

She thought to tell him that she was trying to extricate 18 Jewish Berliners but knew she couldn't. Antisemitism wasn't confined to Nazis. It was as prevalent in French society as it had been in Germany before Hitler came to power. It seemed most European countries were one election away from becoming dangerous to Jews. The requisite latent hatred for them was everywhere.

"I'm in between jobs at the moment," she said, well aware of how mysterious she was being.

The orchestra changed to a waltz. Christophe glanced over at the dancefloor and back at Maureen. "Do you dance?" he said.

"On occasion."

He held out his hand to hers. She hesitated before taking it.

"Don't worry about the drinks," he said. "I'll buy more if someone takes them."

"Generous to a fault."

"I see no fault."

His hand was warm, and his cologne filled her nostrils with a sweet, gentle musk. They didn't speak as they ambled to the dance floor. She smiled as he turned to face her. He took her hand and rested the other on her waist. At least two dozen couples surrounded them on the crowded dance floor. Most were old enough to be her grandparents.

"So, where are you from in America?"

"Just outside New York. Ever been?"

"I've never made the trip across the ocean. Not yet, but I've traveled through most of Europe."

"Berlin?"

"One of my favorite cities. Well, before all this—"

"It's a tragedy. I lived in Germany for several years before I came here. It's hard to believe the changes since I moved there back in '32."

"I was in Hamburg on business during Kristallnacht," Christophe said, shaking his head. "I thought I'd been around and seen some things, but that night opened my eyes. Where did those people come from that night? The Nazis must have emptied out every insane asylum in the country and let the inmates run riot."

"My sister was among the mob that night." she watched his face for his reactions.

If he is an agent, he might take this as a sign of common feelings between us, Maureen thought.

Christophe's face stayed neutral. "She was?"

"As a member of the League of German Girls. They're the—"

"Female Hitler Youth. I'm aware of them. Where is she now?"

"Back in the States with the rest of my family."

"Thank goodness for that," he said with what seemed like genuine relief. Either that, or he was a good actor.

"I'm the only one of my family still in Europe."

"And why didn't you leave?"

"I had unfinished business here."

"Don't we all?"

"What about you, Christophe? What do you do? Where do you live?"

"I'm from the south. Marseille. I'm an art dealer. This is the kind of event where I can extend my list of clients—people with more money than they know what to do with. I make suggestions to them about putting their idle wealth to use." He looked around and then back into her eyes. "I really should be working the room right now."

"Why aren't you?"

"You're quite the distraction, Maureen Ritter."

It took all the fortitude she could muster not to laugh. "So, how did you get into that line of work?"

"My father was one of same type of men you see around you tonight. He was a collector, and I developed an eye at a young age."

"You must travel quite a bit."

"I do."

"And meet a lot of people. Do you have a wife and children in Marseille?" The fact that he wasn't wearing a ring or was dancing with her was no guarantee he didn't have a family at home. Several married men had propositioned her in the past, some with the apparent approval of their wives. Not that she was looking for a relationship. She'd stayed away from romantic trysts these last few years since she'd been torn away from Thomas, her old boyfriend in Berlin. Too many people were relying on her to get involved with anyone.

"No," he said with a faint smile. "I was engaged once but it didn't work out."

"Why not? Did she catch you with other women?"

"She died two months before our wedding day."

She winced, ashamed for mocking him. "I'm so sorry."

"It's quite all right. It was cancer. It was quick and she didn't suffer much. She's buried just outside the city now. It's a beautiful place she would have appreciated."

"When did she die?"

"Four years ago."

"That was the year I moved to France from Berlin."

"It can't be coincidence," he said with a grin.

The song ended. They and the other couples on the dance floor stood stationary for a few seconds, waiting for the music to begin again. The natural thing to do was to stand back, and that's what they did, but she didn't want to. She apologized again, but he assured her it was okay.

"You want to stay out here?" Maureen asked.

"I can't think of anything I'd like more."

The band started up, and they moved with the music once more. His movements were fluid and concise and stood in sharp contrast to hers.

"You're showing me up," she smiled.

"I think you do yourself a disservice," Christophe said in English.

"You speak—"

"A few languages," he answered. "It helps to speak to people in their native tongue in my line of work. Makes them feel special and appreciated. Puts them at ease too."

"Is that what's happening here? You're making me feel special and appreciated?"

"Isn't that what everyone wants?" He switched back to French. She was glad. It made her feel less like he was trying to sell her something.

"You speak German?" she asked in German.

"Yes. I have a lot of clients in Berlin and Hamburg. Or at least I had," he answered in the same language.

"Has the war affected your business?"

"To the point where I came here from Marseilles to drum up some business."

"And yet, you're here dancing with me."

"Yes, I am."

His eyes were rich pools of intrigue, and she was having a hard time looking away from them. Something inside her wanted to open up to this stranger, but she stopped herself. This is how spies worked, getting you to trust them.

"I met him once, you know," Christophe said.

"Who?"

"The Führer—the man at the center of all this consterna-
tion," he said. "It was back in '34. I was naïve as a child back then,
just 22 myself. I had no idea of what the man would become."

"But he was already Chancellor."

"Yes, he was."

"Where did you meet him? What was he like?"

"Hitler's a keen collector. He has quite a good eye. Not that
you'd ever know it from all that horrendous Nazi art they churn
out. I ran into him at an opening in Berlin. He was surrounded
by SS of course, but he was interested in a Gauguin I was repre-
senting so he approached me. He's a small man, and that
mustache is hard to fathom, but the thing that struck me was
his speaking voice—it was much softer than I'd heard in his
speeches. I'm convinced he slips into character when he takes
to the lectern. The man I met seemed different than the ranting
lunatic we've all grown used to seeing on the newsreels. He was
knowledgeable, polite, and stopped to listen when I had something to say. I couldn't say I found him charming, but he wasn't
the thug you'd think he might be."

"Seriously?"

"I'm not saying he's a good person. I'm just telling you that
he was quiet and thoughtfully spoken when I met him. Even
the most dangerous despots have their peaceful moments.
Some other dealers I've met know him better. They say the
same things I did. He seems to have different personalities he
keeps for suitable occasions."

Again, she wondered if he was an agent. She was nearly
sure, but he was so handsome, and she wanted to be certain.
They kept dancing.

"This does feel like the time when the band played on the
deck of the Titanic, doesn't it? The Nazis could be here any
day," he said.

"We'd better keep dancing," she replied.

"What else can we do?"

They danced in silence for a few seconds. He seemed so intelligent and sincere. She remembered the Nazi spies throughout the city. Someone as charming as Christophe would make an ideal undercover agent.

"I should go," she said and stepped back.

"So soon? We were just beginning to get to know one another."

She saw the figure of Gerhard out of the corner of her eye. He would provide the perfect excuse to escape from this man she wanted to dance with all night.

"I have to go," she said and hurried toward Gerhard as quickly as her high heels would allow. Her old friend caught eyes with her as she emerged from the dance floor and held up a hand.

"I see you two have met," Gerhard said as Maureen reached him.

"What?" she said.

Christophe was standing beside her. "You know each other?" he said.

Maureen wanted to hide in the corner, but this was the man Gerhard wanted her to meet. She caught eyes with him again. He didn't seem as embarrassed as she was.

"This is convenient," Gerhard replied. "Come over to the table and sit down. I wanted to introduce you."

The young German dissident led them to an empty table in the corner. Most people were standing to talk or dancing now. Maureen was confident no one would hear their conversation.

"Christophe, this is the woman I was telling you about—with the houses outside Lyon."

"Ah, yes," the Frenchman said with a smile. "You told me you lived just outside Lyon with some friends."

"What does he know about me?" Maureen said. The alarm bells were ringing inside her.

"Just that you're someone willing to help those in need,"

Gerhard replied. "I met Christophe a few months ago in the city. We've been in contact ever since."

"I did come here to hobnob with the fat cats of Parisian society, but also to meet Gerhard and the people he wanted to introduce to me. And you must be one of them," Christophe said.

"Maureen and I go way back," Gerhard said.

"Any luck with organizing visas for the refugees in your houses?" Christophe asked her. "That was your reason for being here, wasn't it?"

Maureen was shocked. "You told this man about me in advance?"

"I didn't want to waste any time, particularly if we're going to be working together."

"Working together?"

"Forgive our mutual friend," Christophe said. "It was my idea."

He took a few seconds as if gauging the atmosphere at the table. "I'll get us some drinks."

Maureen waited until he was gone to begin. "Who is this person?" she hissed. "We've been burned by spies before. I would have hoped you'd exercise a little caution."

"Of course, I did," Gerhard said in a whisper. "I trust Christophe."

"Trust can get you killed faster than a bullet these days. He seems like a Nazi to me."

"Don't be ridiculous. He's from a good family. I spoke to some people from Marseille, and they all trust him. He's from money. His father has his own successful shipping business. All his siblings work for the family company. He's the black sheep but apparently his father would still do anything for him. Christophe knows everyone. The man makes his living meeting rich and powerful people. He speaks four languages and has been traveling around Europe talking to everyone for the last ten years. And he hates the Nazis just as much as we do. I can't imagine a better contact."

The Frenchman returned with three beers.

Maureen took hers without a word and sat back in her seat. "Gerhard told me a little about you when you were at the bar. Since when does an art dealer become a crusader for freedom?"

Christophe's smile was beginning to annoy her. "Is that what you call it? I could ask the same of you."

"But Gerhard knows he can trust me. I don't have to prove myself."

The German didn't speak. It was left up to Christophe to explain himself. "I travel all the time, and I'm aware of the grave threat the Nazis pose to the world. I was in Vienna a few weeks before war was declared. A client of mine sent me on his behalf to attend an exhibition of a new artist's work," he said. "I was walking down Opernring Street on the way to the opening when I saw a crowd gathered. I was curious and stopped to have a look. After pushing through the crowd, I saw some SS men. They'd dragged several Jews out from their hiding places or wherever they found them. They'd shaved them, then took sticky tar and spread it all over their exposed bodies. The feathers were the final touch. Anyone who spoke up was beaten, and several people still did. They took what the SS had to give."

"Did you speak out?"

"No. I was too afraid."

"I'm sure most of the crowd were the same as you."

"No," he said, shaking his head. "Most of them cheered the monsters on. I vowed I'd never stand idly by again while something like that happened."

His story felt rehearsed. She didn't believe him.

"Hitler's an art enthusiast. The Nazis won't stand in your

way. You'll be able to make just as good a living as before," she said.

His eyes flashed with fury. "I think there's more to life than money, Maureen. Why did you stay in Europe? Surely you could have returned to New York and gotten a lucrative job? But why even bother with that? A beautiful woman like you could find fifty men in here, married or not, to take you on. Some you could marry; others would put you up in an apartment in the city and give you an allowance. But you're not about to entertain that idea, are you? And I won't get into bed with the Nazis either, because, just like you, I won't sell myself off to the highest bidder. Some things in life are more important."

"Said like a true child of privilege," Maureen said, but regretted it as soon as the words left her lips.

Christophe's face changed with those words, and he stood up. "I won't sit here and be insulted."

"Sit down, my friend," Gerhard said. "Maureen didn't mean that, did you?"

Maureen locked eyes with the Frenchman but didn't answer.

"I understand that you might be suspicious of outsiders," Christophe said, "but you don't know me. You have no right to make judgments about me. You haven't even heard what I have to say."

"Sit down and tell her," Gerhard said.

Christophe flopped back into the chair, displeasure rippling through his face. He took a breath and began to speak. "I was at an event much like this one in Bern a few weeks ago. I met an official from the Swiss Red Cross. They're operating all over Europe in anticipation of the coming conflict. They've already been to Poland and Czechoslovakia. He told me some stories I wish weren't true. The Nazis have initiated a reign of terror in the east already. First thing they did in Poland was to round up the intellectuals, the politicians, and whoever else might pose a threat. The Nazis didn't bother to put them in camps. They skipped the middleman and shot them by the thousands instead. They're planning on enslaving whatever Polish people are left after their purges and setting them to work feeding the Germans."

Maureen could see the passion in his eyes as he spoke but was still unconvinced. She'd met many great actors before— people who could convince you of their virtue as they held a knife behind their backs.

"But get to the children...." Gerhard said.

"Yes." Christophe swallowed a mouthful of beer and looked around to see if anyone was listening in. Satisfied, he continued. "After a bellyful of beer and champagne this Red Cross official in Bern—"

"What was his name?" she asked.

"Arnaud Brunner. He's about 45 with gray hair and a matching beard," Christophe answered, looking right at her. "He told me about some children in Belgium, in a small town outside Ghent. They're Jews, sent away after Kristallnacht. The original plan was to get them to England or America but someone messed up the paperwork and they got stuck."

"How many?" Maureen asked.

"About 20. Not more than 25. It's hard to say. Some have come and gone."

"Do the Red Cross have a plan to extricate them?" she asked.

"No plan. No budget, and no manpower to get it done."

"And?"

"He asked me to do it."

"How can you when the Red Cross can't?" asked Maureen.

This smelled like a trap to her, to get her and Gerhard into enemy territory. Perhaps he'd found out about Gerhard's father and their plan to depose the regime in Germany.

"He came to me out of desperation," the Frenchman continued. "Those kids are about to be in the eye of the Nazi storm."

"They're directly in the path of any invasion," Gerhard
added.

"Why are you so bothered about these particular children?"

"Why would you ask that question?" Gerhard said.

Christophe looked like he'd tasted something sour.
"Because they're Jewish children, and they need our help. Who
is this American girl?" he said to Gerhard.

"If you're not interested, we can find someone else," the
German said.

Maureen looked at the two men. She could trust Gerhard
with her life and had before. Perhaps Christophe was who he
said he was. She could keep a close eye on him.

"I thought you'd be ideal for this mission," Gerhard said.
The look on his face was somewhere between disgust and
embarrassment.

"I don't know this man," she said, pointing at Christophe.

"Find someone else to help," the Frenchman said and
stood up.

"Wait!" Maureen said, relenting. "What's the plan?"

"We don't have one yet," Christophe said.

"We'll need transport. Gerhard, can you drive a truck?"

"Yes."

"So can I," Christophe answered.

She resisted the temptation to give a snide answer. "I can't,
but I did a couple of years in medical school and can act as a
nurse. We'll have to get past the Allied blockade at the border.
Leave it to me. I'll come up with something."

"It'll take time to procure trucks," Gerhard said.

"Which we don't have. We need to get them out as soon as
we can," Maureen said. "We don't have a moment to waste,"

"I told you, you'd like her, didn't I?" Gerhard said and patted

Christophe on the arm. "When she makes up her mind to do something, she always wants it done straight away."

"Because we have no choice. The Nazis could invade tomorrow," she said.

The two men laughed, but she didn't join them. She still didn't trust the new man but would give him a chance in the hope that Gerhard was right about him. They toasted free France and the children in Belgium. Maureen was already formulating a plan in her mind as the two men drank their beer.

_____

8

Saturday, May 4, 1940

Maureen awoke just after eight, but she hadn't slept much. Christophe was on her mind. Despite her attempts to rid herself of him, he'd been resident in her consciousness since she'd laid eyes on him the night before. The attraction she felt toward him was just what a Nazi agent would have tried to cultivate. Perhaps the whole story of the children in Belgium was a trap. But she trusted Gerhard's instincts, and if it was a ruse, it was an intricate and unusual one with no clear end. She thought about what the handsome Frenchman had said the night before about the Germans wiping out any opposition in Poland to establish their dominance of the remaining working and agrarian classes. It was entirely possible they'd do the same here. Perhaps Christophe was trying to weed out those with enough courage to stand up to them in advance. Or the possibility existed that he was a good man trying to make a difference in the face of evil. Either way, she intended to find out.

A rumor had swept through the ballroom of the Hotel

Lutetia at about one in the morning. Someone had heard from a friend that the Dutch government had received a warning from a spy within Germany about an imminent invasion. No one knew whether to panic, run out of the place, or just keep dancing. Ultimately, dancing had won out because what else was there to do? If the Germans were coming, most people figured they'd better have their fun while they still could. The rumor inspired a different reaction in Maureen. She set a meeting with Gerhard and Christophe for the next morning and left the ballroom soon after. The alcohol was starting to go to her head, and she knew the best-laid plans were not made while half-drunk in a ballgown—at least the ones she'd made in the past. So, she made her excuses and left with an agreement to meet in Les Deux Magots. It was touristy but large and open. It was one of her favorite cafés and only a short walk away in Saint Germain.

After a shower, Maureen slipped into a pale blue summer dress. It was a warm, sunny morning, and wearing it felt like the season was already upon them. She went to the mirror in the bedroom, taking extra care with her makeup and applying a little red lipstick which she might not usually have done.

The arrangement was to meet at nine, and she hurried out the door to be on time. Usually, she'd never be on time to meet a man or two men in a café, but this was different.

If what she'd overheard at the soiree was true, the children in Belgium could be consumed by the Nazi war machine in days or even hours. Gerhard and Christophe were already sitting outside as she arrived.

"You're early," Gerhard said as he stood up to greet her.

"So are you," she replied.

Gerhard was dressed in a simple tweed blazer and a white shirt, but Christophe wore a blue pin-striped suit with a gray hat. He took it off to kiss her on the cheek. His aftershave lingered in her nostrils for several seconds after he pulled back.

"I took the liberty of ordering you a coffee," Christophe said as the waiter placed a café-au-lait in front of her.

"Thank you," she said and took a sip.

"How did you sleep?" Christophe asked. "It doesn't seem long since we were all talking last night."

"I got a few hours," she answered. "But let's dispense with the small talk. Time is of the essence here."

Christophe smiled and turned to the other man. "She said exactly what you predicted she would."

"Children's lives are at stake. Once they're safe I'll laugh and joke with both of you. You'll find me a different person then. Gerhard's seen that side of me."

"I saw it last night, albeit briefly," Christophe answered.

"Is it safe here?" Gerhard whispered.

The people closest to them were a couple in their 80s, holding hands in the morning sun. No one around them seemed to be paying them even the slightest bit of attention. They all agreed it seemed as safe as anywhere.

"The Nazis could invade any day. What do you think the chances are they'll sweep through Belgium?" Maureen said.

"That's what I'd do," Gerhard said. He took a map from a leather satchel by his feet and spread it out over the table. The others moved their coffees to afford him the space. "The Maginot Line is strongest along the border, all the way up to Luxembourg." He moved his finger along the line that separated France from Germany. "But it's much weaker behind the Belgian border here."

"But the Wehrmacht would have to sweep through the Ardennes Forest if they attack through Belgium," Christophe said. "The French generals say that's impossible."

"Perhaps the difference between difficult and impossible is the key definition here. I'd say breaking through the Maginot Line would be tougher than moving the tanks through the difficult terrain of the forest. There are roads," Maureen said.

"One main road," Gerhard said. "But whichever way they attack, the Germans aren't going to forget about Belgium. It'll be occupied, those children will be under Nazi control, and God only knows what will happen to them then."

"Does anyone else know about them?" Maureen asked Christophe.

"My contact in the Swiss Red Cross said they're understaffed and dealing with the crisis in Poland first and foremost. It's a matter of priorities, and what they're able to achieve. He knew I travel all the time, and hoped I'd be able to do something."

"So, we need to get two trucks, drive into Belgium and get the children. I'll take them to the houses in Izieu, and we'll work on getting them out of the country to somewhere safer," Maureen said. "And we need to get organized today."

"Unfortunately, it isn't as simple as merely driving over the border to get them. It's about four hours' drive but we'd be battling a flood of refugees. The roads are clogged already in anticipation of the invasion, and it's only going to get worse. The French Army has tightened the border crossings to the point where you need a good excuse to enter," Christophe said.

"What better excuse than rescuing the children?" Maureen asked.

"Rescuing or kidnapping?" Christophe replied. "Three or four adults have been looking after those boys and girls for almost two years now. You think they'll just hand them over to three strangers who arrive in trucks?"

"They will if we have a telegram from the Red Cross," Maureen said. "Can you contact your man in Bern? Arnaud?"

"That might just work," Christophe said.

"I told you she was good," Gerhard said and lit a cigarette.

"First thing you need to do is contact him," she said. "Can you send him a telegram today?"

"Right after breakfast, but that doesn't get us past the border checkpoints," Christophe said.

"Do you have any contacts in the army? Your father must," she asked.

"He does."

"Tell them you need to rescue some valuable paintings from the Nazis. The French generals are nothing if not snobs. They won't stand for losing artwork to the Teutonic hordes. The town's near Ghent? Is there a gallery in the city you're familiar with?"

"No, but I could find one."

"Do that and ask for a telegram. This time stating the importance of our mission in rescuing these invaluable works. Also, get his friends in the French army to write a letter for us to grant us safe passage through the lines."

"And if the generals won't?"

"You don't think your father can pull the necessary strings?"

"I'm not sure the Prime Minister could in the current climate, but I'll try. I always try."

"What about the way back into France?" Gerhard asked.

"The way back won't matter. We'll just join the line of refugees. If that rumor from last night is true, we might only have a few days to get those kids to safety. At least no one will be checking visas at the border in that case. Once the battle begins the stream of refugees will grow to a tsunami."

"The roads will be clogged," Gerhard said.

"But we'll be able to bring the kids without entry visas into the country. That's why they were stuck in Belgium in the first place—nowhere else would take them."

"That's exactly what happened," Christophe said, putting his coffee back on the table as Gerhard folded the map. "You were right, Gerhard. She's good."

"What did I tell you?"

"You chose the right person to help us," Christophe said

with a smile. "I can provide money to hire the trucks if you do the hiring, Gerhard. You know more about vehicles than me." He pushed a wad of cash across the table. "The delay will be in receiving an answer from my father. I don't know if he's at home right now."

"I'm sure you can sort something out, even if he's away," Maureen said. "You seem like the resourceful type."

Christophe's eyes met hers, lingering for a second longer than expected.

"Your instincts are correct," he said.

They ordered croissants, fresh ham, and fruit salad for breakfast. They didn't discuss the plan again until they finished the delicious food a few minutes later.

"I'm savoring every meal these days," Christophe said. "As soon as the war proper starts, rationing will kick in. The good things in life will disappear."

"Not everything," Maureen replied. Realizing what she'd been thinking, she blushed and blurted, "Gerhard, can you organize the trucks? I'll go with Christophe to send the telegram."

Her German friend threw down his napkin on the plate and stood up. "Shall we meet back here for dinner?"

"At seven," Christophe said. "And hopefully we can travel to Belgium on Monday or Tuesday."

"I just hope that's not too late," Gerhard said, tipping his hat to Maureen and walking off. She was alone with Christophe. He didn't speak as Maureen raised her coffee cup to her lips.

He pulled his wallet out of his pocket and threw down a few notes to cover the cost of their breakfast. Maureen thanked him, but he didn't acknowledge her.

"When are you going to start trusting me?"

"Trust is something that has to be earned."

"Time to go," he said and stood up.

He edged his way past the chairs. The old couple beside

them glanced up. The worry in their eyes betrayed their true thoughts. Perhaps this was their first time out for weeks or months—one last hurrah before the coming of the invaders.

Christophe seemed annoyed by her attitude, but she didn't care. What was worse, irritating him or putting the lives of dozens of innocent people at risk?

"What's our next move?" he said.

"You need to send those telegrams to your father, and your man in the Red Cross."

"And what are you? My babysitter?"

Resisting the temptation to reply in the affirmative was difficult. "Let's do this together," she said. "Better to work as a team."

"So you'll be able to keep an eye on me?"

She stopped dead on the street and turned to him. "I don't trust you yet. That doesn't mean I never will. I don't know who you are. Perhaps if you'd been through half of what I have over the past few years you'd understand."

"Who do you think I am, some high-living dandy wondering what speedboat to waterski behind next?"

"I've told you ten times—I have no idea who you are. But I do know there are Nazi agents all over this city, and I won't put my people in danger for you or anyone else."

"I'm the one who brought this plan to you," he said through gritted teeth. The dance they shared the night before seemed like a long time ago.

"Can we send the telegram please? I know an office around the corner."

Christophe bristled with anger but nodded and followed her.

He sent the first telegram to his father in Marseille and then to the Red Cross official in Bern.

Maureen didn't say a word as he wrote down the message to give to the clerk. Her mind tried to wrestle with the notion that he was like her and Gerhard, but that would have made him too perfect, which was dangerous in and of itself. The sharp end of the Nazi spear was about to strike her adopted homeland. She had too many commitments to begin a relationship with the likes of Christophe Canet.

She repressed her heart's song with thoughts of the boys in Izieu and the heinous acts she knew the Nazis were capable of.

The telegram sent, they convened on the street outside. "Next thing we need to see is if we can call the orphanage. Then plot a way into Belgium. The British and French forces are massed on the border."

"They won't be directing us toward the local Belgian tourist office," he answered.

They strolled through the Parisian morning sun to his hotel, where he assured her they had detailed maps of Belgium and could try to connect to the orphanage. Golden sunlight lit their way. Christophe took off his jacket and slung it over his shoulder as they passed Notre Dame. All seemed normal, and anyone observing them might have imagined she was taking a pleasant walk with her boyfriend on another beautiful Saturday morning in Paris.

"You have brothers and sisters?" he asked, breaking the silence between them.

His words caught her by surprise and pulled her out of deep thought. She had to pause for a few seconds before she answered.

"Yes, they're all in America. Two brothers, and two sisters. One of the girls is a step from my father's second marriage. I'm the oldest."

"And yet, you stayed here."

"What about you?"

"I have two brothers and a sister, but I'm the opposite of you —I'm the baby."

Her instinct was to bite back with another snide comment, but she stopped herself.

She was determined to be nice to him, to seduce him into a false sense of security.

"Gerhard told me your siblings all work for your father's shipping company."

"Down at the port in Marseilles. I never did appreciate the smell of fish, and I prefer fine art to shipping containers. I see my family whenever I'm back. They're all happy in what they do, but terrified at the prospect of war."

"And what about you, are you happy in what you do?"

"Yes. And I'm also terrified at the prospect of war."

"Have you ever thought of joining up?"

"Many times, but the French army is the biggest in the world. They don't need more men. Those children in Belgium —they need me more than the infantry or the navy. I think I can make more of a difference if I stay home, particularly if an invasion comes to pass."

Maureen fought the softening of her heart. This situation was too serious for the likes of that.

His hotel was less luxurious than she'd imagined, and somehow that was endearing.

"This isn't where I expected a rich dandy would stay," she said as they entered the lobby of the still respectable hotel.

"It was all I could find at the last minute," he said with a smile.

After ten minutes of calling operators in Belgium and France, they determined the orphanage didn't have a phone.

According to Christophe, the orphanage was located just outside a town called Kruisem, near Ghent, in central Belgium. It was a country she'd passed through by rail and road many times but had never visited. With the military blockade at the border, time was likely too short to send a letter, but that was what telegrams were for.

"Let's send them a telegram too. Do you have the address for the orphanage?"

"Yes, I do," he said, reaching into his pocket for a small black book. Glancing over, she couldn't help but notice the contact details of several ladies.

"A lot of history in here," he said. "I need to clear out a lot of these names."

"None of my business."

After procuring some writing paper and pen, they found a table and wrote the telegram.

"We don't even know who's running the orphanage, do we?"

Christophe shook his head in response.

"You didn't think to ask?"

"Of course I did. Arnaud didn't know either—just that the children are stuck there. The people who took them in probably didn't want to advertise the fact."

"I can relate to that."

To whom it may concern;

I am a concerned citizen in France with access to a safe haven. I heard about the plight of the boys and girls there from Arnaud Bruner of the Swiss Red Cross. He dispatched us to pick up the orphans and bring them to France. The welfare of the children is my only concern. I will travel to Kruisem in the next week with trucks before the invasion begins.

Yours sincerely,

. . .

"Would you release children in your care on the strength of this telegram?" Christophe asked.

"Perhaps it might be better if we just show up with the telegram from the Red Cross."

"If I was desperate enough, and they had a truck, I might. The people running the orphanage must know what's coming."

They returned to the telegram office. The clerk behind the counter looked them up and down as he read the address.

"Don't you know what's happening in Belgium?" he said through his thick mustache. "You can pay all the money you want, but I can't guarantee that this will make it in a month, let alone a day."

"Just send it, please," Christophe said and handed it over.

Deflated, they left the office together. "Will you have lunch with me?" Christophe said.

"After the way I've treated you these last few hours, you still want to have lunch with me?" she said.

"What other way is there to get to know me than to spend time together?"

Mulling the offer over for a few seconds, she decided to play hard to get. She smiled and shook her head. "We'll have plenty of occasion to speak tonight when we meet with Gerhard, and then on the drive to Kruisem next week. I'll see you at seven, Christophe."

"I suppose I'm just a glutton for punishment." He laughed and walked away, promising to meet to finalize the plan later than evening.

9

Tuesday, May 7, 1940

The letter from the French general, a man Christophe's father had made acquaintance with some years before, arrived in the morning by courier from military headquarters outside Paris.

With no other option and without a reply to their telegram to the orphanage or even the knowledge that it had arrived, they set off for the border before lunch. A steady stream of traffic from the east began at the military outposts and continued all the way to about an hour outside Paris. Gerhard had arranged for two trucks to transport the children. He rode in one with Maureen while Christophe drove the other alone.

Gerhard refused to answer any more questions about Christophe's trustworthiness. He proclaimed that the line between healthy suspicion and paranoia was a fine one, but she'd pole-vaulted over it. She supposed he was right and stopped asking. Christophe's truck was in front as they reached a British Army checkpoint just past the city of Lille, a few miles from the Belgian border. A river of people in cars, on horses and carts, and just walking was traveling in the other direction, but theirs were the only vehicles traveling toward the potential war zone. Christophe's lorry slowed to a halt. Maureen jumped out of the passenger seat right behind him and listened to his conversation with the British soldier on duty.

The soldier, in an olive-colored uniform with a rifle slung over his shoulder, looked at the letter Christophe had handed him before passing judgment.

"I don't know who this General Altmayer is," he said in a heavy cockney accent. "But no one's coming through except military personnel."

"Read the signature," Maureen said.

The soldier seemed almost startled to see her at first but then smiled. "It says you're going to "rescue priceless artworks?"" the soldier said, reading from the letter. "I'll have to speak to my commanding officer."

The young private disappeared, leaving them waiting for about 20 minutes before a stout man with an impressive bushy mustache barreled up. He introduced himself as Captain Gowan before asking what he could do for them.

"We need to cross into Belgium," Maureen said in English. She'd applied some lipstick while they were waiting and tried to smile at the stern Englishman as he took the letter from Christophe. "I understand the pressure you and these other brave soldiers must be under, but we only need to drive two hours and then come back."

"Two hours east is about equivalent to ten hours west these days," he murmured without looking up from the sheet of paper signed by General Charles Altmayer. "This says you're on a mission to rescue some art from a museum."

"A gallery," Christophe said.

"Well, wherever you're picking it up from, I can't let you across the border."

"We have permission in that letter from a high-ranking French general."

"And where is he now? The French have relinquished control of this part of the Belgian border to the forces of His Majesty. We're running things now, and I say you're not crossing. The Jerrys are coming any day now. It'd be suicide."

"Please, sir," Gerhard said, stepping forward.

The Englishman's face contorted at the sound of his voice.

"You're German?" Gowan said. He stood back and reached down toward his sidearm.

"Swiss German," Maureen said, but she knew any hope they had of crossing had evaporated.

They argued with the junior officer for a few minutes. "I don't care if you have a signed letter from God himself," the captain said to finish the conversation. "You're not crossing into Belgium anytime soon. And don't try any of the other border checkpoints; you'll hear exactly the same thing!"

Maureen ignored his advice and tried two other checkpoints, but Gowan was right—the British officers they met all said the same thing. The letter they'd waited days for counted for nothing. Dejected and bristling with frustration, they climbed back into the trucks as evening drew in. They turned around to make the short trip back to Lille. Maureen rode with Christophe this time to keep an eye on him.

"We're not beaten yet," she told him as the night closed around them. "We set plan B into action as soon as the invasion begins."

"As soon as the invasion starts? You want to wait until the Nazis flood across?"

"Plan A was a little safer, I admit," she said. "But as soon as the fighting starts the avalanche of wounded will follow. The army will be desperate for ambulances to evacuate their men back to field hospitals in France. That's when we slip across. And let's hope Gerhard keeps his mouth shut this time."

He shook his head and kept driving.

They parked the trucks on the street outside the hotel on Rue du Réduit. Lille had been occupied by the Germans for the entire duration of the first war, and some of the scars of the artillery bombardments that flattened much of it were still visible on statues and old buildings. The locals must have been living in terror since war was declared. The nightmare of the Great War seemed set to repeat itself, and soon the armies of Germany would march through again. The city was just 12 miles from the front lines and had become a massive field hospital during those years. The streets were empty as she, Christophe, and Gerhard jumped out of their trucks.

The hotel was still open. A nervous-looking clerk booked them two rooms, and after a dinner where they went over the plan for the next day, they retired to bed. Gerhard was already in the room when Christophe stopped her at the door to hers.

"Do you have to go to bed?"

"Yes." She put her hand on the doorknob and turned to him. "I still don't trust you, and if you put a foot wrong when we're in enemy territory I'll shoot you myself."

"I've only known you a week, Maureen Ritter, but I can already say I've never known anyone like you. You're the most stubborn person I've ever met."

"Any more compliments to send me off to sleep?"

"You have wonderful self-control...for a woman."

She could see from the sly smile on his face that he was goading her, but she decided to respond anyway.

"And you are a typical man, trying to conquer every female you meet."

"Don't ladies love to be conquered?"

"Oh, yes, tell yourself that. Men have started every war in history, but it seems to me women are the ones who suffer most. Perhaps it's time we took control of everything, not just of ourselves."

Her eyes flashing, she bid him goodnight and closed the door behind her.

~

Friday, May 10, 1940

They had breakfast of soft rolls smothered with jam, sliced ham, and coffee in the hotel. Christophe read the paper while the other two ate. He held it up, showing them the headline on the front page.

"Look who the new Prime Minister of England is," he said.

"Winston Churchill. It's been a long time coming. He said his whole life had been leading up to this trial and this moment."

"I should hope so," Gerhard said. "England is going to need him."

"He was the only one arguing against the policies of appeasing Hitler in the 30s," Christophe added. "If he'd had his way this war would have started when the glorious Führer invaded the Rhineland back in '36."

"It's funny," Maureen said. "The fear of another war led us here, to one that might even dwarf what happened between '14 and '18."

"Nothing so powerful as fear to impair judgment," Christophe said, placing the broadsheet on his lap. "Although I wouldn't say you've much experience with that, Maureen."

"Fear?" she replied. "I'm afraid all the time, my friend. I just do what has to be done anyway."

Christophe laughed so loud that the few other diners in the almost empty room looked over.

The first task at hand was to turn their vehicles into ambulances. Maureen had a steady hand and volunteered to paint the sides of the trucks with the familiar symbol of the Red

Cross. The two men gathered as many medical supplies as they could in pharmacies with little left on their shelves. The trucks were ready just after lunch—about the same time Germany invaded Belgium, Luxembourg, and the Netherlands as a prelude to their invasion of France.

Maureen turned to the two men as soon as the ambulances were ready. "Teach me how to drive one of these things."

"But you're the nurse," Gerhard said.

"What if one of you gets killed? We need a third driver."

All three sat in the cabin as Christophe drove out of the city to somewhere she couldn't hurt anyone. An old parking lot, emptied by the coming of the German hordes, proved perfect, and Christophe volunteered to show her the basics of driving the heavy vehicle.

"Please don't crash it," he said as she sat behind the wheel. "It was expensive."

Maureen's heart was thumping in her chest as she let the clutch out, but soon she calmed down to the point where her hands weren't so sweaty as to slide off the wheel. After an hour of practicing in the parking lot, she turned to the two men in the cabin. "You trust me to take her back into the city?"

"If we're trusting you to perhaps drive it in a warzone, we should do the same on empty roads back into the city," Gerhard said.

They arrived back at the hotel 30 minutes later. The clerk at the front desk told them the invasion had begun.

Maureen couldn't quite believe it. Somehow, despite every-thing she'd seen since moving to Berlin in '32 and everything Hitler had said, despite hearing stories of the Nazis' lust for weapons, and the remilitarization of Germany, part of her had believed it was all a bluff. A voice within her had said this couldn't be. These things happened to other people. Her father was in the Great War, but something like that could never happen to her. Now it had. It was real, and she and her friends were venturing into the belly of the beast the next day to rescue children none of them had ever met.

"Will anyone join me in a drink to dull the pain of the outbreak of war?" Christophe asked. Both agreed. After persuading the young man at the front desk to act as their bartender in the deserted hotel, Christophe ordered a bottle of the most expensive champagne in the house. "We could all be dead tomorrow," Christophe said as he poured the drinks with a shaking hand. His debonair façade showed signs of cracking, but his resolve remained intact. "But we're going to get those children out of Belgium if it's the last thing we do."

They clinked glasses and downed the effervescent golden liquid.

"What about dinner tonight?" Gerhard asked Bruno, the young clerk who seemed to be the only employee left in the hotel.

"I don't know," the young man answered. "The chef went home this afternoon. I'm the only person here."

"Why didn't you run with the rest of your colleagues?" Christophe asked.

"I thought I should finish out my shift. I don't see the point in fleeing. Hopefully, our army will stop the Germans in Belgium and they'll never even get here."

"An optimist," Christophe said, holding up his glass. "I'll drink to that! Join us," he said to Bruno, and a few seconds later, the front desk clerk was drinking the 1930 Bisquit Dubouche with them.

Bruno let them into the kitchen, and Christophe and Gerhard made dinner while Maureen sat in the bar with Bruno, discussing what he'd do if the Germans did arrive in Lille, as they had almost 30 years before.

"My father talked about the occupation when I was a kid. He said the Germans were brutal savages without a care for anyone but themselves."

Maureen nodded without passing comment. She'd seen the best and worst of humanity during her time in the Reich, but now it seemed the dregs of German society had taken over completely.

"What will you do if the Wehrmacht does break through and arrive here?"

"I'll stay," he replied. "At least I know this place. I have a home. And I could never leave my grandmother."

Christophe and Gerhard emerged with the ham steaks and fried potatoes they'd cooked. The food was better than Maureen had thought it would be. The four of them ate together and downed another bottle of, this time cheaper, champagne.

Bruno stayed until his shift ended at midnight. They all knew how hard the next day would be and decided to say good-night too.

The knock on Maureen's door came just as she was about to get changed. Still in her clothes, she answered the door to Christophe.

"Since we're driving into a warzone tomorrow, I thought I might ask for one last dance," he said with a devilish smile.

Knowing that she shouldn't do it didn't stop her—it never had. "Okay," she replied. "I'll meet you downstairs in the bar in five minutes." He replied with a nod, and she walked back into her room to reapply some of the lipstick she'd just cleaned off.

He was putting a record on the gramophone in the corner of the room as she arrived at the deserted bar area.

"You like Tommy Dorsey?" he asked.

"Who doesn't?"

"I was hoping you'd say that because it's all I could find."

The first song was a fast-paced number, and they broke out in happy grins as they danced the rhumba together. The song ended, and another one followed in its wake. They danced for 30 minutes or more without saying a word until the inevitable slow number followed. Maureen put her hand on his shoulder as he put his on her back.

"I knew you were trouble the second we met," she said.

His face was only inches from hers. He laughed before responding, "Only the best kind."

The gap between them faded to nothing, and she felt his lips on hers, somehow both rough and tender at the same time. The kiss lingered as seconds stretched into something more. It was he who drew back first, his eyes fixed on hers.

"So, do you trust me yet?"

"Do you want the honest answer to that question?"

"Probably not. Sometimes ignorance is bliss."

The record finished, and he walked to the gramophone to turn it over.

"Ready for side two?" he asked.

"Maybe we should get some sleep."

"What if tomorrow is the last day of our lives?"

"That's a line men have been taking advantage of in warzones for thousands of years," she said with a smile.

He responded by laughing. "You're right. I have no intention of dying tomorrow, and I know you don't either."

"Too much to do, Christophe, and we're only going to get busier."

"You know, I might prove a useful ally to someone like you."

"Let's just see how tomorrow goes, shall we?"

"You're taking it one step at a time. Seems sensible." The music was still playing. "One last dance before bed?" he asked with a tilted head.

"All right then," she said and took his hand.

They danced until the record ended and then returned to their rooms. Maureen shut the door with a strange concoction of joy and fear swirling around inside her. The war she'd been preparing for since she arrived in Berlin eight years ago was beginning, and all she could think of was Christophe.

10

Saturday, May 11, 1940

Maureen woke expecting to hear the sound of artillery in the distance, but the city was quiet. Bruno wasn't at reception as they arrived downstairs. An older man stood in his place, and he greeted the hotel's only guests as if they were royalty. Gerhard was pale and fidgety at breakfast. Even Christophe was silent. They ate yesterday's bread and drank coffee they'd brewed themselves. Last night was forgotten, for the time being at least. Time for such things could come later. Matters of life and death had to be taken care of first. Maureen knew it was the least of the hardships that the day would bring.

They stepped out into a dull, gray day. The sun was hidden behind a thick blanket of clouds from which there seemed no escape.

Maureen turned to the two men before they reached the trucks. "Gerhard, do you know where we're headed if we get separated? The roads in Belgium are likely to be bedlam."

"I have the map," he said.

"On a regular day, it's less than an hour to the orphanage at Kruisem from here, but today, it could take... a lot longer," Christophe said.

"Good luck to us all," Maureen said.

She was so terrified that the mere act of speaking was about all she could manage. Entering a warzone was close to her definition of insanity, but what choice did she have when the Nazis would get their claws on those children if she didn't?

Christophe and Maureen rode in the first vehicle in their little convoy, with Gerhard behind. They made directly for Kruisem, stopping at the border at the small town of Neuville-en-Ferrain, a different crossing point than they'd tried previously. It was silent in the truck.

The border was quite a different scene than the last time. The checkpoints were down, and a steady stream of traffic inched into France unchecked. Maureen directed Gerhard to stop by a small crowd of British troops who seemed to be supervising the traffic. Maureen poked her head out the window. "We're part of the volunteer ambulance corps," she said.

A young private with red hair and freckles who couldn't have been more than 19 stopped to look up and answer. "You want to see Colonel Armitage. He's at the church in Halluin, about a mile up the road." He pointed in the direction of the French town a little further north along the border. Maureen thanked him, and they were off.

She kept the window down as they drove and heard gunshots echoing in the distance and the crump of what she could only assume was artillery. The phony war was over, and the dreams of the optimists who had tried to argue that the war wouldn't materialize had been shattered. The worst-case scenario was in the mail, and almost nothing would stop it now.

They arrived at the church on the outskirts of the town in

minutes. A massive flag with a medical red cross flew from the steeple. They pulled up short among a mess of trucks and ambulances and jumped out. The smell hit her nostrils as soon as she stepped inside. It was like nothing she'd experienced before. The thick odor of blood and misery wafted through the air. Wounded people of all ages lay sick and dying, spread all over the floor where the pews had been removed. Dozens of them. Already.

"The war's not more than a day old," Christophe said.

Several children lay together in the corner with blood-stained bandages. Several doctors and a dozen nurses were rushing around, their white uniforms dashed with crimson. Gerhard reached out to stop one of the nurses, a pretty young woman with chestnut brown hair and matching eyes.

"Who do we speak to about volunteering for the ambulance corps?"

She pointed through an open door.

A tall, middle-aged man in a British Army uniform with a clipboard under his arm stood outside smoking a cigarette.

"Colonel Armitage?" Maureen said in English. "We have two ambulances."

He looked back at them and threw down the cigarette. "We need everyone we can get. Even a woman."

"What's being a woman got to do with it?" Maureen snapped.

"Nothing," the English officer said, taken aback. Armitage seemed too tired to make the usual joke men liked to crack in these situations and looked down at his clipboard instead to escape Maureen's glare. He looked at the two men standing behind her, but both knew better than to step forward.

"Will we be able to enter the country?" she asked.

"Without any problems. Drive east but don't stop at the first group of refugees you come across. We're here to help those who need it the most. Look for the ones who can't walk, who won't make it without you."

"Where are the Germans?" Christophe asked.

"Hard to say. Last I heard, just outside Brussels, but they're moving fast. *Blitzkrieg* they're calling it."

"Lightning war," Maureen said under her breath.

"Good luck," the Englishman said. "Bring the wounded here. If we fill up, we'll make.... alternate arrangements."

The trio returned to the trucks in silence. Maureen took Gerhard's hand before he got back in. "Be careful," she said.

He returned the sentiment with a tight smile. "You too."

They were in Belgium within minutes, the border guards parting like the waters of the Red Sea when they saw the markings on the sides of the trucks. Everyone in the entire country seemed to want to be in France. The other side of the road was thick with vehicles of every variety. The traffic jam snaked along for miles.

The sound of gunfire was growing louder with every mile they traveled. It seemed like they were driving into hell.

Planes roared above their heads, at first only with Allied markings on their wings, but after 20 minutes of driving, Christophe spotted a Luftwaffe fighter. He stopped in the middle of the empty road to watch it fly by.

"He's not stopping," the Frenchman said.

"You don't think they'd strafe an ambulance?" she asked.

"I wouldn't put anything past them."

Maureen ignored the refugees and the wounded by the side of the road. They had to focus. The children in Kruisem had to be their sole emphasis. If they started picking up others, they'd never make it to the orphanage on time. It became harder not to stop with each bloodied civilian and burning army truck they passed. But time was of the essence.

Christophe let out a muted cheer as the sign for Kruisem came into view. Maureen drew the paper with the directions to the orphanage out of her pocket. The town itself seemed untouched, but all the stores were closed, and what people they saw were peering out from behind closed windows.

The orphanage was outside the town, set among green fields with a stream flowing through. It was like a painting hanging above a fireplace.

The trucks rumbled through an open gate into a courtyard already in a frenzy. About ten children were standing in line with small suitcases in their hands. A nurse emerged from inside the large, gray house with a girl of about 12, and then another woman followed her with a boy about the same age.

Gerhard pulled up with a hiss on the loose stones outside the house. The woman stopped and walked over. "What are you doing here?" she said with a stern, frightened voice. "This isn't a medical facility."

"We're here to evacuate the children," Maureen said and jumped out. "Did you receive our telegram?"

The woman, who was about fifty, looked at Maureen as if she had two heads.

"I didn't receive any telegram—"

"I spoke to Arnaud Brunner of the Swiss Red Cross. He told me you were marooned here. We came to help evacuate the children." She presented the telegram from the Red Cross.

A German plane roared overhead. The sound of artillery sounded again, except it seemed much closer this time.

"I don't know where you came from," the nurse said. "But thank God you're here."

"We don't have much time," Maureen said. "I run a safe-house in France near the Swiss border. I can take the children to it if you let me."

The woman seemed not to know how to answer.

"What was your plan?" Christophe said. "To join the tidal wave of refugees?"

"I had no other way of evacuating them," she said. "All the others left. It's just Claire and I now."

Maureen introduced herself and the two men with her.

"I'm Antoinette," she said.

"Come with us," Maureen said. "Make sure your children are safe."

Claire, the other nurse, was standing a few feet away. "Let these people take the kids," she said. "My husband is driving to the border in an hour with my children. I'll be with them."

She said goodbye to a few boys and girls in the courtyard and walked through the gates and back toward the town.

"All right," Antoinette said. "But I'm coming along with them."

"Of course," Maureen answered.

Antoinette took it upon herself to divide the kids into two groups—one group for each truck. The question of travel documents was raised, but all agreed it didn't matter. With hundreds of thousands of refugees streaming across the border, the police wouldn't have the time or the inclination to check everyone's papers. Maureen was confident they wouldn't be stopped, and if they were, the French authorities had better things to worry about than Jewish orphans from Germany.

The sound of artillery was audible as they led the first batch of children out to the street to pile into the back of the truck.

"You think that's ours or theirs?" Christophe asked.

"Judging by the fact that we can hear the explosions more than the guns, I'd say that's Nazi artillery," Gerhard said.

The 24 children were already packed, and within minutes, Christophe and Gerhard were shepherding them into the trucks, where they sat with their small suitcases at their feet. The sound of fighting continued in the distance. Maureen had visited her father's factory many times in Berlin and had seen the ammunition as it was produced by the ton. But she'd never heard it used before and had never witnessed the carnage it could inflict.

Soon, the trucks were all full. Antoinette banged on the cab when they were ready to leave.

Half an hour after arriving, they drove out the front gate, knowing that getting to the orphanage had been the easy part.

The journey back through town was uneventful, but the traffic jam began just outside. They joined a line of cars, trucks, buses, and carts. People on horseback slalomed through the slow-moving vehicles, all seeking sanctuary in France.

"I don't know why they're bothering," Christophe said. "The Wehrmacht will be in Paris in a few weeks."

Maureen saw an old couple pushing a hand cart, their meager belongings on top. Guilt flooded through her. "I wish we could do something for these people," she said.

"We're here to help the children. By the grace of God, we found them. Stopping to help anyone else would be putting everyone at risk."

An hour into the journey, they arrived at a French checkpoint. But the nine soldiers manning it could do little other than wish the thousands of refugees passing on foot good luck on their travels. The vehicles were a different story.

"We're with the Red Cross. We were assigned the task of collecting these orphans and transporting them across the border." Christophe said as he handed over his personal papers. Like all the best lies, a kernel of truth in the center made it easier to deliver.

The soldier asked for their papers, and Maureen leaned across to speak to him. "The Nazis are coming. Listen to that!" she said as another explosion sounded in the distance. "What are you about to do, send us back toward them?"

The soldier folded his arms, looked away, and motioned for them to keep driving. Just as he did so, a terrifying screech filled the air. The private who'd been speaking to them looked up with terror in his eyes and raised his rifle. The crowd around the checkpoint scattered into the fields as a German Stuka dive bomber began its descent with a horrific squeal. Maureen looked out the side window and saw the lone plane, then shouted at Christophe to get off the road.

Gerhard had already turned and was driving through a ditch into the open field.

"Get away from the checkpoint!" Maureen roared.

Christophe put the truck in gear and pushed down on the accelerator as the French soldiers opened fire with the small arms they carried. He burst through a hedgerow just as the first bullets hit the ground around them. The truck struggled to pick up speed on the muddy ground as rounds struck French soldiers and refugees alike. The ping of metal striking the bonnet brought screams from the children in the back.

"Floor it!" Maureen shouted as a massive explosion rocked the checkpoint behind them. Bodies were tossed in the air and fell to the ground with a sickening thud. The Stuka pulled out of its dive and ascended again.

Christophe craned his head to look up and out the window. "It's coming back around," he said.

Gerhard's truck was a hundred yards ahead of them, driving full speed over the rough ground toward a clump of trees on the other side of the field.

"Follow him!" Maureen shouted.

The Stuka's scream began again. Hundreds of panic-stricken people were running for whatever cover they could find. The French soldiers leveled their guns and fired but were obliterated in a cloud of smoke, blood, and dirt as another bomb struck. Bullets dug up clouds of dirt in lines along the field just behind the truck.

"Don't they see we're an ambulance?" Maureen roared above the din.

"They don't care," Christophe responded.

This was the moment the Stuka pilot had been training for. He wasn't about to let markings on the side of a truck ruin his glorious attack.

Gerhard's vehicle was stopped under a large tree at the end of the field. He had nowhere else to go. The Stuka seemed to switch its attention to the other lorry and flew toward the trees. A line of bullets pelted the ground leading up to the cabin and hit the door, shattering the window and tearing up the seats inside. Maureen looked on in silent horror as the fuel tank sprung a leak and ignited. The entire truck erupted in a ball of flame.

"Gerhard!" Maureen screamed. "The children!"

A British Hurricane appeared over their heads and opened fire on the German bomber, which turned tail, fleeing the fighter. Seconds later, a plume of black smoke extended from the Stuka's fuselage, and the Hurricane moved in for the kill. The Stuka plummeted to the earth just beyond the trees in an empty field.

Christophe stopped, and they both jumped out to run toward Gerhard's stricken vehicle. Another explosion rocked the truck. Antoinette was beside them now, running toward the inferno.

They reached the burning wreck together, but the charred bodies she'd expected to see weren't there. The vehicle was empty.

"I don't suppose you'll get your deposit back now," Gerhard said as he walked out of the trees with several children. Antionette hugged them. Some had tears running down their faces, and several girls held each other as they wept, but all were alive.

Maureen ran to Gerhard, throwing her arms around him.

"We thought you were—"

He wore a wide grin as she pulled back from him. "Dead?" he said. "We would have been, but for the cover of the woods. I got everyone out in time. I figured the Nazis weren't too concerned with respecting the Geneva Convention, and we'd be safer in the trees."

Antoinette arrived beside them and started hugging the children. Christophe ran a hand through his hair and pushed out a breath. His cheeks were flushed, and he took a moment to sit on the dry ground.

"We do have the problem of only having one truck now," he said.

"And the road is littered with wounded," Gerhard answered.

The checkpoint was obliterated, and several French soldiers were dead. Only one was untouched and approached Maureen as they arrived back on foot.

"I am Private Marchand of the French Army and I need your truck."

"It's full of children," Maureen replied.

"I have wounded men here who'll die if they don't see a doctor," the soldier said. He was in his mid-twenties with a brown mustache and a deep scar along his cheek. Five of his comrades lay on the grass beside him. Two were covered in blood and seemed not long for this world. The other three were sitting up, tending to the dying men, but had visible wounds themselves. Several dead civilians littered the road also, women and children among them. Maureen counted seven wounded among them, including a girl of about eight with blood running down her arm. The little girl's mother was trying to stem the bleeding. Her three other children, all younger, were unhurt.

"Let me," Maureen said. She ripped a piece of discarded clothing she found on the ground and tied a tourniquet around the girl's bicep.

"I was in medical school for a couple of years," she explained to the girl's mother, who nodded and thanked her.

"What's your name?" Maureen asked the girl.

"Beatrice," came the reply through gritted teeth.

"Well, Beatrice, you're going to have to keep this knotted tight around your arm until we get you to a doctor, can you do that for me?"

The child nodded, and Maureen stood up to tend to the next person, a man with a gaping hole in his side who was beyond help. He reached up to her with gnarled, bloody fingers, grabbing onto her shoulder like hooks into her flesh. Christophe stepped in and wrenched the dying man's hands off her.

"Nothing you can do for him," he said. "Focus on who we can help."

The French soldier appeared once more. "Bring that truck back. I'm commandeering it."

"We have 24 children to transport back across the border, some of whom can't walk," Gerhard said.

"My men will be dead in an hour if we don't get them back."

"He's right," Maureen said. "Let them use the truck."

"What about our kids?" Gerhard asked.

"I'm not asking," Marchand said, lowering his rifle to aim at them.

"No need for that my friend," Christophe said and pushed down the barrel of the weapon.

"You can have the truck, but my two friends drive," Gerhard said, turning to Maureen and Christophe. "I'm the one who got my truck blown to smithereens, so I should be the one who has to walk. It's only about six miles to the border from here."

"I don't like the idea of leaving you," Maureen said.

"I'll go with Antionette and the kids. It's okay," he said. "We'll see you in a few hours."

It didn't seem right, but Maureen looked around and realized they had no choice.

"I'm not letting you bring the children back alone," she said.

"Antionette will be with me. And look around you, no one's alone here."

"I am looking and I see what happened to the crowd here."

Gerhard put his hand on her shoulder and then gestured at Marchand. "You can come back for us. And he isn't in the mood to compromise, anyway."

"Get that ambulance back here now," the French private said.

"Of course," Christophe answered and went with Gerhard to get it.

They returned two minutes later and jumped out of the vehicle, the engine running.

"No stretchers?" the soldier said. "What kind of an ambulance is this?"

"The kind with four wheels and an engine," Christophe said. They laid the soldiers who couldn't walk along the floor and gave them what medical supplies they had.

"What about my dead comrades?" the French private said. "We can't just leave them here."

"Count the wounded civilians we have to bring," Maureen said. "We don't have room for people we can't help. I'm sorry about your friends."

The Frenchman seemed to accept her answer but didn't help as she, Gerhard, Christophe, and Antoinette helped the seven wounded civilians into the crowded ambulance.

The little girl, who had to be separated from her mother, was last.

"Would you like to sit up front with me?" Maureen said to her.

The girl nodded through agonized tears.

"I'll take care of her. We'll be at the church in Halluin. Come find your daughter."

The young mother nodded. She kissed the little girl before Maureen helped her into the cabin. Christophe sat behind the wheel and reversed onto the road. The crowd parted to let them through, and they inched toward France, a few miles away.

The French soldier cursed the crowds swarming across the roads. He shouted at them as Christophe honked the horn.

"My men are dying in the back!"

The people on the road moved, but the pace was slow. The little girl beside Maureen was growing pale from the loss of blood.

"Beatrice is such a pretty name."

Maureen examined the tourniquet. It was doing its job, and Beatrice would likely already be dead without it, but she'd still lost too much blood.

"Can we cut through the fields?" Maureen said in desperation as another vast crowd of people pushing carts and carrying children stood before them.

"In this vehicle, with wounded people inside?" Christophe asked. "We'd never make it. They'd all die. I'm doing my best."

"I know you are," she said.

Her heart was thumping in her chest. No noise came from the back. She banged on the metal frame behind her head. "How are you doing back there?"

"Most of us are okay," came a woman's voice. "But I think one of the soldiers is dead."

Hearing her words stoked a flame in Marchand, and he began roaring at the refugees on the road. He opened the door, raised his rifle, and fired in the air. The refugees scattered, and he jumped back in. "Now, drive," he said.

He got out three more times to fire over the fleeing people's heads before they reached the meaningless line that now constituted the border between France and Belgium. The stream of refugees dissipated upon reaching France, and they were able to speed up to Halluin.

Beatrice hadn't spoken in a few minutes and was cold to the touch.

"How are you feeling, sweetheart?" Maureen said.

"Tired," the little girl replied.

"No time for sleep now. The doctor will see you in just a few minutes.

"I just want to sleep," Beatrice said in a voice so low Maureen barely heard it.

"Stay awake, and with me. We're almost there. Christophe, can't this thing go any faster?"

The Frenchman stepped on the gas.

They pulled up outside the church just after five o'clock. It had been more than an hour since the Stuka attack. Marchand jumped out before the truck came to a halt, shouting to attract the attention of the doctors and nurses inside the makeshift medical center.

"Let's go, Beatrice," Maureen said, but the girl didn't respond. Her body was limp. "Help me, Christophe!"

He ran around the front of the ambulance and carried Beatrice out of the cabin. Maureen ran beside him. The other walking wounded were struggling out of the back. A nurse emerged from inside the church.

"She took a bullet to the upper left arm. Her name is Beatrice. She's lost a lot of blood."

The nurse nodded and escorted them inside. They laid the girl down on an empty stretcher.

The doctor stood up and strode past them. He was in his fifties, slim, with thinning gray hair. Maureen stopped him with a firm hand.

"How is she?"

"Weak."

Maureen looked at Christophe and then back at the doctor. "But she'll live, won't she?"

"Hard to tell right now. The next 24 hours will be vital. She needs blood but we don't have any. The best we can do is make her comfortable, and make sure she gets plenty of water."

He hurried off to the next patient.

Maureen ran after him. "I'll give her my blood. I'm O negative—a universal donor."

"That could save her life."

"Let's not waste any more time."

The doctor called over a nurse who tapped into a vein in Maureen's left arm. Soon rich crimson liquid was surging through a tube into a bag. Twenty minutes later, the doctor connected the same bag to Beatrice's arm, and Maureen watched as the life-giving blood flowed into the little girl's body.

Christophe stood with her. "I know you don't want to leave her, but we have to go back for the others. "We can't wait here any longer,"

"I know," Maureen said, holding back the tears. "The war's just started," Maureen said, shaking her head. "The Nazis haven't even made it into France yet and we're already faced with choices like these?" Christophe didn't answer, just stared back at her. "Let's just wait a few more minutes for her mother to arrive, okay?"

"Ten more minutes," he answered. "Beatrice's mother knows where she is. She'll be here."

They went back to the truck. Two of the French soldiers inside were dead. Marchand and Christophe lifted them out and disappeared around the other side of the church to where a mortuary had been set up. Maureen didn't follow them. She spared herself that much, at least.

The time disappeared in the blink of an eye, and they went back inside to see the sleeping little girl.

"Goodbye, little one," Maureen said. "Be strong and make it through the night."

Christophe took her by the hand and they walked out. Marchand was sitting on the steps of the church, smoking a cigarette.

"Another man died," he said without looking at them. "Another one of my comrades. Maybe I'll be next."

"I'm sorry," Maureen said, but had nothing more to say to him, so they got back into the lorry. Colonel Armitage appeared with his clipboard again. He already looked defeated.

"Where's your other ambulance?"

"We lost it. A Stuka attack," Christophe answered.

"Are you heading back over the border this evening?" the Englishman asked.

"We have to get the rest of our companions and bring them out," Christophe replied.

Armitage shook his head. "Okay, good luck. Come back when you're done. We don't have the ambulances to deal with the scale of the attack we're seeing," he said, and strode back toward the church.

Christophe backed the truck out through the narrow gates, and they were on the road in seconds. The sound of artillery, like distant thunder, echoed in their ears. Maureen didn't speak at first, just thought about Beatrice and all the other citizens they'd seen mangled by German bullets and bombs. Christophe might have been talking to her when she spoke. It was hard to tell.

"Do you think she'll be all right?"

"The little girl?" Christophe shook his head, his eyes on the road. "She's young and strong and in good hands. And she has your blood in her now—the best there is. But this is only the beginning. I hate to think of all the children like Beatrice who are going to get caught up in this horror, but we have to focus on what we can achieve."

Maureen pressed the side of her head against the glass. It was still light out, but the air was gritty now, as if you could reach out and feel the fading of dusk between your fingers.

11

Saturday, May 11, 1940

The crowds of fleeing refugees were on both sides of the road. With no word from the government on what they should do, they had stayed true to their instincts and fled, even when it made little sense for most of them. Perhaps they thought this war would be like the last, even though it was already apparent that the German Army had moved on from 1914, even if the French hadn't. Christophe weaved the truck through the masses of horse-drawn carts and trolleys. Some people were on horseback, but many just walked with as much as they could carry on their backs. It was impossible to count how many, but Maureen guessed the number had to be in the hundreds of thousands in this small part of Belgium alone. Every person they saw wore the same terrified look and cringed at the slightest noise. They knew that death was only seconds away at any time.

Neither Maureen nor Christophe spoke for the hour it took them to drive three miles back to where they'd last seen Gerhard and the children from the orphanage.

It was Maureen who broke the silence. "I see them!" she roared. "Up ahead on the left." Christophe pulled the truck over to the side. It was swamped in seconds by refugees begging for a ride.

"We're here for the children," Christophe said as he got out.

"What about my child?" a mother holding a two-year-old said.

"And mine?" said another young mother.

Maureen looked at Christophe. "We have to stay focused," he said. "We came here for the orphans. The non-Jewish kids will have a better chance."

Maureen waved to Gerhard, and he and the bedraggled bunch of children struggled toward them through the thickening crowd.

Gerhard was covered in sweat and dirt, but he smiled as he turned to her. "We're all okay. It was just one heck of a walk."

"Did you see any more attacks?"

"One or two. Thankfully we didn't get caught up in any. This is Amelie, by the way," he said, gesturing to the girl beside him. "We've had quite a time together, haven't we, my dear?"

"You could say that," she said, shaking Maureen's hand.

Antionette arrived a few seconds later with the rest of the children. She lined them up and had them count off. Christophe stood up on the hood of the truck to speak to the crowd of 50 or more, trying to catch a ride.

"We came for these children. They're Jews. The Nazis will send them to camps or ghettos in the east if they get their claws into them."

"You won't let us on, and you're taking filthy Jews?" one man said.

"Don't you realize they come for the Jews one day and for us the next?" a woman beside him said.

"This is not a negotiation," Christophe said. "Get on the

truck and you will be removed. But we will be back. Keep moving. We might see you later."

"You're worse than the Nazis," someone said, and Christophe jumped down.

He and Gerhard stood facing the crowd as the children climbed into the truck. Most of the people returned to their handcarts and resumed walking. Only a stubborn few remained to watch the ambulance leave. Gerhard sat up front with Maureen and Christophe. Antionette insisted on sitting in the back with the children.

"How are we to get the kids to Izieu?" Gerhard said. "We only have one truck now. The other is a burned-out hulk in some field a few miles back."

"We'll try to take some or all of them on the train," Christophe said. "They're still running into Paris from the station in Lille."

"I'm sure that's where half the people we just met on the road are headed too," Maureen said.

"But we can only try, can't we?" Christophe replied.

"In the event that we can't get on, I say we drive straight down to Izieu."

"That's eight hours in normal conditions," Gerhard said. "And these days are far from that."

"The kids can't ride for ten hours back there. They're packed in so tight they can hardly breathe," Christophe said. "The train ride will be far easier, particularly after the change in Paris."

"Let's see what we can manage," Maureen said.

It was after six in the evening when they arrived at the train station in Lille. The crowds were visible from the outside.

"Let me see what's going on," Maureen said as she jumped out of the truck.

She joined the crowd, pushing through the mill to get into the station. The refugees were here but also the locals.

Everyone was determined to escape the inevitable. Few had as much reason to flee as the children in the back of her truck.

Each platform was thick with people but in orderly lines which snaked up and down. Four trains sat waiting. She found a ticket inspector. "Will everyone get on trains tonight?"

"I don't know," he said. "Do you have tickets?"

She shook her head. "I need about 27."

"You'll be lucky to get half that amount. Go to the booth over in the corner."

After fifteen minutes of standing in line, Maureen bought the last 15 tickets for the last train leaving in two hours.

She returned to the truck and shared the news. The younger and sicker children would travel with Antoinette and Gerhard. She, Christophe and the rest of the orphans would follow in the truck the next day. The children greeted the news with muted cheers. After all, she was a stranger bringing them somewhere they never knew existed. They spent the next two hours finding somewhere to buy food and then eating it. By the time they were finished, it was time to board the train.

Antoinette got on first. It was standing room only, and each child inched forward, clinging to their small bags of personal belongings. Maureen stood on the platform, watching Christophe pick the children up to lay them down in the luggage racks.

One little girl stopped to speak to Maureen before she got on.

"Excuse me," she said in a tiny voice. She was about six with bitumen eyes and chestnut-colored hair. "Will our parents know where to find us when we arrive?"

"What's your name?" Maureen had no idea how to answer the little girl's question. Lying would have been the easiest recourse, but how could she?

"Rebecca."

"I know you're missing your parents very much. Do you have any brothers and sisters too?"

"My brother is inside," she pointed to the train. "His name is Max. He's 11."

"I'm sure your parents are eager to see you wherever they might be."

"Do you know where they are?"

"I'm sorry, my sweet, I don't. You saw all those people on the road out of Belgium, didn't you?" The little girl nodded. "Lots of families are spread out all over the place right now because of this horrible war that's starting. We'll be somewhere safe soon where the Germans won't find us. Not for a long time."

"If we hide my mother and father won't find us either."

Tears were welling in Rebecca's eyes, and all Maureen could think to do was to put her hand on the little girl's cheek. "I'll keep an eye out for your parents every day. And if I find them, I'll bring them straight to you. How about that?"

"When will I see them again?"

Christophe emerged and took the child's hand. "All the other kids are on the train now, Rebecca. It's a long journey," he said in a tender tone Maureen had never heard him use. "And I promise, you'll love it in Izieu."

"It's so beautiful, and we have plenty of room for all of you," Maureen added.

The girl wiped away her tears with the back of her wrist and climbed on board. She was one of the last. Maureen stayed on the platform to shepherd the rest on. The train's whistle sounded, and the doors began to close. The train was packed beyond capacity.

The eleven children from the orphanage who were left behind stood on the platform and waved until the train disappeared.

They were back in the truck when Maureen turned to Christophe.

"Why didn't you leave on the train?"

"You didn't think I'd let you go back alone, did you?" he said.

"No," she replied with a wry smile.

"Or let you drive the one truck we have left alone in the dark?"

"I'm an excellent driver."

"You'd never sat in a six-wheeler before a few days ago. I grew up driving them for my father at the port."

She couldn't help but smile as she started the engine.

"There's somewhere I have to go before we bed down for the night," she said. "I have to see how she is."

"Let's drop the kids off at the hotel first. They're old enough to stay without us for an hour or two."

They went to the hotel. Christophe parked and disappeared inside for 20 minutes before emerging with the key to the last room. "It'll be a tight squeeze with 11 of them," he said.

The exhausted children were grateful for anywhere to lay their heads. Four lucky ones took the bed, while the other seven made the floor their bed for the night. Most of them were asleep by the time Maureen shut the door behind her.

The roads back to the border were emptier than earlier. In the far distance, flashes of white light illuminated the black skyline, and the thumping sounds of those explosions rolled like waves through the night.

They returned to the church in Halluin. It was a small border town— somewhere she'd never heard of until a few hours before, but that night it became the center of her universe.

She jumped out of the lorry before her friend had brought it to a complete stop. The courtyard outside the medical center was full of ambulances halted until dawn. One had bullet holes tacked down the side as if some giant needle had punctured it in a perfect line. Inside, the fetid stench of blood and death filled her nostrils. Armitage, the British officer, was nowhere to be seen, and the French soldier, Marchand, was doubtless back at the front by now.

She pushed the heavy wooden doors open, and her heart sank like an anvil as she saw that Beatrice's bed was empty. Dozens of wounded patients lined the interior of the once holy place, and Maureen ran up and down, searching for the little girl. A nurse with two-inch bags under her eyes appeared from behind a pillar.

"What are you doing here?" she demanded.

"I'm looking for a little girl. Her name is Beatrice. Is she still here?"

"Are you her mother?"

"No. I just brought her in a few hours ago."

The nurse looked at her a second and, likely because she didn't have the time or energy to argue, led them to the altar, where Beatrice was lying on a stretcher alongside several other children whose wounds were so grisly Maureen could hardly bring herself to look at them. The girl was asleep, her sandy brown hair bloody and matted by the side of her head. Her face was still caked with mud and grime.

"How is she?" Maureen asked.

"Better. She was awake about an hour ago, and the doctor said she was healthy enough to move over here. This is our children's wing."

"She'll live?"

"It's looking more positive."

"What about her mother?"

"No sign yet. We wouldn't have known her name if you hadn't told us when you brought her in."

Maureen took scant solace from the nurse's words. The girl might live, but who would care for her if her mother didn't show?

Back outside, it was still warm, and the stars shone like

diamonds on a cloth of black satin. She sat beside Christophe on the steps.

"She needs us. I have a place for her in Izieu. She could be safe."

"How do you know her father isn't waiting for her in Lille? She could have cousins in Paris or anywhere else for all we know."

Maureen kept arguing even though she knew he was right. "What if they don't? She'll be alone, and ill, among strangers. I can't bear the thought of it. It shouldn't have taken her mother this long to get here. We'll give her the night, but if Beatrice is still alone by lunchtime tomorrow, we have to take her."

"You don't know her, not even her last name."

"She needs help. What more do we need to know?"

"Perhaps if we were going to be here a few more days, we could wait to see if her parents come for her."

"And I know we can't just take her too, not until we know for sure she's alone," Maureen said as a tear rolled down her cheek. "It's just.... leaving her feels so wrong." He opened his mouth to speak, but she cut him off before he could utter a word. "Don't give me that line about wanting to save the world. I'm not a fool, Christophe."

"Believe me, Maureen, that was very much apparent from the first moment we met."

He reached over and took her hand. It felt good.

"I know I can't just take every child that needs help. The fighting's only a few days old. Europe will be full of Beatrices soon."

"You already do so much. We wouldn't be here if it wasn't for you."

"The idea was yours. You brought it to us."

"But you agreed to help, even though you didn't trust me at all. People love talking. Doing is something different altogether. I've never met anyone like you before."

"You just wanted to kiss me."

"That was one factor," he said with a grin. "But the passion you instill in people is like nothing I've seen before. I'm here because you convinced me it was the only thing to do, and you did that without saying more than a few words." He put his arms around her and drew her into his body. She wrapped her arms around him and rested her head against his chest to hear the thumping of his heart.

"Perhaps her mother will come for her tomorrow morning, and bring Beatrice to a beautiful house in the country."

"She'll be better in days," Christophe whispered. "And running around with all those other children, laughing and playing."

Maureen let that dream sit in her consciousness for a few seconds, savoring it like the taste of an exquisite meal.

"We should go back to our hotel. We have a long drive ahead of us tomorrow, remember?"

He held her hand as they walked back to the lorry.

The urge to run back inside the church and see the little girl she knew nothing about one last time was almost too strong to resist, but she climbed into the passenger seat and shut the door behind her. Maureen rested her head against the glass and peered out into the darkness as Christophe drove back. He parked on the street outside the hotel among a slew of carts and cars. The city, which had been almost entirely deserted the night before, was bustling with exhausted people.

"I'm sure we'll be fine here. I don't think the Nazis will march through the streets of Lille tonight," Christophe said. "The fighting seemed to be a few dozen miles behind us all the way. The Luftwaffe was the only sign we saw of the invading German forces, and they were high above us and few and far between."

"Not when it counted. Do you think they'll have space?" she

said gesturing to the hotel. "We're not going to fit in with the kids upstairs."

"Give me a few minutes. I'm sure they'll have a broom cupboard or something."

Christophe struggled up the steps, moving like an old man. He hobbled inside and reappeared five minutes later. "We can sleep in the bar, on the long seats."

His words elicited a feeble cheer from Maureen, who stood up and walked into the lobby. After a little gentle persuasion, the clerk behind the counter agreed to open up the kitchen, and Maureen and Christophe made sandwiches from the scraps of food they could rustle together.

"Have a drink with me," Christophe said as they finished their food.

"Okay, but just one."

"Does such a thing as "one drink" really exist? I thought the notion was like the Loch Ness monster—often spoken of but never seen."

"You'll find out tonight that it's a reality."

"Say it isn't so," he said.

He looked as if he were about to keel over with tiredness but still insisted on ordering a bottle of Bordeaux from the bar, which was full of people drinking and sleeping. He poured them each a glass and sat forward. The look in his eyes was somewhere between anticipation and exhaustion. He clinked glasses with her.

It was obvious he wanted to kiss her. She could see him trying to work up the courage in his eyes. The sound of bombs and bullets came like distant hail. The Germans would be here within weeks. She knew that, despite what every French general said in the newspapers. She debated in her mind whether to toy with him for a few seconds longer before she relented and kissed him on the lips.

Someone wolf-whistled.

As he drew back, she took his head between her hands and kissed his lips again, lingering for a few seconds.

"In case we die tomorrow," she whispered.

"I'd be a happy man," he answered.

They slept with their arms around each other on the last available bench, crushed together, the sleep of the dead.

12

Sunday, May 12, 1940

Christophe was still asleep beside her as Maureen opened her eyes. A dozen others were rousing around them. Her first thought was of Beatrice. Not wanting to shake Christophe awake, she stood up and stretched out the pains from sleeping on the long chair she'd shared with the man from Marseilles overnight. Who was he now? A friend? A comrade? Something else? It didn't matter at that moment. All that did was getting back to the church in Halluin. She used the bathroom and returned to shake him awake. The children were already up and waiting for them in the lobby.

"Sleep well?" he asked.

"Better than I could have expected."

"You want to go to see her right away, don't you?"

"I spoke to the kids. They're all up and waiting for us in the lobby. We have to feed them too."

They set about finding some food, but the hotel's larders were bare. After taking some time to wash the best they could, Maureen and Christophe set out with the 11 children to seek out breakfast. After 20 minutes of looking, they found a bakery selling fresh croissants. Christophe bought four dozen and handed out two or three to each child, depending on their appetite.

They walked back to the hotel and Maureen gathered them to talk.

"We have a long journey ahead, but rest assured, it's to a better place." Her words were greeted with blank stares, and whispers. She wondered if they would have agreed to come at all if they hadn't heard the sounds of the invasion in the distance.

The question of travel documents was raised, but all agreed, with hundreds of thousands of refugees streaming across the border, the police wouldn't have the time nor the inclination to check everyone's papers. Maureen was confident they wouldn't be stopped, and if they were, the French authorities had better things to worry about than Jewish orphans from Germany.

The sound of artillery was audible as they led the children out to the street to pile into the back of the truck.

"You think that's ours or theirs?" Maureen asked.

"Judging by the fact that we can hear the explosions more than the guns, I'd say that's Nazi artillery," Christophe said.

It was an unsettling thought but nothing surprising. Somehow, Maureen had slept through the night, but now in the bright sun of the early morning, a great tiredness descended upon her. It was as if the weight of everything they'd seen and experienced the last few days brought itself to bear on her all at once. She sat on the hotel steps as, one by one, the children from the orphanage climbed in and took their seats along the benches at the side. Soon, the back was full.

"Let's check on Beatrice one last time," Maureen said.

"We can't take her today." Christophe said and pushed a hand back through his hair. "What if her parents are unconscious in some other hospital?"

"We'll leave notes. We can't leave her all alone! She's just a kid."

"Who you'd never even heard of 24 hours ago!"

"What has that got to do with anything?"

Christophe slammed the wheel with an open palm. "It doesn't matter how many times I say you can't save the world, does it? You're still going to try."

"If I see a wrong, I have to at least try and right it."

"Okay, Maureen," he said. "I'll drive you, but we're not going to do anything rash."

"Thank you," she said. "I have to know."

The Red Cross flag over the church at Halluin came into view 30 minutes later. Maureen's hands were wet as she opened the door and jumped out. Half the ambulances parked the night before were out in the field, and Armitage was prowling the courtyard again.

"Mademoiselle? Are you back to drive for us?" he asked, but Maureen ran past him and inside the church. The situation was all the more horrible in the day when the grotesque wounds were more visible in the light. She weaved in and out, past dozens of people laid out on stretchers, to where the makeshift children's wing had been set up. And she felt the same sinking feeling as the day before—Beatrice wasn't there.

"Where's Beatrice?" she said out loud, hoping someone would answer.

"Are you family?" A passing nurse replied.

"No, just an ambulance driver. I was concerned her parents might not show."

"Don't be," the young woman said. "Her mother took her an hour ago."

Relief flooded through Maureen's veins, and she almost collapsed on Christophe's shoulder.

"Thank you," she said.

Christophe took her hand and led her toward the truck, where the kids were waiting for them in the back.

Armitage was prowling around outside with the clipboard in his hand. "I need you out in the field. We have hundreds of wounded," he said.

"I'm sorry, sir, but we have to bring these children south," Christophe said.

Maureen didn't speak, just stood watching the British officer's face contort in frustration.

She followed Christophe onto the truck—he was right. Their first responsibility was to the children in the back.

Another ambulance arrived behind them and swerved around to the entrance of the church. Two men and a woman jumped out and seconds later were carrying in more wounded on stretchers. Maureen stared in silence as Christophe backed the lorry out onto the street. He took one last somber look at the church and drove away.

They stopped for lunch and bathroom breaks somewhere south of Reims at about noon. Maureen picked up a newspaper after they'd eaten. The front page was splashed with stories about the German invasion of the low countries. Nazi tank divisions were pushing toward the River Meuse. They were mechanized and moving fast. It seemed they'd learned the lessons of the last war, even if the British and French hadn't.

The late afternoon sun was bathing the mountains as they arrived at the houses outside the village in Izieu. Maureen jumped out and walked around to the back of the truck.

"We're here!" she said to the exhausted faces inside.

Several children from the orphanage who'd come by train were outside as they arrived and greeted them with hugs as they jumped down into the dirt. Abigail and Martha ran out seconds later. Soon, all of the original 18 refugees from her father's factory in Berlin were helping the children with the luggage they'd brought. Everyone was there except Gerhard, who'd stayed in Lyon to meet some contacts. He was moving south too.

Rudi, Adam, and Abel ran into Maureen's arms, and she kissed each of them.

"Oh, I missed you," she said. "And I have so many new friends for you to meet."

The new arrivals, Christophe included, were looking around in wonder, just as she had the first time she'd seen the awe-inspiring beauty surrounding the houses.

"Welcome to Izieu," Maureen said to the crowd of newcomers. "This is a safe place. Somewhere for you to stay until the madness that's consuming the outside world ends. Treat this place as your home and respect our rules and you'll enjoy living here as much as we do. I'm sure you're tired and hungry. We have food for you and a warm bed."

Maureen took a young girl called Sandrine's hand and showed her the room in which she and four others would be staying.

"Thank you," she said.

"You're welcome to stay as long as you want."

"Until my parents come?"

Maureen smiled. "Of course."

Abigail and Martha prepared bread and cheese for the new arrivals, and a few minutes later, they shuffled inside to sit at the massive dining table. The other children they knew joined them at the table as they sat in nervous silence.

"They'll get used to it here," Maureen said to Antoinette, who was standing beside her in the doorway. "They all do."

By the time the meal ended, the newest children were laughing and talking and were ready to explore outside. Rudi took it upon himself to show them the playground out back and the fields that lay beyond it. Within minutes almost all of the new arrivals from Belgium were outside playing.

One of the boys on crutches who'd come on the train met her at the bottom of the stairs as she returned inside. "Rebecca still talks about her parents all the time," he said. "The rest of us stopped a long time ago. What's the point when they're all dead?"

"You don't know that," Maureen answered.

The boy didn't respond, just hobbled back toward the back door and the view of the mountains in the distance.

Christophe seemed in awe of the place, and Maureen found him shuffling around after the children had gone to bed with a smile on his face. "You've been living here for how long?"

"Over a year. It's not much, but we've done the best we could."

"It's incredible. A haven for the lost under the mountains. Thank you for bringing me here."

"What are your plans?" she asked. "How long do you intend to stay?"

"I hadn't thought about it yet. A night or two if I'm welcome?"

"As long as you want."

"What about you? Are you settling in here for the summer?"

Maureen shook her head. "No, I'm heading back to the front."

Christophe's mouth dropped open. "Wait, you can't be serious."

She pointed at the lorry parked outside the house. "We have an ambulance. And they need them on the front lines."

"We almost died picking up all these children and you want to go back?"

"I can't not," she said. "It's something I have to do." He looked at her in bewilderment. "Will you walk down to the river with me?"

"Of course," he replied.

She took his warm hand in hers and led him out the back door, past the swings and see-saws the men had built, and toward the river. Holding his hand felt right. They walked through fields and pushed open a gate that led to a dirt track. The river came into view as a broad swath of black on the horizon, and the sound of the water rushing and lapping at the sides was all they heard in the still of the night. The neighbors' farms, the road back into town, the old church, and the schoolhouse were all outlined in the ghostly white light of the moon.

"I spent one summer on the Rhône when I was a boy," Christophe said as they reached the river's edge. He picked up a stone and hurled it out. It broke the water's shimmering surface with a splash and then disappeared. "At a cabin in Switzerland. I swam in it every day. I don't think I've even touched it since." He got down on his haunches and pierced the surface of the water with his thumb and forefinger, rubbing them together as he stood up. "This is such a beautiful place. Why would you want to leave it for a warzone?"

"Because of Beatrice and all the others in Belgium. That little girl would have died if we weren't with her when the Stuka attacked. The only reason she had a chance is because we brought her back to the medical center. We have a truck. I know the roads now, and where to bring the wounded. I can't just stay here waiting for the Nazis to come. People need my help and I have the means to do so. Children are caught up in that horror."

"I understand the instinct to dive into whatever situation you see, but this war could balloon into something bigger than we've ever imagined. It'll touch everyone's lives. If you go around trying to help every child and lost soul you see, you'll...." He trailed off and stared out at the river.

"I'll what?"

"End up dead. And I don't want you to die, Maureen."

"How many ambulance drivers must there be in Belgium? Dozens? Hundreds? It's not like I'm trying to infiltrate the German lines or blow up their headquarters. I only want to help the wounded, and that's what I'm going to do."

"I could tell you how much you've already done by bringing the children here, couldn't I? But you've already made up your mind and nobody's going to change it back, are they?"

"I'm glad the time we've spent together hasn't been wasted. You're getting to know me now," she said.

He chuckled to himself but shook his head at the same time.

"What's next for the great Christophe Canet? Hobnobbing with millionaires on a yacht in St. Tropez?"

"No, I've exceeded my quota for hobnobbing already this month. It looks like I'll have to fill my time in some other way."

She smiled and knew it was time to ask the question. "It's your truck. Can I take it back to Belgium?"

"Yes, but on one condition."

She tilted her head a few degrees, unsure of what he would say. "What?"

He took a breath and spoke. "You take me with you."

"Are you sure?" she replied, incredulous.

"What choice do I have? I could stand here and argue with you for the next six months but you'd still go anyway. The only option I have to try to keep you from getting yourself killed is to tag along. And I was meant to have a meeting with a client in Marseilles next week."

"Maybe you should tend to your business. I can look after myself."

"But can you look after the truck? You've never driven one for more than a few miles at a time."

"You really want to come with me? Back to the front?" He nodded. "Okay," she said with a beaming grin. "Let's set out tomorrow morning. I'll talk to the ladies about looking after the new arrivals. They're well used to it by now. Although this is quite the amount of work I've landed them with."

"They have Antoinette to help them."

"One extra person and 24 new children."

He put his arm around her shoulders, and she reached up and took his hand, holding it against her. They stared out at the flowing waters for a few seconds.

"It's so peaceful," she whispered.

"Not where we're going."

"Sometimes I wish we could bring the leaders here and show them this. There's so much beauty in the world, and all they seem to want to do is destroy it."

"Hitler, Stalin and Mussolini? They'd be scoping out the riverbank for defensive positions, where they could place artillery and build bunkers. Conquest is in their blood. It's all that drives them. They have no regard for the people they claim to represent, just for glory for the nation—which means themselves. No, I don't think bringing them here or to that cabin my family rented in Switzerland when I was a child would make the slightest bit of difference. All they'd want to do was to plant their flag in the ground."

Maureen took him to a large flat rock she liked to sit on. She'd often wondered what sitting on it with a man would be like. She told him about her family, how they'd been poor before they moved to Berlin, and how their lives had changed. She spoke in detail, only stopping to answer his questions. She told him about her mother and how her father met her just after she immigrated to America from Ireland. She remained calm as she told him about her death and how her father had left them to find work afterward.

"Do you still think about her, even after 11 years?"

"Most days. I try to remember her so she's still in my life. I think that if you still love someone and keep them in your heart then a part of them lives on through you."

"I couldn't agree more."

"I'm sorry," she said at last. "I've been talking about myself for an hour. You must be bored out of your mind."

"Quite the opposite," he said. "I don't have anything like your family story. My mother and father are both still alive. I was born into money. My father worked hard, as my grandfather did before him, but the truth is I've never had to wonder where my next meal was coming from, not one day in my life."

"Until you came to Izieu. We're out of food!"

"Grass for breakfast, is it?" he said.

"We'll rustle something together. We get fresh eggs most mornings and we have the ingredients to bake bread." She paused for a few seconds to look at him. "Is that why you're doing all this, because you've grown tired of your life of privilege?"

"Who said I'd grown tired of it? There's a lot to be said for privilege, you know."

She laughed. "I do know. We lived in a mansion in Berlin. I remember what it's like."

"It is good, isn't it?"

"Oh, yes. Definitely."

"But it's not the most important thing," he said as their laughter died. "Maybe I just want to make my father proud."

They sat on the rock together, talking and watching the moonlight-tipped waters of the Rhône drift past. If Maureen could have stopped time, she might have. Midnight came, and she realized they were driving into a warzone again the next day, so she stood up, and they walked back to the houses.

"What do you think the other adults in the house will say when you tell them you're heading back?" Christophe asked.

"I don't think they'll be surprised at all," she replied.

The house was quiet but for the sound of a child crying. "I'd better go," Maureen said. "We always get some criers on the first night, but they get used to the place eventually." She kissed him again, lingering for several seconds before she left him in the darkness of the hallway outside his room.

13

Sunday, May 21, 2006

The Grand Canyon amazed them both. Amy was amazed that her grandmother still had the capacity to experience that much wonder after such a long life. She'd seen so many things but still expressed that she'd never witnessed anything like the majesty of those countless miles of red canyons that rolled into the horizon as far as their eyes could see. Amy hadn't been since she was a kid, and like everything else, experiencing it as an adult was something far different. Being there with her grandmother made it precious. Now they were back in the car, leaving the hotel and heading north to Utah. Surrounded by desert, they were the only car on a lonely stretch of road. Her grandmother had been talking for several hours, but the old woman's voice faltered. Amy glanced across and could see she was remembering. The voice recorder was running on the center console between them. She asked a question to begin the conversation again.

"So, did you go back to Belgium to drive the ambulance?"

"Yes. We both did."

"We drove out every morning, and more bodies were strewn on the roads and fields, some soldiers but mainly normal citizens, trying to flee the carnage."

"What happened to them?"

"It was the Stukas and the other bombers. They'd dive at anything that moved, and most of the time it was just a family pushing their belongings on a cart or a bus full of refugees. We found burned out vehicles every day that hadn't been there the day before. The worst was when they blocked the roads and we had to witness the carnage up close. We both wanted to stop and bury the bodies we saw every day, but that wasn't our job. It was up to us to find the wounded and bring them back. We forced ourselves onward, past the corpses that littered the roads."

"Were you able to help the people you found?"

"I'd done a couple of years in medical school, and I was able to stitch them up, and resuscitate some. I could tie a tourniquet to stop someone from bleeding to death on the side of the road."

"Like you did with Beatrice."

"Yes. But we couldn't help most of the people we found. There's not a lot to be done for someone who's taken a bullet in the chest or lost a limb. I tried to focus on helping children, but most of the time we had to pick up the first people we found and then slalom through the crowd back to the church. People bled to death in the ambulance, and we had to unload the bodies. I saw things no person ever should—people burned in vehicles, mutilated beyond recognition."

"But you kept going back."

"Yes. Day after day. We slept in the front seat of the ambulance, collapsed on top of one another. All pretensions were gone. I didn't bathe. My hair must have been like a rat's nest and Christophe's beard was thick with filth, but we didn't care. All that mattered was finding more people, and we were always able to, wherever we went. We must have taken hundreds back to the church with no idea of who lived or died."

"Did you bring any other children back to Izieu?"

"No. Christophe was right. We had to be practical with whom we could help. I began to think like the doctors and nurses after a few days. I didn't mourn the dead we brought in, just moved on. And I knew the ladies in Izieu were swamped with all the new arrivals. I did what I could."

"How long did you carry on?"

"After four weeks of driving in and out we were told the church was being evacuated. We were instructed to pick up anyone we could, civilians, soldiers, wounded or not. We picked up the last people on June 10—a group of exhausted British soldiers fleeing for their lives. The whole attack on Belgium was a diversion. The cream of the British and French forces was massed on the Belgian border and moved in when Germany attacked on May 10. It seemed the Nazis wanted to grab the channel ports to gain access to the open sea. Otherwise, they would have been bottled into the Baltic. But it was a ruse. The invasions drew the Allied forces into the low countries to leave the way free for the Blitzkrieg through the Ardennes in the south and over the River Meuse. The real attack encircled the British and French in Belgium. It was all about speed and surprise, and they caught the Allied forces with their pants down."

"How could that happen?"

"Just thinking about it makes me angry now," Maureen said. "The Allies were prepared for the grinding attrition of the first war, not wave after wave of German bombers. The French morale broke like a wishbone, and the legacy of World War I was complete."

"What about the Maginot Line, and everything said before the war began?" Amy asked.

"The Germans went around it, through the Ardennes Forest —something everyone said was impossible. It wasn't. Thinking about the incompetence of the French generals, and all the suffering their mistakes caused, makes my blood boil. It was all so preventable. I heard a report after the war of a French reconnaissance plane, sent to spy on the German troop movements. That pilot witnessed the mother of all traffic jams behind enemy lines as the cream of the Nazi tank divisions lined up behind one another on the one road into the Ardennes. They could have sent bombers and destroyed the German military in hours, but the French generals dismissed the report. An attack through the forest had already been deemed impossible so they ignored the information the pilot had given them. Hitler's tanks moved through unmolested."

"How could the French have been so idiotic?" Amy asked. Even she found herself getting angry at something that had happened 66 years before, 3,000 miles away.

"Arrogance? A refusal to accept reality or that they weren't living in the 1800s anymore? I don't know. It was a joke—one that cost many lives. The French commander-in-chief, General Gamelin, was holed up in the Château Vincenne outside Paris for the entire invasion. The man didn't have a telephone anywhere in the château, because he deemed it a security risk. By the time a message reached him about the Germans breaking through, it was already too late. And the Nazi tanks and soldiers rolled on day and night, never stopping."

"Day and night?"

"They had a secret weapon. Are you familiar with a drug called crystal meth?"

"Not intimately, I'm glad to say, but I've heard of it."

"A Berlin drug company produced it by the truckload and supplied it to all the troops. It was given out like candy. Drugs like that were commonplace in German society back then. They were legal and available over the counter as a well-known way to fight fatigue. I remember seeing it on the shelves among a slew of others we now know to be harmful."

"What effect did it have on the soldiers?"

"It dulled empathy and gave them the feeling of being superhuman. The morale of the Germans was quite low before they took the drugs, but it immediately went through the roof. For the first time in human history invading troops didn't have to stop overnight. They just kept rolling on through the French countryside."

"What about you, what did you do when it all collapsed?"

A strange look came over her grandmother's face as if the old woman had tasted something sour. "We stayed as long as possible, but when the Nazi forces swept through Lille, we knew it was time to leave. I had my three boys and the others in Izieu. Christophe wanted to return to his family in Marseille. Retreat is a miserable thing. We knew what was coming."

"You must have been proud of what you did, transporting all those wounded back to receive the attention they needed?"

"We weren't in the mood to pat each other on the back. The entire country was imploding. The smell of blood and death was still thick in my nostrils. We drove south, away from the fighting."

"Didn't you have to return the truck?"

Maureen laughed. "Christophe was past the point of caring by that stage. All he cared about was getting home and taking a shower. We reached Izieu the next day."

"Did Christophe stay?"

"Not long. He drove back to Marseilles with a promise that he'd come back again soon. As he was arriving home, Paris was declared an open city. The Germans entered without firing a bullet, otherwise the place would have been destroyed. Then the occupation of France began."

The story ended. Amy pressed stop on the tape recorder, and Maureen settled down to rest for the remainder of the journey.

Amy was in constant awe of her grandmother, but could sometimes almost see the energy fading from her like steam from wet clothes left in the sun. She wondered about the older woman's fortitude as the sign for Moab, Utah, came into view. The woman had been talking for most of the five hours it had taken to drive here. Asleep now, her eyelids looked like petals resting on her face. Amy felt invigorated by the story and had gone through three tapes already. Editing it down would be a job, but she couldn't wait to get started or, indeed, to hear the rest of what her grandmother had to say. She knew a little about the war from school or glancing up at the television screen when one of the countless documentaries about Hitler came on. But talking to her own grandmother, who'd seen and done so much, made it real. It was humbling to be in the presence of a war hero. Why hadn't her parents talked about Maureen's exploits during the war when she was growing up? And why had she never heard of Christophe?

Maureen began to stir and raised her head off the large pillows propped against the window as they pulled up outside the hotel in Moab. Amy took care of the bags. Ten minutes later, they were in the room.

They were both sitting on the bed, about to go downstairs for dinner when Amy suggested they get room service. Her grandmother was exhausted and agreed. Amy propped up pillows against the headboard, and Maureen lay back on them, letting out a gasp of what Amy hoped was relief.

"We've spoken about my past all day," the older woman said. "I want to hear about what you want, how you see the world."

"What I want right now is to write your story. It's one that deserves the be told."

"Mine's almost at an end."

"Don't say that."

"My body might be failing me but my mind is still good. No one lives forever. Death is as much a part of life as birth itself. Every star fades in time."

A pang of frustration at all the time they'd wasted stabbed at Amy's heart, but she didn't want to show it.

"Tell me, dear. What do you want?"

Amy took a few seconds. It was easy to dismiss questions like these as she'd done a few seconds before. Answering them required introspection and courage.

"I want to live a life that matters, and to love and receive the same in return."

"And how do you think you can achieve those goals?"

Her grandmother stared at her with earnest green eyes.

"I don't know," she replied.

"Yes, you do. Look inside yourself. The answers are in your heart."

"I'm still in love with Ryan Smith. I can't stop myself."

"I understand. Love isn't something we can turn on and off like a water faucet, but we can control our reactions to those who inspire those feelings, and then they'll fade in time."

"Ryan is like poison in my veins. I wish I could rid myself of him."

"Have you had other boyfriends in the past you regret?"

Amy laughed. "Only all of them; well, Jimmy Anderson was a sweet boy. We held hands for three weeks in middle school until I dumped him. Apart from him, they're all regrets."

"But at one time these other men, or boys, occupied you. They had you in their grasp."

"Some did."

"And you moved on. You'll leave Ryan Smith behind too. It just doesn't seem that way right now." Amy wanted to ask about Christophe but decided not to push her. "But the most important thing is not to let the hurt he inflicted on you guide your future. Don't let him scar your heart so that when the right man comes along—and he will come, believe me—you're not ready to welcome him."

"It's hard to see that," Amy said.

"It seems counter to every instinct, but you have to live with an open heart, ready to accept love, otherwise you'll deflect it like water off an umbrella."

Amy closed her eyes. She hadn't heard from Ryan since he left New York to visit his brother, but he was still resident in her mind. Squatting. "What about my career?" she asked.

"We're working on that every day, aren't we?"

Dinner arrived a few minutes later. It wasn't quite fine French cuisine, but her grandmother seemed more than happy with eating her chicken sandwich, even if she kept half for the next day. They talked about the road trip and all the places they'd already seen as they ate.

Being in the car for so long had taken its toll on Maureen, and she brushed her teeth and went to bed for the night straight after dinner. It was only nine, and Amy toyed with going out for a drink but decided against leaving her grandmother.

She was ready for an early night and about to settle into bed when her phone buzzed. Her heart leaped when she saw the name Ryan Smith come up.

I'm sorry I haven't texted. It's been full on here. My brother died last night, and my ex and the kids are flying out for the funeral in a few days. I hope you're doing okay. I know this must be a hard time for you too.

Amy gasped and looked over at her sleeping grandmother, remembering her words. But she had to respond. The man had just lost his brother, and maybe what people said wasn't true. He referred to his wife as his ex. She brought her fingers to the phone and began to type.

I'm so sorry. I'm glad you were with him.

The response came seconds later.

It's been awful. What about you? How are you doing?

I'm on a road trip with my grandmother. In Moab, Utah, of all places. She hit the send button and immediately questioned her decision, but it was too late.

Just six hours from Denver! We need to talk. Are you coming this way?

Amy threw down the phone. The desire to see the man she still loved fought with her instincts to stay away from him. For all she knew, he had an explanation for all this. Was her relationship with him not worth that chance? But then she remembered Sara and what Ryan had done to her. This was a pattern. She picked up the phone, unable to commit to either thought.

I don't know. I'll call you in a day or two. You should be with your family until then.

He didn't reply, and five minutes later, she settled back down, tortured now. It took almost two hours of tossing and turning to escape her thoughts and spiral into sleep.

The sound of screaming cut through the stillness of the hotel room, and Amy's eyes shot open, her heart thumping like a hammer in her chest. It was her grandmother. Amy turned on the light and leaped out of bed. The look of terror in the old woman's eyes was contagious. Amy ran to her grandmother and wrapped her arms around her frail frame, and Maureen's long gray hair draped over her forearms. Her grandmother was shaking and looking around as if she had no idea where she was.

"Where are we?"

"It's okay, Grandma. You're with me in the hotel room. You're safe here."

"Marie?" the older woman said.

"No, that was my mother. It's Amy, your granddaughter."

Something seemed to click in her grandmother's brain, and the fear subsided. Her breathing slowed, and she sat back against the pillows Amy propped up behind her. Amy didn't speak for a moment, letting the older woman find her bearings.

"Are you okay now?" she asked.

Maureen nodded, pushing ragged breaths out through pursed lips. It took her another minute or so to begin talking. Amy held her the entire time.

"It's been a while since I had those dreams. I thought I'd banished them, but they were just lying dormant in my subconscious. I was back in Belgium, driving that ambulance again, except I was alone and I came across a burning vehicle. Your mother and father were inside. I tried to reach them. I thrust my hands into the flames but they were too far inside. That's when I woke up, and I didn't know where I was. Did I call you Marie?" Amy nodded.

"I'm so sorry."

"No, don't say that. It's fine."

"What time is it?"

The digital clock beside the bed said it was 2:14.

"This is all my fault. I'm so sorry." She hugged her grandmother again and felt the tears forming in her eyes. "You don't have to talk about the past anymore, not if it's going to affect you like this."

"Can you get me some water?"

Amy raised herself off the bed and went to the mini-fridge. She returned with a bottle of cold water and opened it for her grandmother. "No more talk about the war," Amy said. "You've told me enough. I know what kind of a person you were and still are. You don't have anything to prove to anyone."

"Except myself, perhaps." She placed the bottle of water on the nightstand beside her bed. "One thing I've learned over the years is to never make decisions in the middle of the night. The mind plays tricks during witching hour."

"Are you all right now?"

"My heart is still thumping."

"Take some deep breaths to calm down."

Amy held her hand as her grandmother calmed once more. A few minutes passed before she turned off the light and sat on the side of the bed, watching her until she knew she was asleep. Amy let go of Maureen's hand, placed it back on the comforter, and returned to bed.

A great weight descended on her in the dark. This was all her fault for pushing her grandmother. Some secrets were best left buried. Sleep was long in coming, and she woke several times to check on Maureen, who was peaceful for the rest of the night.

Amy got up first the next morning. Her grandmother seemed normal and asked her to get a table for breakfast. After procuring a seat in the dining room for two, Amy sat alone, staring out at the garden until her grandmother arrived a few minutes later. She looked resplendent in her checked blazer and black skirt and showed no sign of the previous night's stress.

"Isn't this lovely," the older woman said as Amy held her chair for her. "I'm looking forward to seeing the red rocks today." She pulled out a pair of gold-rimmed reading glasses and squinted down at the menu. The waitress arrived a few seconds later, and they ordered.

Amy waited until they'd both handed the menus back to say what was on her mind.

"I'm so sorry again about last night."

"About what? You mean the dreams? Why on earth would you need to be sorry about that?"

"It was my fault for making you talk about the past, for bringing up what you'd buried."

"Nonsense," Maureen said. "It's no one's fault but Hitler's, and the enablers who let him unleash his madness. I've been living in fear of the past too long. It's part of who I am, and I intend to confront it head-on like I did with everything else my whole life."

"I don't think it's wise to talk about the war anymore. I'd never have started if I'd known—"

"If you'd known what, that there's still hurt inside even after all these years? What should we do then, just forget? Your parents are both dead and gone, should we disremember them, just go on as if they never existed because talking about them is too painful?"

"No, of course not."

"Do you still feel pain over the loss of your parents?"

"Every day."

"So did I for many years—the likes of which I hadn't felt since the war. Losing a husband is one thing, but a child is something no one should ever have to face, but we're still here, and talking about our grief is the only way to confront it. Otherwise, we shrivel up and die inside."

"It's not a good idea. I can find something else to write about."

"If I don't confront this now, then when? I've never been one to run from anything and I'm not going to my grave with this still hanging over me."

"Why didn't you tell anyone about your experiences in the war sooner? Why did you wait to tell me?"

"Perhaps I tried to hide from them, to shield the ones I love from what I experienced. I know to you, it must all seem so noble and brave, but living through it was horrific at times. I experienced so much joy too, but most of it was in the face of evil greater than I ever could have imagined."

"My life seems so insignificant compared to yours."

"Oh, no. All lives are valuable. Without you, I'd be lost. You were the rock we all relied on when your parents died. I was a coward. I couldn't face the sorrow, and stayed in France with my dogs and my flower garden. You were the one who faced the situation head on, who stayed and made a life for yourself."

"A life which fell apart."

"How many times do you think my life has fallen to pieces over the years? When your grandfather died, when your parents passed. And many times before that. Life isn't about calm. It's about how we handle the storm."

Their eggs benedict arrived. Amy didn't know how to answer what her grandmother had said, but she was glad to be sitting here with such a powerful woman.

"Do you still want to go out and look for where your father might have worked in Ohio?" Amy asked.

"No, what's the point? I only know he was in Akron, nothing more. Just being with you is enough."

"The reason I ask is I might want to visit Denver, maybe. That might affect our route."

"Oh, okay. I've never been there either."

"What was your father like back then?" Amy asked, eager to change the subject.

"He was a complicated, imperfect man, but he was a hero to hundreds. I wouldn't be the person I am today without him. I owe him everything."

"I hope someone will say the same about me someday."

"Oh, they will sweetheart, and much more besides."

They finished their food and went to the car. They spent the day at the magnificent Arches National Park and left the following morning, driving in the direction of Denver. Amy hadn't contacted Ryan since the night in Moab or told her grandmother yet. She wanted to make the decision to see Ryan or not alone.

They were on their way out of town when Amy asked her grandmother if she was ready to speak into the tape recorder again. She replied without hesitation, and they were back in 1940 once more.

14

Thursday, July 18, 1940

Maureen presented her new papers to the policeman on duty at the railway station in Lyon. His thick mustache moved back and forth like a massive caterpillar on his upper lip as he read them. He looked her up and down, and received a smile in response. She was dressed in a light summer dress, white with blue flowers and a belt to finish the ensemble, carrying a handbag and a newspaper. He handed the papers back and wished her well on her journey. She found a seat by the window and opened the newspaper to read the latest proclamation from the new government.

The new country set up after the invasion was officially called the French Free State, but from what Maureen could ascertain, the liberté made famous during the revolution had evaporated after the Nazi occupation. The government had adopted an alternative motto—Work, Family, Fatherland. It sounded like something she would have heard while attending school in Berlin, where portraits of Hitler stared down from the wall with beady eyes, and the teachers had to be members of the National Socialist-controlled union to do their jobs. The French government had collapsed when the Wehrmacht took Paris, and a new Prime Minister was appointed when Paul Reynaud refused to sign the armistice with the Germans. Marshall Pétain, a decorated general from the Great War, took over in his stead. It soon became apparent that he had no intention of doing anything other than lying down in the face of the Teutonic conquerors. Lines were drawn across France, dividing it into Occupied and Free Zones. The German army gained complete control of the north and west of the country. Paris was the capital of this new Occupied Zone, while the rest of France would be administered from the small city of Vichy, a place previously known for its spas.

The new Vichy government promised benevolence and loyalty to the Führer and made it clear who the actual power in France would be. Pétain and the other leaders, former heroes of the last war, were now seen as lackeys of the insidious Nazi overlords, who were already installing a new system. Freedoms fell away like autumn leaves. Papers were now required to move from one part of the country to another, and rationing would be brought in within a few months. Northern France was under Nazi control. It seemed only a matter of time until the rest of the country fell under the same spell.

Already, everywhere, everything felt changed. It didn't matter that the Nazi flag wasn't flying above the station or anywhere else in Lyon. It was clear who was in control here now. The French police seemed to take to their new role with little hesitation and checked citizens' papers thoroughly and without the slightest hesitation. She thought of her home country. Two weeks ago was the 4th of July—America's national day celebrating the freedom enshrined in its constitution. No one would be celebrating similar sentiments in France this year. The only ones rejoicing were the Nazis. The invasion of France had been Germany's greatest military triumph ever. Hitler was being acclaimed as the most brilliant strategic mind in history. It seemed he could make the impossible possible.

Laying down the newspaper, she stared out at the countryside and, for a short while, forgot about everything that had dominated her, and everyone else's, thoughts these last few weeks. Tiredness descended on her, and she fell into a deep sleep.

Awakened by the slowing of the train, Maureen glanced up to see the man standing waiting for her on the platform.

Christophe was dressed in a pristine white shirt with gray slacks and holding a beautiful flower bouquet. A bright smile lit his face. Trying to remain calm, she reached for the bag she'd stowed above her head and joined the line to alight from the train. He was at the door as she stepped onto the platform, and he pushed the flowers toward her.

"How did you know what door I'd be getting out?"

"Just lucky, I suppose."

"Why do I feel like that's the answer to most questions I could ask you?"

"I have no idea where one could garner that impression."

She took the flowers and kissed him on each cheek. He took her suitcase, and they walked out together. It was the first time they'd seen one another since the government collapsed.

It was a bright, sunny day, and the heat struck her like wave as she walked outside. Christophe had put back on some of the weight he'd lost when they'd driven the ambulance together. She hoped she had too. He put her bag in the back of his car and held the door open as she climbed in. The windows down, he started the engine.

"Did I tell you how beautiful you look?" he said as he pulled out.

"Even better than when we were driving those roads in Belgium?"

"Of course, but you were beautiful then too. I hope I look better now. I don't think I've stopped eating since I got home."

"Better get your fill while you still can," she answered. "Rationing's coming soon."

"Don't remind me."

"What's it been like here since the armistice?"

"In Marseilles? I arrived back from Izieu just in time for the bombs from the Italian planes to drop. I heard the explosions and saw the damage the next morning, but I wasn't in any of the damaged areas. Many others weren't so lucky. What about you? Have you seen any changes in Izieu?"

"Nothing. We'll be the last place they get to—I hope. Any German presence here?"

"Not officially, but you'd have to be blind not to notice the sudden influx of square-jawed, blue-eyed pale men flooding the city. If they're not Gestapo I don't know who is. Most of them don't even bother trying to speak French. They shout in German across hotel lobbies and bars to each other as if no one would ever notice."

"Seems like the arrogance of people who think they can't lose."

"And why shouldn't they think like that? They conquered the biggest army in the world, scurried around the Maginot line and cut off hundreds of thousands of Allied troops."

"But let them escape."

"For now. I'm sure you've heard the name for the bombing campaign on England."

"The Blitz," she said.

"Yes. Maybe they're so arrogant as to assume they'd destroy the British Army on their own soil. We can only hope they're wrong."

He pulled over and parked on the side of the road.

"I've missed you," he said and cupped her cheek.

"Me too," she said and reached over to kiss him. She put her hands on his face, reveling in the feeling of his lips against hers. It was hard to know how long they lingered, but when he finally pulled away, it seemed too soon. He got out and held the car door for her.

Maureen looked around. Marseilles was a place to fall for in seconds. The Old Port stretched out in front of them. Hundreds of yachts bobbed on the azure surface of the sea. Luxurious villas gazed down from the peaks and hills surrounding the ancient city. It was thick with cafés and bistros, fishing boats, and casinos. Fishmongers carrying their wares to market brushed past tanned sophisticates on their way to lunch in cafés overlooking the Mediterranean. City parks brimming with colorful flowers were found every few blocks, and the ancient streets were fresh with the smell of sea air.

Christophe took her by the hand and led her to a place he knew of by the harbor. He ordered mimosas, and they sat on the sidewalk, beholding the beauty of the bay.

"How are the children settling in?" he asked.

"Well, for the most part. We've had a few who struggled but that's always the way."

"I can't imagine how hard it must be for them to be apart from their parents at such a young age."

"I know. I'm amazed at their fortitude, although some are a little more delicate than what we're used to. The journey to Izieu took a lot out of them. We've had more visits from Doctor Mitte in the last two weeks than the previous year. I think the old man's getting sick of the sight of us."

"What about Gerhard? I thought he'd be with you. Isn't he coming to our rendezvous?"

"I told him to come down tomorrow to give us some time together."

Christophe beamed at the news. "That's my girl. I was planning to introduce you to my family tonight."

Maureen was taken aback, but took a gulp of mimosa

instead of verbalizing her first thoughts. "That would be love-ly," she said, putting the glass back down.

If Christophe realized she wasn't entirely comfortable at the prospect of meeting his family, he didn't let on.

The waiter arrived, and they ordered fish so fresh it melted in her mouth. Christophe ordered a bottle of wine from a vine-yard not more than an hour away, and they sat in the shade, luxuriating in each other's company. He reached his hand across the table and took hers. Maintaining self-control in the face of such an intoxicant as Christophe was a challenge.

She'd been in love before, but he was different. Despite her efforts not to do so, she'd thought about him every day since last they'd met. Heaven only knew how much she'd muse over him if she let her thoughts and desires run free. Soon their conversation turned to business once again.

"Things are getting worse by the day for the Jews especially. Those still left hiding out in Germany and Austria are cut off and getting exit visas is close to impossible for them now. Their only realistic hope is to escape over the border or through Switzerland and then to get as far away from the Nazis as possi-ble," Christophe said.

"Have you anything to tell me I don't already know?"

"My proposal is that we set up a series of safehouses all the way from the border to Marseille and even to the Pyrenees— places of refuge from the Nazis for escaping Jews, political dissidents, and eventually the inevitable French, British, and maybe even American servicemen. It's time we started to prepare for the inevitable. I got the idea when I saw what you're doing in Izieu. You've taken in refugees coming across the border before for a night or two?"

"Yes. Several times."

"And where did you send them when they left?"

"Into Lyon, or on toward the Marseille."

Christophe smiled. "A place I know well."

"And you'd like to use my houses?"

"Only as a port of call. The people passing through would be completely separate from the children living there."

"Wouldn't that invite extra attention to our secret place?"

"No more than to any of our other secret locations. If any of the houses are rumbled, we're all in trouble."

She took a few seconds to digest his words before continuing. "The great debate in Izieu is whether we should get the children out of France while we still can. But even Gerhard thinks staying put is less of a danger for the children, because the travelling will be so hard over the mountains. Many of the little ones are weak and injured."

"Have you heard anything about visas?"

"If I never heard that word "visa" again it'd be too soon. Those stupid stamps on paper are life and death these days. Abigail and some of the others won't flee without them. They think the houses are so out of the way that the Nazis will never find them."

"And what do you think?"

Maureen took a few seconds to answer, savoring the view before speaking. "I don't know, but how can we hide so many for so long? The village school is overflowing with children who speak German to each other. Wouldn't it be better to be in Spain or Switzerland than in the hands of the Nazis?"

"I can see both sides," Christophe said, offering her a cigarette. She declined, so he lit up his own. "Hitler has some heinous obsession with Jews, but what will he do about it? They've lost their rights as citizens in Germany, and I read about the ghettoes set up in Poland, but will the Nazis come hunting every Jew in France? Outside the Occupied Zone?"

"I don't have answers to your questions, Christophe... but I don't trust the Nazis. If they've proven one thing over all these years, it's that their intentions are always worse than you could ever imagine. All I know is, I care about those people in Izieu," she said. Her emotions were bubbling up inside her. "I care about my boys."

"Rudi, Adam, and Abel. Yours?"

"Yes. They're my responsibility now," she said. "I can't risk their lives by keeping them in France."

"So once we set up this network...."

"I'm not sure I can wait that long. I'm starting to think I should get them out sooner rather than later."

"Where would you take them?"

"Switzerland is the closest place, but if we could get them into Spain somehow, and then onto Britain or even America, I'd feel truly at ease."

"England? The Nazis are preparing to invade."

"They won't make it across the channel. And I'll take them to America if they do. Once we get to Spain we'll have several options."

"When?" he asked. His voice was stripped of the joy that had swelled it just minutes before.

"Soon."

"Who would look after them in those foreign places?"

"I would have to." She let go of his hand and slumped back in the chair. She stared out at the undulating surface of the sea, rippling with gold. She steeled herself, trying not to cry.

"Maureen, have you thought this through? Perhaps they are better off where they are. It's difficult...."

"Difficult isn't impossible," she said.

"Don't pretend you're the only one who cares about your boys!" he said with a fire she hadn't seen in him before. She liked it. He needed to get angry. He dropped his voice again. "I understand what they mean to you. I just think they're in the best place they could be—with you in Izieu. Leaving isn't always the answer."

"I was in Berlin for almost four years. I've seen what the Nazis are capable of firsthand. You think Hitler's hatred for the

Jews is going to cool off now that he's taken France? He's already started persecuting them in Poland. It's only a matter of time before it starts here too."

"Appreciate what you have and what you've done," he said. "It's a miracle those other children made it down to Izieu in the first place."

"Perhaps it was only the first in a string of miracles they're going to need."

Christophe shook his head. He finished his glass of wine. "Let's not fight, we're on the same side. Let's just appreciate today's miracle—you and I together in Marseilles."

"I came here to see you, Christophe. I thought about you every day since you left," she said. "And I thought about you. But now, I'll show you my beautiful city."

He threw down enough money to cover their meals and drinks with a generous tip.

"Are you Catholic?" he asked.

"My mother was Irish, what do you think?"

Her comment brought the smile back to his face. She walked up and took his hand in hers. He looked down at her, and she wrapped her arms around him.

The reason for his question became apparent a few minutes later when the massive Notre Dame de la Garde Basilica came into view. Set on a hill overlooking the city, its white limestone walls shone in the afternoon sun.

"I didn't think any building could top what I saw in Paris," she said. "But this is something special."

Christophe brought her back into the city, and they walked the narrow streets together, peering in at luxuries in the windows most could never afford if they lived ten lifetimes. Maureen kept a hold of his hand as they walked.

Evening came, and he brought her to his parents' house, a tasteful villa a few minutes outside the city center. His father shook her hand at the door. He was in his early sixties with a thick white mustache.

"So, this is the girl I've been hearing so much about," he said with a wide grin.

"Woman," came the voice of his wife behind her. She was petite with the same dark eyes Christophe had. She invited Maureen through the marble foyer into the living room, where glasses of exquisite 1930 Château Cheval Blanc awaited them. They sat on the balcony overlooking the city and the harbor. The blue of the Mediterranean stretched out to the horizon. Christophe's brother and sister arrived soon after, and the six of them soon sat down to dinner.

Christophe smiled at her and forked some fresh mackerel into his mouth. His father made a toast to their guest, and they all clinked glasses. They spent the rest of the evening regaling her with stories about Christophe as a boy.

"So, you wore dresses?" Maureen asked.

"I found my sister's," Christophe replied. "It's been a few years since I've worn one—about 25. I was three."

"What about my makeup?" his mother asked. "I caught you in that more than a few times." They all laughed.

Maureen looked over at Christophe as he shook his head with a smile. Something was blossoming inside her. Something dangerous. She took a sip of wine and poured herself another glass. The scene around her seemed to be moving in slow motion. Christophe threw embarrassing stories back at his siblings, but he was outnumbered, and his were far worse. The boys in Izieu appeared in her mind, and suddenly she was back there, planting carrots, potatoes, and green beans. The rich tapestries on the wall stood in stark contrast to the cracked walls of the houses she was used to, but as much as she was falling for Christophe, she couldn't fall into this life. Not now.

After dinner, Christophe's siblings made their excuses to leave and shook Maureen's hand. Both were married. She

wondered how many other women their brother had brought
home to meet them.

Madame Canet showed Maureen the spare room before she
and her husband departed to bed.

"Join me for one last glass of wine before bed?" Christophe
said from the end of the hallway.

"Of course," she replied and followed him.

He led her back to the balcony. The city was a dark mass
below them, illuminated by golden spots of light with the black
carpet of the sea beyond. He handed her a glass of red, and
they went to the rail at the edge.

"What did you think of my family?"

"They were wonderful."

"I wish I could meet yours."

"They're all in New York now."

"Have you heard from them lately?"

"I get a letter most weeks," she said.

The intoxication that this view and this man should have
engendered within her was missing. Her head was spinning a
little, but only from the wine. Christophe was standing within
touching distance from her, handsome, warm, and noble. She'd
already been through more with him than some people experience in a lifetime, so why couldn't she surrender to the feelings
coursing through her? Why was it always necessary to build a
fortress around her heart?

"What's the matter, Maureen? Was bringing you to meet my
family too much? Is it too early?"

"I don't know," she said, staring at the Mediterranean. "Perhaps you're leading me to a place I can't follow. I have so many
other responsibilities, Christophe."

"I know who you are, that's why I love you."

It took her five long seconds to answer him. The words hit
her like a fist. It wasn't how she'd expected this to go. She
wanted to say the same back to him. She felt it. But all she

could see were the dead bodies in Belgium and the boys in Izieu.

"I wish I could stay, I'm so torn between taking the children and staying here with you, and to help with the network of safe houses. But if something happened to my boys because of something I chose.... I could never live with myself."

He stood staring out at the sea. "I had no idea you were planning on leaving the country until today."

"Only to protect the boys. I'm not running away from the war."

"I was with you in Belgium; I'm under no illusion as to who you are."

"You were right beside me the whole time. I couldn't have done any of it without you."

"We make quite the team, don't we?" he said with a smile and a shake of the head. He hadn't looked at her in a minute or more. "Do you want to stay as a team, Maureen?"

She wanted to reach out and grab him, to wrap her arms around him, but she didn't. "It seems we might have different paths, Christophe. You and Gerhard, and the rest of the resistance. Me with my boys in Spain or England."

"So, this changes my plans a little," he said.

"Your plans?"

"Yes, I was going to ask you to marry me."

Maureen felt a flaming dagger in her heart, like she was the worst person in the world.

"Oh, Christophe, I'm so sorry. With our divergent paths.... I do wish it was different."

"No, it's okay," he said, struggling to look at her. "Not to kiss you now seems like a waste of this view," he said. "But maybe you don't want me to if you're leaving me."

"I'm sure you'll find plenty of girls to bring back here to meet your parents and take in this view," she said and immediately regretted it.

"No," he answered and looked at her with a wry smile. "You're the first since Sophie, my fiancé. I wouldn't bring just anyone to meet my parents, Maureen."

"Perhaps it's best if I get to bed now," she said. Like everything else, it wasn't what she wanted, but she knew it was what she had to do.

"I'm going to stay here a while and enjoy all this," Christophe said, gesturing toward the city below.

"I'm so sorry, Christophe."

"So am I, Maureen. So am I."

Walking to the spare room, she managed to shut the door behind her before the tears she'd been holding flooded down her cheeks. She cursed the Nazis and the war they'd begun, pounding the pillow in frustration. She half-expected a knock on the door and had no idea how she would have reacted if it had come, but it didn't, and she fell asleep curled up in a ball, shaking as she sobbed.

Maureen woke at the sound of the knock on her door. After a couple of seconds of grappling with where she was, she responded to Christophe's call. She washed up and put on a different dress from her suitcase, then joined them for breakfast on the balcony. It was hot already, and sunlight shimmered on the turquoise surface of the sea, flecking it with gold. Christophe did an admirable job at the meal with his parents, somehow remaining jovial and friendly. It was more than she would have been if the roles were reversed. Maureen made an excuse soon after they finished.

"I'll give you a ride into the city," Christophe said.

"No, It's fine. I can walk," Maureen answered. Her heart was breaking being around him.

"Not at all, it's way too far," Monsieur Canet said.

"It's decided," Christophe said.

Christophe carried her bag to his car and loaded it in the back. He started the engine and drove toward the city.

"I wanted to talk about last night—"

"I've had some time to think since we spoke," he replied. "You're right about everything. You need to tend to your responsibilities and get those little boys to safety. Nothing else matters."

"I think—"

He interrupted her again. "This isn't your country, but it's mine. So, you're right, I can't come with you. I don't have an option but to fight for it."

"I'm grateful for that. You are very important here."

"And you're going to get yourself killed. I know you now. You're too reckless. You don't care about your own safety, only that of others. You need to leave before the Nazis invade the rest of France, because one day you'll make one mistake too many. Even cats only have nine lives. So, go, Maureen. Get your boys out and take them to America."

He kept his eyes on the road. She had never seen him like this. The warmth had vanished, but she understood why. The car came to a halt in the middle of the city.

"Is this okay?" he said. "You can walk down to the harbor again, or window shop. I know a park around the corner."

"Thank you, this is fine. I'll see you at the meeting with Gerhard later. We can plot together again."

"It's what we do best," he replied and drove off.

15

Friday, July 19, 1940

Maureen felt the sting of sunburn on her face as she entered the hotel Christophe had chosen as the rendezvous. He was already sitting in the lobby, staring into his drink.

"You look like someone who's been walking the city all day," he said with much of the charm he usually exhibited. It was clear that whatever they'd had was over now, but she was grateful he was still warm. She'd run through the sad conversation she'd had with him the night before a hundred times in her head as she strolled the streets of Marseilles that day. It was easy to see all the reasons she should give her own happiness a chance and say yes to him, but the facts remained, and she couldn't escape them.

"I enjoyed it," she said. "Being a tourist for the day helps you forget your troubles." It was hard to tell if he believed her lie or not.

"Take a seat," he said. "I have a room upstairs for us once

the others arrive. You never know who's listening in Marseilles these days."

Two square-jawed, blue-eyed Aryans were sitting across the lobby drinking beer, not paying any apparent attention.

Maureen excused herself to visit the bathroom.

Gerhard was at the table with Christophe when she arrived back, along with two other men she'd never seen before. All stood to greet her. Before she had a chance to sit, Christophe directed her toward the elevator and brought the group upstairs. They were in the hotel room he'd hired when he introduced her to the men.

"This is the person I trust most in all of France," Christophe said. "I'd like to introduce you to some friends." She turned to face the others. "This is Arnaud Brunner of the Swiss Red Cross."

"Who told Christophe about the children in Belgium," she said and shook the man's hand. He was in his mid-forties with gray hair and a beard to match.

"And this is Jean Villiers."

The balcony, with a view of the harbor, was open. Jean closed the sliding door leading to it and gathered some chairs together inside. They sat in a small circle. Christophe reached for a bottle of wine on the counter, and soon they all had glasses in their hands.

"To continue what Christophe just said, I'm a member of the new resistance—the *Maquis*, based in Lyon. We're planning a network of safe houses all the way to the Spanish border, and we were hoping we could use your place in Izieu as one of them," Jean said.

"Christophe mentioned this to me yesterday. At the moment, it's almost entirely for Jewish children being hidden from the Germans. Who do you expect to come?" Maureen answered.

"Allied servicemen, escaped soldiers who want to get back

to England to fight," Arnaud said. "I'll have plenty of suitable candidates. Airmen from Poland, political refugees from Germany and Austria. The list goes on."

"From what I hear, your houses are rural, safe, and equipped for visitors," Jean said.

"Am I being railroaded here?" she said. "I need safe passage for the children first, before we start taking in soldiers."

"You're overreacting," Gerhard said. "No one's trying to take over the houses, just to use the spare rooms from time to time. Most of all we need you, though."

"Will you help me get my boys out first?" she asked.

"And you too?" Christophe said.

"Most likely."

"In time," Jean answered.

"Your location is ideal, and it'll only be a few adults at a time. We can get them from the Swiss border to you. There's a not a whole lot between you and Switzerland. A few towns. Some ski resorts."

"You might think the security presence there is minimal as it isn't in the occupied zone," Gerhard said. "But we'll need to be careful. The Germans are still patrolling the border, and the French police aren't much friendlier. They'll arrest anyone they find crossing illegally."

"We were also thinking about the port here in Marseilles," said Jean, looking at Christophe, who shook his head.

"It's a bureaucratic nightmare since the armistice," Christophe said. "My father is at his wits' end. The city is flooding with refugees, but to get a residence permit you have to prove you don't intend to stay, and to get an exit visa you need a foreign entry pass—into France." He counted the steps on his fingers. "They also need a foreign entry pass for whatever country they're sailing to and a steamer ticket. Juggling them all is like trying to keep fifteen plates spinning at once, and if one comes crashing down the ship leaves without you.

I've seen it happen more often than not. France has become a prison for these people."

"Have you considered smuggling people out?" Jean asked.

"The police are at the harbor all the time. My father's ships are checked by the police. Every container, everything. Getting anyone out by sea without papers is impossible. For now, at least," Christophe answered.

"So, we're looking at crossing into France from Switzerland and then out through Spain illegally as our best option," Arnaud said. "For that we'll need safe houses, an ability to manufacture and distribute false papers, money."

"Everything takes money," Christophe said.

"And guides to bring our people over the Pyrenees into Spain," Arnaud finished. "Once they're in the Basque Country, or Galicia, they can wait for visas or travel to Lisbon or Gibraltar and take their chances there. Better stuck in Spain, Portugal or Morocco than in the hands of the Nazis."

"How close are we to getting the network of safe houses set up?"

"Hard to say," Jean said. "But we're aiming to begin moving Allied soldiers trapped here in Marseilles in a few weeks."

Maureen felt her acceptance was being taken for granted.

"Let me know whatever I can do," she said. "And anyone coming across will find safe haven in Izieu. But my children need safe passage before this happens," Maureen repeated. "Otherwise by agreeing to this I'm putting them in danger. German agents and the French police will be looking for these servicemen, in a way they might not as yet be hunting down Jewish children. Arnaud, could we bring them into Switzerland?"

"The children?" Arnaud shook his head and let his eyes fall shut for a moment. "The official position of the Swiss Red Cross is that the borders are closed. The country's not equipped to deal with the flood of refugees entering every day. Evacuating children or any other refugees from France into Switzerland would put all our operations at risk. We'd be openly defying the Vichy government."

"And the Nazis. Don't forget about them," Maureen added with more than a little vitriol in her voice.

"Like it or not, they're the most powerful force in Europe today. If the Red Cross is to do even the slightest bit of good, we have to play within the framework they give us. Otherwise, we could be branded an illegal organization, and risk being shut down or even being used as an excuse to invade. We can't risk offending the Nazi regime."

"You can't.... what? This is a bad joke. It must be," Maureen said.

"We can't oppose the legal actions of sovereign nations."

Maureen jumped to her feet, hands in fists by her sides, flushed with fury.

Gerhard stood up and took her arm. "I know how it sounds," he said. "But think about what would happen if the Swiss Red Cross started acting illegally. They'd never gain access to another concentration camp or warzone again. The Nazis would outlaw them and they would cease to exist."

Arnaud also stood up and faced her. "That's the official position of the Swiss Red Cross, not mine. I'm here to help, not to throw up barriers. I appreciate what could happen here. It might not be long before Jews, and other so-called "undesirables" are treated the same here as in Germany or Poland."

She took a deep breath. "Can we move children into Switzerland illegally, if not officially? Sneak them across and then the authorities will feel they have to protect them?" she asked.

"That's going to be as difficult as crossing any mountainous border," Jean said. "Word is the Swiss police have doubled their patrols."

"But at least they'd be going somewhere the government doesn't fawn to Hitler!" she said.

"But where do we house them once they arrive? At least they have beds and a roof over their heads here. Dumping them in Switzerland and hoping for the best isn't a strategy—even if they do make it across."

"Couldn't you arrange somewhere for them to stay? What about in a refugee camp?"

"Not officially, and there's no other way to do it."

"So, you're saying if I brought two dozen Jewish children into Switzerland, smuggled them in, the government would deport them back to France or even Germany?"

"I don't know," Arnaud said.

"That's knowledge I need!" Maureen said. "These are children we're talking about."

"I won't sit here and be accused of playing with people's lives by you or anyone else," the Swiss man growled. "I'm here to help. But we need to respect the rules of the Red Cross as much as we can."

Maureen went to the window and stared out for a few seconds. The men murmured among themselves for a few seconds, agreeing about something. She found it hard to believe the Swiss authorities would send children back to Germany. That would be tantamount to locking them up in concentration camps themselves. But what about sending them back to France? The Swiss Red Cross had already recognized the legitimacy of the Vichy government. Their intentions in doing so were sincere. If they didn't, the puppet government wouldn't allow them into the country, and thousands would suffer even more. Would their ties to Vichy force their hands to deport children back to France? Perhaps the Swiss Red Cross official had a point. She rejoined the four men. She wasn't about to give up.

"The problem with Switzerland is your options once you

arrive," Christophe said. "Spain is harder to reach but once you're over the Pyrenees the world opens up. You can travel to Barcelona, or Gibraltar or Lisbon and get a steamer to England, Palestine or even America."

"That's why we'll send the servicemen there," Jean said.

"So, we're to take in people from Switzerland, not the other way around?" Maureen said.

"Yes, but we'll move the refugees on as fast as we can. The best way to do that would be through the safehouses, starting with yours, all the way to the Pyrenees," Arnaud said. "Perhaps your children could go the same way."

Maureen took a deep breath and sat down. "You talk about crossing those mountains into Spain as if it's a jaunt in the park on a Sunday afternoon. Many of the children from the orphanage in Belgium are sickly and weak ...."

"I'm fully aware of the difficulties," Arnaud said. "But in that case Switzerland won't be any easier."

"I've spoken to some locals already, men who grew up in the Pyrenees, and know those mountains," Jean added. "None said it would be easy, but it's certainly possible."

"Won't the Spanish just deport the children back to France like the Swiss?" Maureen asked. "I'm struggling to see the difference, bar the even more arduous journey into Spain."

"The Spanish authorities haven't cracked down on refugees as much yet," Jean said.

"How do we know the Spanish won't get invaded by the Nazis in time also?" Christophe asked. "No point in sending them into exile there, if the Wehrmacht is right behind them."

"I don't see that as a possibility. Spain is officially neutral even if Hitler and Franco are politically aligned. The Germans won't upset that apple cart, and even if they wanted to invade, they'd be stretching themselves thin," Gerhard answered.

"So how do we transport people to the Pyrenees?" Maureen asked.

Jean said. "Don't you have a truck? And cars?"

Christophe said. "But what about when rationing comes in? Petrol will become as rare as hen's teeth."

"Get yourself a coal-powered vehicle. They're common enough in the area, and you won't have any problems finding the fuel to run them," Jean said.

"I'm in the process of setting up a new printing operation in Lyon," Gerhard said. "But we're moving on from pamphlets and focusing on identification papers. We're still trying to get the formula right, but I think we'll be able to start churning them out in the next few weeks."

"Where is all the money to come from?" Maureen said.

Christophe held up his hand. "I have some. Not enough to sustain the operation indefinitely, but to get us off the ground. I've also been in touch with a friend of mine in London. He's putting a good word in for us with the War Office. I think they'll start supporting us in time, with both materials and cash."

Maureen looked at the other men in the room and felt a stab of excitement despite her anxiety for her boys. This seemed like the beginning of something important.

Jean took out a map of southern France and spread it over a table by the window. Maureen and the other men watched him point to the towns, villages, and tiny hamlets where the safe houses would be located.

"We need someone reliable to run this network," Jean said. "Maureen, are you willing?"

"I would but I won't be here much longer. I have to get the young boys in my care out of France, and then I'll probably have to stay with them, wherever we end up," she answered.

"I only found out yesterday," Christophe told Gerhard.

"I was afraid this might happen," Gerhard added.

"The children have no one but me. France is becoming too dangerous for them and I can't send them over the mountains into Spain alone."

The French resistance fighter seemed annoyed, but then his face cleared. "How about testing out the route into Spain?" he said. "You and those kids could be the first ones across once the passage is ready."

Maureen wasn't sure she liked the idea of using her boys as guinea pigs. "I don't know...the boys are young. They're 8,5 and 3."

Jean looked shocked. "Then it's not a suitable route at all. Children that young would need to be carried across the mountains. You can't do that alone, and no guide would agree to that."

"So, the young and the sick children —they're stuck in France?"

"They have a secure home in Izieu," said Gerhard. "The locals have proven we can trust them. It doesn't seem the Nazis will find the houses."

"Tell yourself that all you want. But I know you don't believe it," she answered.

"I'm not giving up on getting the boys out."

"You're not the type to quit just because someone tells you something can't be done," Gerhard smiled.

"People can be wrong," she said.

They went over the map of France again. The occupied zone reached along the border with Germany and Switzerland, down to where Geneva jutted out. The city was surrounded by Wehrmacht. Anyone trying to enter Vichy France would have to do so from the south through the mountains and forests. It was a sobering thought.

"Maureen, you can expect the first refugees at the houses in the next few weeks," Jean said. "Will you still be in the country?"

"I don't know," she said.

"We'd rather you stayed where you are, with the children," the resistance fighter said, folding up the map. "We need all the trustworthy people we can get."

The meeting over, the others began filtering out of the hotel room. Christophe waited until the others were gone to approach her. "Can I still come up to the house to see the kids? Not many people are considering upgrading their art collections at the moment."

"Of course," she said. "I could let you know when I won't be in Izieu if you wanted to come then."

"Is that what you want?" he said.

"No," she said. She didn't want to hurt him, though it was obvious that was what she'd done. "I just thought.... You know what? Never mind what I thought. It's important we can still work together while I'm in France."

"I agree."

"And the kids would love to see you. Come whenever you like, and we can have a glass of wine together."

"I'd like that," he said, and walked out the door.

Maureen arrived back in Izieu the next afternoon, more confused than ever about what to do. Perhaps the others were right, and the boys would be safer here until the war ended. For all anyone knew, the Allies would sweep down from England in the next few months and, with the elusive support of the Americans, would vanquish the Nazi invaders...She couldn't even hold that ridiculousness in her mind for five seconds. The British were a shambles, and the public in the States had no interest in joining what they saw as a European war that was nothing to do with them. Little realistic hope existed of ridding the continent of Hitler's scourge.

Adam and Abel were playing in front of the house as she

pulled up. They ran to the car, bashing on the door until she got out. She picked up three-year-old Abel in her arms and kissed him on the cheek. He wrapped his arms around her neck as his five-year-old brother did the same with her legs.

"We missed you," Adam said.

"Don't leave again," his brother said in her ear.

She didn't answer, just carried him inside while holding Adam's hand. Marseille was beautiful, but it was better to be home.

Rudi was out back playing with some of the other kids. His love was less forthcoming than his younger brothers, and he waved at her before throwing the soccer ball in his hands to one of the Nusbaum boys. Abel didn't make putting him down easy, and she had to unfurl his arms from around her neck. She kissed him again before sending him back to play with his brother and some other kids their age from the Belgian orphanage. Amelie, one of the girls from Belgium, was in the dining room with another boy called Stefan. They both greeted her as they would a teacher, with respectful nods.

Abigail and her husband, Herschel, were in the kitchen starting dinner with Hans Ohlmann.

"How was the trip to Marseilles?" Hans asked.

"Confusing," Maureen replied. She told them about the conundrum of getting the children to a safer country.

"It seems clear to me the best option is to stay put," Abigail said. "Without visas we've nowhere to go safely. You could go to Spain, and then England, or back to America. We'd be fine here."

"I'm sorry, Maureen," Hans said. "But none of us agrees with you. We can't get into Switzerland, or America, or almost anywhere else we'd ever dream of moving to. This seems like the safest place."

"No one's coming," Abigail said. "Not for a long time. If ever. We're comfortable here. This is our home."

"I respect your decision, even if I disagree with it," Maureen said. She was torn, but still leaning toward taking no chances.

Abigail put her hand on Maureen's shoulder. "We're all so grateful for what you've done for us."

"What you still do," Herschel said.

Their gratitude came only as a sprinkling of cool water on the flames inside her. "I'm getting the Bautner boys out as soon as I can. I'll stay in Spain with them for the entire duration of the war if I need to."

Abigail started rummaging around and came up with an envelope. "This came for you while you were in Marseilles," she said and handed it to Maureen.

With nothing else to say, she took the letter and brought it to the dining room. It was hard to find somewhere private when the house was this full. Still, it was nothing compared to what it'd been like when they first moved here when over a hundred packed the place. Without the energy to retreat to her room, she opened it then and there in front of Amelie and Stefan. It was from her father in New York, and her heart skipped a beat as she unfolded the paper.

MAUREEN,

I HOPE THIS LETTER FINDS YOU WELL. WE'RE ENJOYING LIFE IN OUR NEW HOUSE. BROOKLYN IS AN INTERESTING PLACE I'D NEVER PAID MUCH ATTENTION TO UNTIL WE FOUND A HOME HERE. LISA IS STILL A LITTLE PARANOID OVER HER GERMAN ACCENT, AND TRUTH BE TOLD, SHE SOMETIMES SUFFERS BECAUSE OF IT. BUT ONLY ON RARE OCCASIONS. MOST PEOPLE SEE HER AS THE GOOD PERSON WE KNOW HER TO BE. YOUR SIBLINGS ARE ALL WELL. FIONA'S ENJOYING COLLEGE IN THE CITY, AND MICHAEL HAS A JOB IN AN EQUITIES BROKERAGE DOWNTOWN. HE'S ENJOYING IT SO FAR—TWO WEEKS IN. MY OWN CAREER IS

FINE, AND I'M STILL ENJOYING BEING HERE. WE ALL ARE, BUT WE MISS YOU EVERY DAY.

I KNOW I'VE ASKED YOU THIS BEFORE, BUT I THINK IT'S TIME YOU CAME HOME TO NEW YORK. BY THE SOUNDS OF THINGS, THE FAMILIES IN IZIEU ARE SETTLED AND HAPPY. WHETHER THEY LEAVE OR NOT IS THEIR CHOICE, AND WHATEVER MAY OCCUR BECAUSE OF THEIR DECISIONS IS ULTIMATELY THEIR RESPONSIBILITY. NOT YOURS, MY LOVE. YOU'VE ALREADY DONE SO MUCH. IT'S TIME TO ARRANGE SAFE PASSAGE FOR THE BOYS TO ENGLAND. THE HOUSES THAT TOOK IN THE CHILDREN FROM THE KINDERTRANSPORTS WILL WELCOME THEM. THEY'LL LIVE SAFELY AND HAPPILY. YOU WON'T HAVE TO WORRY ABOUT THEM ANYMORE. BUT PLEASE, COME HOME. I KNOW YOU DON'T OFTEN LISTEN TO MY ADVICE OR URGINGS, BUT MAKE THIS AN EXCEPTION. WE'RE ALL WAITING FOR YOU HERE AND STILL SET A PLACE FOR YOU AT EVERY FAMILY DINNER. I WILL ARRANGE ANY MONIES YOU REQUIRE FOR YOUR PASSAGE.

YOUR LOVING FATHER,

SEAMUS RITTER

Maureen let the paper fall and put her hand up to her forehead. The children at the table looked concerned but didn't speak out. Returning home meant leaving Izieu behind forever. But was it time? The parents in the house were well able to look after their own children, and Antoinette was used to corralling her group, who were well-behaved and loyal enough to listen to her. Perhaps her work was done here, and she could return to her family in New York with the clear conscience she demanded.

She stood up with the letter still in her hand and walked over to where the two children were sitting.

"What are you playing?" she asked them in German. It was

the most commonly spoken language in the house, though some spoke French.

"Gin rummy, Fräulein," Amelie said with a respectful smile. Maureen stood waiting for them to tell her a little about the game. When it became clear they weren't going to, she spoke again. She asked them who was winning and to run the rules past her again. Once Stefan had told her, she asked the question on her mind.

"Do you like it here?"

"Very much," he said, and his friend agreed. "We have the open fields, the mountains and the river. I've been swimming with the boys every day."

"The place in Belgium felt...more dangerous than this one," Amelie said. "No one will ever find us here."

"Of course not," Maureen said and left the room. Dinner came and went and soon the hallways in the house were crowded with children playing, but the curtain of bedtime would soon fall and bring some respite until the next day. Her boys were still playing with the other kids behind the house as she called them.

"Time for bed," she said to grumbles and moans.

"It's not fair, no one else has gone yet."

"It's ten minutes until all the children go. I want to read you a story before all the others crowd the rooms."

The prospect of a book lightened the boys' moods, and with a little cajoling and some gentle threats, they did as she asked.

Sitting on her bed in the room she had to herself for now, Maureen reached into the bag she'd brought back from Marseilles. The boys arranged themselves around her as she pulled out a new book. Abel and Adam clapped their hands at the sight of it.

"It's called *The Story of Ferdinand*," she said. "I'll give it to Frau Ohlmann to read at story time tomorrow, but I thought you might like to see it first."

"Oh, please read it," Rudi said.

Maureen opened the cover and began. The boys sat with rapt attention and called for her to read it again as soon as she finished. The sound of the other children in the hallway outside her room signified that bedtime had come for all.

"Tomorrow," she said. "I'll read it to all the children again."

The boys accepted that and hopped off the bed, inspired by the bull who'd rather sniff flowers and make friends than fight in the ring.

Maureen tucked the boys into bed, not forgetting to do the same for the six others who shared the room with them now. She left the door ajar so a sliver of light cut through the darkness inside. She stepped into the hallway when she heard a tiny voice from one of the beds.

"I love you," Adam said.

"Oh, and I love you too," she replied with tears in her eyes.

16

The Swiss border, near the village of Vallorcine,
Wednesday, July 31, 1940

Maureen lay on her stomach, binoculars pressed to her eyes. Gerhard and Jean Villiers were beside her, squinting to peer through the darkness around them. It had been several minutes since they had spoken. The trio was lying beneath some bushes, watching the tree line a hundred yards ahead of them that comprised the invisible line separating France from Switzerland. Even in summer, it was cold at night at this altitude, and Maureen was glad Jean had insisted she wear a coat. The ground was damp, and she could almost feel the mud seeping through her clothes, but she didn't say a word, just stared down. The terrain was mountainous woods, ideal for skiing if one were so inclined or had the time for such pastimes. Jean had told them on the journey out here that some of France's most famous winter resorts were a stone's throw away from the rendezvous point. It was hard to believe anyone could meet here. It seemed impossible to differentiate one clump of trees from another, but the

French resistance man was confident they'd be in the right place at the right time.

"How long have we been here?" Maureen whispered to Gerhard.

The German looked at his watch and showed her the time. It was almost 10:30, meaning they'd been lying on the cold ground watching the same cluster of trees since 8:30. They were deliberately early, which meant the refugees coming across were almost an hour late. The network of safehouses from the Swiss border to Spain was now ready, and the people they were waiting for were to be the first to use it. They were German dissidents who'd escaped concentration camps and then made it into neutral Switzerland. No one had mentioned why they didn't want to stay there, but Maureen guessed they wanted to make it to England to help with the war effort. Or else perhaps, as Arnaud had warned, they couldn't find refuge and had nowhere else to go. Maybe because of its neutral stance, but more likely because of the mountainous terrain that made up its border, Switzerland hadn't been invaded by the Nazis. Hitler had shown his disregard for international norms like neutrality when he invaded Denmark and Belgium a few months before.

Maureen was still here because she couldn't figure out the best way to get the Bautner boys out of the country. She'd come on this mission not just to help the refugees crossing but also to check out the terrain so that she might help the boys cross here. From what she'd seen so far, she'd need a lot of help getting them over these mountains into Switzerland. And then she and they would be stuck there. Taking them alone was a daunting prospect, and she'd found herself making the same excuses as the others these last few days. Perhaps they really would be safer in Izieu.

Gerhard poked her in the arm and brought Maureen back into the moment. The trees were rustling. The Germans were patrolling the border, with the Swiss guards on the other side.

Being caught by either would be trouble. The night was still and silent until a birdcall sounded. Jean whistled back, and two figures emerged from the foliage. Both men were covered in mud, with their faces blacked out.

"Stay here," Jean said.

Maureen and Gerhard did as they were told as the resistance man descended to meet the refugees. The next step was to ask them the agreed codeword. Maureen watched without hearing any of the words the men exchanged, but the handshake they soon shared made the operation's success apparent. Jean gestured for them to come down. The men were covered up. Maureen could barely make out their faces behind their scarves.

"We'll save the introductions for later," Jean whispered. "Safe to say, we're all friends here. You'll be in a warm bed in less than three hours," Jean said.

The refugees didn't move. Maureen chuckled under her breath as it became clear they couldn't understand what the Frenchman was saying. She repeated his sentiment in German, and the men laughed and patted each other on the back.

"We have a car waiting, about 30 minutes' hike away," Gerhard said.

"Let's get going," one of the refugees said. "If I stop for too long my legs might seize up."

The group of five left together. Gerhard had walked the trail several times the previous week, and the broken branches he'd left guided them along.

One of the new men was slow and walked with a noticeable limp. The walking stick he'd fashioned from a branch helped him along. "I'm sorry," he said from behind his scarf. "I slipped on a rock earlier. I don't think it's broken, but it's painful."

"It's probably just a sprain," the other man said. "I checked it for him."

Maureen wondered how a man with a sprained ankle

would climb the Pyrenees into Spain but shelved the concern for later. She dropped back and offered to help the man, who took the opportunity to introduce himself as Otto. She and Jean put his arms over their shoulders to allow him to hop along but soon discovered he was happier and faster alone.

The 30-minute hike took them closer to 45, but the car was parked at the end of the dirt road where they'd left it.

"We took the car as far as we could," Maureen whispered to Otto. She was sure she wouldn't feel safe until they were in the houses in Izieu.

"What about the headlights?" Otto said.

"We're in France now, past the Germans," Maureen answered. "And we'll never make it to the safehouse without them."

Maureen fumbled with the keys for a painful few seconds before opening the door. The refugees got in the back, with Gerhard beside them. Maureen drove. It was her car, after all. The two men were asleep in minutes. She concentrated on the narrow mountain roads watching out for patrols or checkpoints as they went. But none ever came.

A little under three hours later, they crossed the Rhône, and moments after, the houses at Izieu came into view like an oasis in the desert. It was well after midnight, and all inside were asleep, at least Maureen hoped. Some of the older children had taken to sneaking down to the river at night to swim and do whatever boys and girls that age did. It wasn't something she liked to think about.

The refugees in the back woke up as the car stopped. Otto and the other man limped inside.

"You can take a day or two to rest before moving on," Gerhard said.

"I don't want to think about walking through mountains and forests for a while," Otto said. "How about a drink to celebrate our arrival?"

To Maureen's surprise, the other man was also amenable to the idea. "I have some wine," she said.

"Sounds heavenly."

Gerhard showed the two men to the room Maureen had kept for them before taking a few moments to change into some of the other clothes they'd brought in the packs strapped to their backs.

Maureen prepared a small meal of bread and cheese and laid it out on the table.

Gerhard appeared with the two refugees a few minutes later, and they sat down at the table. Jean made his excuses and, unable to communicate with the new men, retired to bed.

"I haven't introduced myself yet," the other dissident said. "My name is Heinz Kier." He shook hands with his rescuers, making his introduction official.

"Otto and I escaped from the concentration camp at Dachau along with a few others."

"What happened to them?" Gerhard asked.

"We split up, promising to meet up later if we ever got out," Heinz said before continuing.

The three men devoured the food in seconds before Maureen proposed a toast.

"I'd like to congratulate all of us for getting this far."

"Still a long way until Spain," Otto said.

"Why did you leave Switzerland?" she asked. "It seems like a safe place. Could you not find anyone to take you in?"

"We have information we'd like to share with the War Office in London. Staying put in Basel or Geneva would have meant sitting out the war."

Maureen raised her glass again, and the other three followed suit. "Here's to the first of many weary travelers through our escape route to Spain. May your journey be safe and your reward tangible!"

They clinked glasses. "Here's to the memory of Tony Neuer and Klaus Bautner!" Heinz said.

Maureen held up her glass with a smile before something in her mind stopped her.

"Wait," she said. "What was that name? Who are you toasting?"

"Two fallen comrades, shot while we were escaping."

Maureen's heart felt like it was about to burst. "Did you know this Klaus Bautner well?"

"You form close bonds inside those horrific places," Heinz said. "I considered him a true friend."

"Did he have children? Three boys?"

"How did you know that?" Heinz said with a look of puzzlement on his face.

Maureen grabbed Gerhard's arm, still staring across the table. "From Berlin?"

"He was from Wedding. What's this about?"

"His children's names are Rudi, Adam and Abel. They're asleep upstairs."

"What are you talking about? This can't be. Klaus's kids are here?"

"For the last year. Where's Hilde, his wife?"

"In a camp somewhere in Germany. The Gestapo came for them both a few days after they sent their children away. I had no idea their children were...."

"I could bring you to them right now," Maureen said. Her pulse was racing. It was impossible to stay calm, and the words couldn't come quickly enough. "Most of the other people here were from my father's factory in Berlin, but the boys came separately. I never knew who their parents were. And you're sure Klaus is dead?"

"I saw the bullets hit him with my own eyes."

A great wave of sadness came over Maureen at the thought that her sweet boys' father was dead. But her mourning was replaced by something else as an idea struck her.

"What are your intentions from here, gentlemen?" she asked.

"To leave as soon as possible. We have information for the War Office in London," Heinz said.

"Time sensitive information, unfortunately, so I won't be able to rest my ankle too long," Otto added.

"Where did you get this information?" Gerhard asked.

"You could say that is on a need-to-know basis," Heinz said. "But I was only in the camp a week before I escaped with the others. The only reason I'm not in England now is because they caught me in Germany."

"Our steamer's leaving on August 4 at 3pm. Any later than that and our information will be useless," Otto said.

"For England?" Maureen asked. "That's where you're headed, isn't it?" Otto nodded.

A thousand thoughts crowded her mind. But one drowned out all the others. "I want to come with you," she said. "With the boys—your friend's sons. They're in danger here. It's only a matter of time before the Nazis swarm south. You know that as well as I do. They're Jews. They won't survive the camps. Will you help me with them?"

"I don't know. We only have four days," Otto said. "How would we get such young children over the mountains in such a short time?"

"We carry them," Maureen said.

"Impossible," Gerhard said. "You'd never make it."

Maureen turned to her old friend, disappointed he'd use that word. "Impossible is a perception. Just because it hasn't been done yet, doesn't mean it never will."

"Listen to yourself, Maureen. This is insane," Gerhard said. "You'll never make it to Barcelona in four days. You might not make it there in 15 days."

"We can drive," she said.

"The chances of making it all the way to the Pyrenees without being stopped are astronomical. And if you drive at night you'll be out after curfew."

"Then you're going to have to forge some papers for the kids, aren't you?"

"We can't risk the mission," Otto said. "I'm sorry. And I won't be able to help you with my ankle."

"Three children, right? I'll take one, and so will Gerhard."

"I will?" her friend said.

"Of course, you will. You're not going to let me do this alone, are you?" she said.

"No," he said.

Heinz cursed and threw down his fork. It clattered on the table and fell to the floor. "Klaus used to talk about his family every night. He made me swear before the escape that if he didn't make it that I'd look for his children one day." Heinz said and turned to his friend. "Otto, we have to do this. What choice do we have?"

"Is it even possible?" Otto asked.

"Shall we find out, or do you want to retreat to England never knowing if you could have saved your friend's children or not?"

They were all staring at Otto.

"We have to try," Heinz said.

"Okay," Otto said. "It's insane, but so is all this."

"How bad is your leg?" Maureen asked.

"I think I sprained my ankle. I can walk, but not quickly. I'll be fine in a day or two if someone helps me."

"I'll help you when I can, but you're going to have to do most of the walking yourself," Heinz said.

"Perhaps it might be best if you stayed a little longer, and let your ankle recover," Gerhard said.

"I'll make it," Otto replied. "I won't slow you down. I just won't be able to carry any of Klaus's kids."

Maureen felt exhilaration she hadn't experienced in years. This was the answer she'd been waiting for. This chance was a one-off. She had to make it work. It didn't matter that they had to leave the next day. The boys would be safe.

"How old are the boys?" Otto asked.

"They're eight, five and three," Maureen answered. "They're slight, and strong. They'll make it."

"But will *we*?" Gerhard said. Maureen glared at him again, and he shut up.

"I'll help Otto," Heinz said. "Will you be able to take the three-year-old?" he said to Maureen.

"Abel? Yes. I'll carry him on my back."

"I'll take Adam, the five-year-old," Gerhard said.

"And Rudi is eight. He can walk on his own."

"I'll take him when I'm not helping Otto," Heinz said.

They set the plan. Gerhard would return to Lyon first thing in the morning and prepare the ID papers for the boys. Maureen would have the rest of the day to pack up and prepare for the arduous journey ahead. The other women would help her design harnesses to carry three-year-old Abel and for Gerhard to do the same for Adam. Rudi was a strong child, and she was confident he would make it. He had to. She asked Jean, but he had too much to attend to in Lyon to help them across, and besides, he had no desire to leave France.

"What are you going to do after we get to Spain?" she asked Gerhard.

"Turn around and come back. I'll bring you and the children to the peak of the mountain, and let you take them the rest of the way."

"Thank you, my friend."

"I'll be sorry to see you go."

"I'll miss you too."

The two refugees went to bed, and a few minutes later, Jean and Gerhard departed for their respective rooms. Too hyped up to sleep, Maureen walked out into the cool air, savoring the absolute quiet of the night. A rogue thought of Christophe appeared, and much as she tried to sweep it out, it stayed stuck in the forefront of her mind. She couldn't afford to feel like this. Not now. Not when those little boys were counting on her. The next few days could set them up for the rest of their lives. Her personal feelings for some dandy in Marseilles were nothing more than a distraction. She remembered walking through the fields with him and to the river. It seemed like a dream now.

17

Thursday, August 1, 1940

Maureen took the boys aside after breakfast. They listened with stoic, solemn faces that would have made her laugh in almost any other situation. She told them the time had come, and she would make sure they were safe. They nodded when she told them it would be hard and pretended to understand, but how could they when she had no comprehension of what they were about to go through herself? They ran off to play as usual, and soon Maureen realized her mistake when almost all the other children came to her either to ask her not to leave or to beg her to take them too. It broke her heart, but it was easier to lie. She told them she'd be back in a week or so, and the boys were only meeting someone far away. Few seemed to believe her, but at least it stopped them from asking.

She had little time to cherish her last morning in Izieu and even less for long goodbyes. Abigail, Martha, Antoinette, and Ella were shocked to hear the news but eager to do whatever they could to help. So, the five women, with the help of her boys themselves, set about designing backpacks to carry little Adam and Abel over the mountains. It was the ideal time of year to attempt the climb, and they would have to contend with heat more than the frozen temperatures one would have to deal with during winter. But Maureen was trying not to think about the travails ahead of them at the border so much as the ones they would have to face in getting there. On either side of the man-made line dividing the two countries lay an area called the forbidden zone. It was 20 kilometers deep in France and 50 kilometers deep on the Spanish side. People living in it needed special permits, and anyone caught without those papers would be shot on sight.

Before he left, Jean had provided her with the details of the safehouse in Perpignan. The average journey would take longer, but since they were in a rush and needed to begin the ascent over the mountains as soon as possible, they would skip several stages of the journey.

The few quiet moments she had that day were filled with fear, doubt, and trepidation, but thankfully she was so busy that those instances were few and far between.

Gerhard had made the arrangements with her before he returned to Lyon. Promising to work all day, he'd pledged to have the false travel papers the children would need by the afternoon. Heinz and Otto had the documents they needed to pass any French security checks, but once they reached the forbidden zone near the mountains, only residency passes would do, and no one had them. They'd be illegal once they crossed into Spain, but the authorities there weren't nearly as draconian as the German border patrols and their newly empowered partners in the Vichy police.

Maureen packed the clothes she couldn't do without, knowing that every ounce of weight would add extra agony to her journey over the mountains. Jean had warned her to bring as many pairs of socks as she could carry. Abigail arrived at the door with the harness she and the other women had designed. It wasn't more than a rucksack with a hole for Abel's legs, but it fit him and would do the job. They had one for Adam also, designed for Gerhard to bear. Maureen hugged her friend but had time for little else. The clock was ticking. Once she was alone again, Maureen went to her underwear drawer and rooted around for the cash she had remaining. She packed it into a money belt which she attached around her waist and walked out.

The boys were lined up in the hallway, saying their good-byes. Several girls were crying as they hugged them, and so too were Abigail, Ella, and Martha. Their husbands kneeled down and gave the Bautners words of encouragement, telling them to be strong no matter what occurred. Adam and Abel looked lost. Only Rudi seemed to have any idea of what was about to happen, and he, too, was soon sobbing. The two German dissidents stood with their hands in front of them, not knowing what to say. They got into the front seat of the car.

Without the time to say the goodbyes she wanted, Maureen decided to act as if she was leaving for a few days, even though she knew it was forever.

"Good luck," she said to the group gathered in the hallway. "Stay safe. I'll be in touch."

She took Adam and Abel by the hand and led them to the car, fighting back her tears. Maureen took one last look at the house and started her car. *Don't look back,* she thought as they accelerated along the dirt road. *Never look back.*

∽

"Keep your heads down back there," Maureen said as they entered the city of Lyon. "Lie down. Make sure no one can see you."

The boys did as they were told but giggled as they pressed their cheeks against the back seat. Maureen suppressed her instinct to tell them to keep quiet and kept driving instead.

Gerhard's apartment and the basement he used to print his forgeries were in the city center. Maureen was wary of being stopped before they reached it. With no travel papers, she had no idea what would happen.

She knew the roads well and kept to the smaller streets to reach Gerhard's place. Pulling up on the street outside, she jumped out. The door to the basement came ajar as she knocked on it. A sudden sinking feeling brought bile to the top of her throat. The place had been ransacked. The printer was on its side, and papers were strewn all over the concrete floor like confetti. She stepped inside, hoping that what she knew had happened wasn't true. The place had been raided, and Gerhard was nowhere to be seen. A knock behind her made her jump, and she was shaking as she turned around, ready to explain that she had no idea what had happened in this place. She breathed again when she saw the figure of Michel, Gerhard's partner in crime, standing at the door.

"The police came about three hours ago," he said.

"Where's Gerhard?"

"They took him."

"Is he okay? What will they do to him?"

"He's fine. I was down at the station with him a few minutes ago. He told me to come here to look out for you. His lawyer is convinced he'll be out in a week. This isn't Nazi Germany. Not yet anyway."

"A week?" Maureen said.

"It's a slap on the wrist. Not much more. They didn't catch him with much. He destroyed a lot of it when they were breaking in, and luckily, we didn't have much contraband lying around. We'll have to start over again somewhere else, however. I don't know what we're going to do."

"Does he have the papers I need?"

Michel shook his head. "He said to tell you he was sorry."

Maureen covered her face with two hands. Losing the papers was one thing, but not having Gerhard beside her would make this mission even more difficult. Without her friend, she'd have to cross the mountains with just the two men, one of whom couldn't help her, and she and the other man would have to carry the two little boys – and hope Rudi was strong enough to make it himself. It seemed impossible.

She stumbled past Michel back onto the street but remembered what she'd said to Gerhard the night before when he'd used the word "impossible."

A deep breath calmed her a little before she ran back to the car. She jumped in and turned to the men. The boys were still lying down in the back.

"Change of plan," she said. "I couldn't get the travel papers. Gerhard's been arrested. We're going without him." Heinz and Otto looked at one another and then back at her. "But I don't want you travelling with me and the children. You have papers. It's too much of a risk for you."

"Nonsense," Heinz said. "We can work something out—"

"I don't have time to argue," she said. "Just do as I say. Take the train from here to Perpignan. It's a small city about ten kilometers outside the forbidden zone. When you arrive go to 136 Rue des Archers, and ask for Madame Camara. She'll provide you with everything you need. And I'll meet you there. Got it?"

The two men nodded.

"Good luck," Otto said.

"We'll wait in Perpignan as long as we can," Heinz said.

"I'll be there," she answered. "You two are my one chance to get these boys out."

The two men got out of the car. Once they'd disappeared around the corner, she turned to the boys, who poked their heads up. "It's just us now," she said. "I have to make a phone call. Can you keep your heads down for a while longer?"

"I'll make them," Rudi said.

She knew a hotel around the corner and was red-faced and panting as she arrived in the lobby. The line of telephones was at the back wall, and she picked up the receiver of the first one she reached with a shaking hand. She asked the operator to patch her through and prayed as the phone rang.

"Hello," came the voice on the other end.

"Christophe?" she said as relief flooded her body. "It's Maureen."

"I know who it is. I wasn't expecting your call. Is everything all right? You sound panicked."

"I need a favor. The biggest one I've ever asked of anyone."

"You have my attention now."

"I'm getting the Bautner boys out, on a steamer from Barcelona in three days."

"Where are you?"

"In Lyon."

"In three days? You'll never make it."

"Gerhard was meant to help me, but the gendarmes hauled him in."

"Is he okay?"

"I heard he was fine, but I need someone to take his place. He promised me he'd help me carry the boys over the mountains into Spain. I have two German refugees with me. Grown men. But one is injured, so the other man has to help him."

"Wait, what's the hurry?"

"They have time-sensitive information to share with the War Office in London. Please, Christophe, I can't do this alone. I couldn't think of anyone else I trust enough."

Two seconds of silence greeted her request until the sound

of laughter came down the line. "You really are something else, Maureen Ritter. You call me up out of nowhere and ask me to carry children on my back over mountains past German patrols that will shoot us on sight?"

"That about sums it up," she replied. "I need you. Will you help us?"

He chuckled again before he spoke. "I must have been dropped on my head as a baby, but yes. I'll do it. Where should I meet you?"

Maureen couldn't help but burst out laughing herself. She told him about the safe house in Perpignan but also warned him about none of them having any papers.

"I had dinner plans tonight, but I suppose I'll just have to cancel. It's been a while since I wore my hiking boots."

"Bring at least ten spare pairs of socks," she said.

"I'll see you in a few hours. Good luck."

"I'll need it." The urge to tell him she loved him shocked her. She shook her head, wondering where it came from, as she hung up the phone. Despite everything they still faced, it was hard not to smile as she returned to the car.

The boys were still lying down as she opened the door. She took a blanket from the back and spread it over them, wondering why she hadn't thought to do so earlier. Peering at a map, she asked herself what the best way to travel to avoid traffic stops might be. It took a few seconds for her to realize that she just had to drive to Perpignan and hope for the best.

"Here goes nothing," she said in English and pulled out of the parking spot.

Maureen made it as far as the beautiful ancient city of Montpellier on the Mediterranean coast before her luck ran out. She joined a line of cars on the highway. It wasn't until she was boxed in that she realized they were all headed to a traffic stop, and the police manning it were checking papers. She took a deep breath, fighting the instinct to scream, run, or turn the car around and drive through the field beside the road. The boys were asleep on the back seat, covered by the blanket, but the sound of their breath was clearly audible.

"Only one thing for it," she said. She just had time to reach into her bag for some lipstick and used the mirror to apply it. Distraction was her only chance of making it through. She unbuttoned the top three buttons of her blouse, exposing enough cleavage to give her father a heart attack.

She smiled as she inched up to the checkpoint, even as the gendarme shone a flashlight in her face.

"Hello," she said with a smile, pushing out her chest in an unnatural way.

The policeman was about 40 with a thick mustache and a generous belly no doubt cultivated over time. "What are you doing out so late all alone?" he asked.

"Heading back home. I had a fight with my idiot boyfriend! Some men don't know how good they have it," she said. "He cheated on me with my best friend. Can you believe that?"

"If you were my girl, I'd never dream of anyone else," he answered. "He must be crazy."

She couldn't help but glance at his wedding ring before returning her eyes to his. "I need a man, not a little boy. You want to see my papers?"

The policeman paused a second and then seemed to remember where he was. "Oh, yes, your papers, please."

She had identification papers, but not the ones required to travel. She handed over what she had, and he glanced at them for a second or two.

"Where are you off to?"

"Just down the road."

He moved to shine the flashlight in the back, but she spoke first. "I need an older man, like you, maybe. I've always admired men in uniform. So brave and selfless."

He smiled, revealing yellow, crooked teeth. "You come through here often?"

"Every few days," she answered.

"I'll look forward to seeing you again, Genevieve," he said, reading the name on her false papers.

"Me too," she said and moved the car forward. The relief almost brought tears to her eyes, but she left her blouse unbuttoned for the next stop.

The boys were still asleep when they reached Perpignan two hours later. She'd used the same trick at another traffic stop outside the town, but it was easier this time. The young policeman had hardly been able to speak when he saw her.

Finding her way in a place she'd never been in the dark was difficult, and locating the street took almost an hour. It was well after curfew when she stopped the car, and the roads were deserted. The boys were bleary-eyed and whiny as she forced them onto the road opposite the safe house. Holding Adam and Abel's hands, she crossed the suburban street and approached a red door. She knocked as loudly as she dared and stood back. A stocky woman with short brown hair peeked through a chink in the door and ushered them inside.

"Are you Maureen?" the woman asked.

"And these are the boys."

"I'm Madame Camara," she answered. "Your other friends arrived a few hours ago. I sent them down with my son to the foot of the mountain to spend the night in a barn. It's too late for you, however. You'll have to stay here tonight."

"That's fine," Maureen answered. "Two men?"

"Was there meant to be someone else with you?"

"It's okay," Maureen replied. "Let's get the boys inside and into bed."

The woman looked at her as if she was insane to even attempt bringing children over, and perhaps she was.

Christophe must have come to his senses and decided to stay in Marseille. It was hard to blame him, but she didn't see how crossing would be possible without his help.

Dejected, she followed the woman into her house. The front door closed behind them. The woman brought them into the kitchen, where a meal of bread and cheese awaited. The boys demolished theirs in about five seconds. Maureen didn't take much longer. Once her belly was full, the yoke of exhaustion bore down on her, and the woman showed her to their beds upstairs. The boys were asleep in seconds. Maureen went to the window to peer down at the moonlit street in some vain hope that Christophe's car was outside, but the road remained as it was when she pulled up. She went to her bed, a small cot in the attic, with little hope for the next day.

18

Friday, August 2, 1940

I t was still dark outside when the call came. Maureen jolted awake, ready to fight. The tiny figure of Madame Camara stood with a candle that illuminated her in a ghostly, ethereal light. Maureen moved her wrist, searching for enough brightness to read her watch. It was 4 a.m. The boys were still fast asleep as she put her feet on the cold floor. It took her several minutes to wake them. The sound of a truck pulling up outside told her time was short—it was their ride to the foot of the mountains. The lady of the house was growing impatient, stomping her foot to rouse the boys while Maureen tried gentler methods. In the end, she had to pull them out and drag them to the bathroom. Once they'd used the toilet, they regained themselves enough to get dressed, and that would do for now. Maureen tried not to think of how on earth she'd get the three of them over the Pyrenees alone. Perhaps Otto had improved, and Heinz could help. Should she just give up and submit to the fact that she couldn't do this?

Madame Camara was in the kitchen preparing food to bring on the journey when Maureen approached her.

"I have something to ask," Maureen said. The older woman raised her head without speaking. "Is it possible to leave one of the children here while I travel to Spain with the others?"

If she could double back for Abel or Adam, it might make the journey possible, but what about sailing from Barcelona? Who would take care of the boys while she doubled back if Otto and Heinz were in such a mad rush. The plan didn't make sense.

"This isn't a nursery, my dear, just somewhere to stop off before attempting the climb."

"I was meant to have someone helping me—"

"I'm sorry. I can't. More travelers arrive tomorrow, and I have to look after my sister in Toulouse on Sunday for a week. Maybe if you keep to the lower trails—"

"The ones crawling with German patrols? Is there anyone else who can take one of boys for me? I'll never make it."

"You'll need to ask the guides for help," the older woman said, getting irritated. "I'm sorry."

Maureen wasn't about to take that for an answer and followed the woman to the front door and then out onto the street. A coal truck stood waiting, its engine running.

"This is my son, Patrice," Madame Camara said. "He'll take you to meet the others."

Maureen was about to start arguing again when a car pulled around the corner.

"You weren't about to leave without me, were you?" Christophe said and stepped out.

It was hard to know whether to hit or hug him, but Maureen stood with her hands on her hips, shaking her head. "You made it just on time!"

"Forgive me, I had some business to attend to and then got stuck."

He was dressed for the climb in an old working shirt and pants to match.

"Have you slept?"

"I got a few hours before I left."

"It seems your problem is solved?" Madame Camara said. Maureen nodded, and the older woman continued. "My son will take you to the guides."

Maureen didn't know whether to hug Christophe or not but decided on the traditional two-cheek kiss to greet him. She reintroduced him to the boys and was just about to go over what she knew about the upcoming journey when Patrice began speaking.

"You can expect we'll be stopped at least once or twice by German patrols. Nothing has gotten past them since the capitulation. Stay still and quiet no matter what you hear or think might be going on. They sometimes search the trucks but haven't checked my cargo in detail yet. They don't want to get dirty. I'm used to it, myself." Maureen looked at the filthy lorry packed with bulging bags. "Don't worry, girly, the coal won't kill you. The Nazis just might, though." He gestured to Christophe to help him with the bags, and the two men began unloading the truck.

Maureen went back inside for the children, the doctored rucksacks, and the measly amount of luggage she could bring.

Christophe was already in the back of the lorry when she returned. He reached out a hand to help the boys in. "Isn't this exciting?" he said as they huddled beside him. "We're about to go on an adventure you'll never forget!"

His words didn't elicit the response he would have wanted. The boys seemed to want to sleep and nothing else. Maureen sat on the other side with the boys in the middle before Patrice loaded the bags back on. Soon the sacks were all they could see, and the smell of coal dust filled her nostrils and settled in her clothes and hair. The boys coughed and sneezed until Patrice shouted a warning.

"We have to be so quiet," Maureen said, and they nodded in agreement.

Only after they started moving did Maureen realize she'd forgotten to thank Madame Camara. A letter would be sufficient, and besides, Christophe would have to return for his car. That wasn't something they'd discussed yet, and they couldn't now as talking was prohibited.

A few minutes passed before Maureen felt the car slow to a halt. She held her finger up to her mouth, confident the boys could see her even in the half-light of the back of the truck. They all sat in silence, Maureen holding Abel and Adam's hands, as Patrice's voice cut through the silence. He was talking to Wehrmacht soldiers.

"How are you doing, boys?" he said.

He received a muffled reply. Footsteps on gravel became louder, and a soldier's voice called out in German from the back of the truck. She heard him stabbing one of the bags and some coal spilling out. Abel looked like he was about to cry. Christophe held his hand over the little boy's mouth as they silently begged Patrice to start the engine. Thirty agonizing seconds passed before the sound of the engine came again. Christophe released Abel's hand as the lorry picked up speed. Abel hit him, but remained quiet. Maureen held her finger to her lips just as he seemed about to start fussing.

Ten minutes later, they were halted once more, and Patrice went through the same charade of presenting his papers while pretending to be happy to chat with the guards. The second stop was shorter, and they were soon on the road again.

It was just after 5:30 and still dark when Patrice pulled off the main road and turned off the engine. "We're here," he said and banged on the side.

He shifted just enough sacks of coal to allow them to jump out. They were at the end of the road, beside an old barn.

"Where are we?" Christophe asked.

"In the foothills. Your two friends are inside," he said, pointing to the barn. "Your guides should be here any minute. Remember, there is no status up here—only survival or death. Do whatever they tell you when they say to, and you just might get to Spain alive."

"Thank you," Maureen said.

He shook their hands and drove off just as Heinz and Otto emerged from the old barn. Otto's limp indicated that the miracle Maureen had hoped for had not occurred, and he'd be lucky to make it. He was using a large walking stick. The two Germans shook hands with Christophe after Maureen explained what had happened to Gerhard in Lyon.

A few minutes later, two figures arrived, silhouetted against the sunrise behind them. The four adults and three children stood watching as they approached. A man around 50 with a thick gray beard and a boy of about 16 stopped before them.

"The children will never make it," the man said.

"We're carrying them," Christophe replied.

"Then you won't make it either."

"They're coming with us, and we're crossing those mountains with or without you," Maureen said.

The man laughed and turned to the boy. "Okay," he said. "Your funeral. We'll soon see if you can keep up. I'm Pierre and this is my son, Charles. Don't tell us your names. The less we know, the better."

Pierre was built like a barrel and looked like he could carry several over his head. His son was wiry and several inches taller. Both had the battered complexions of men who had spent their entire lives outdoors.

"How are you planning on carrying the kids?" Charles said with a sneer.

Maureen put one of the special backpacks on. "Like this," she said. The young man shook his head and stood back, deferring to his father.

"You have spare socks?"

"Several pairs for each of us," Maureen answered.

"You'll need them. Pack up and let's get moving. We'll stick to the higher peaks. The Germans have begun patrolling the lowlands the past few weeks, and they have dogs to sniff you out!" He pointed at Rudi, who recoiled a little, much to the older man's amusement. "We move out in two minutes."

Maureen put the rucksack on her back and kneeled down as Heinz lowered Abel in. The boy fit it well. Christophe was next. He slipped the makeshift harness over his shoulders and let Adam climb in.

"You okay back there?" Christophe asked the little boy. Adam flashed a thumb in front of his face. "I think we're ready," the Frenchman said.

"Can you walk for a while?" Maureen asked Rudi. The eight-year-old nodded, not knowing what he was about to take on. "You're such a resilient boy."

"Father told me I was the man of the house before he sent us away. I'll be strong for my brothers—even after you leave us."

"Who said I was going to leave you?"

"No one, but we have parents. You're not our mother."

Maureen pushed the boy's hair back over his ear. "No, I'm not, but I might look after you—for a while anyway."

"You can't leave the others, can you? What will happen to the houses without you?"

"Oh, they'll be fine."

"What about your friend?" he said pointing to Christophe.

The call came before Maureen had a chance to answer, and she stood up, feeling Abel's weight on her back. Heinz walked with his friend, who didn't seem to need help yet. They walked in single file behind Pierre, with Charles in the rear. Abel said little as they went, and Maureen soon realized the boy was asleep. Even cushioned as they were, the straps on the rucksack began to cut into her shoulders after a few minutes. The agony of carrying the little boy seemed to increase periodically as if someone was squeezing her in a vise. Rudi kept on, trudging the narrow path in front of her.

Two hours later, they stopped, and Pierre called out instructions. It was a ten-minute rest, and they were to change their socks every time they stopped to guard against chafing and blisters.

"I've seen men die up here for lack of fresh socks," Pierre said as he walked among them. Maureen hoped he was joking for the children, but his face didn't suggest as much. Before she knew it, Charles was barking out instructions to begin again. She hefted Abel up onto her already aching back and followed Pierre.

The sun grew hotter as the day wore on, but merciful clouds hid them from the worst of its rays. Rudi began to tire at around noon. They'd been hiking for six hours. Maureen went to Christophe, who was changing his socks again.

"It works to some extent, but I'm still getting blisters," he said.

"Imagine how bad it'd be if you didn't change your socks every two hours."

"I don't want to."

Rudi was lying on the ground a few feet away. "I'm worried about him," Christophe said. "I might have to carry him for a while. How are the little boys?"

"The other two are fine," she replied.

"Are you?"

"Never mind about me," she replied.

Christophe stood up, moving like an old man, and limped to where Otto and Heinz sat. The injured man's ankle was holding up well. He had it strapped up, and he was making good progress with the aid of the walking stick.

"Can you take Adam for a few hours?" Christophe asked Heinz. "I have to carry Rudi."

The German nodded. Christophe put the backpack on him, and when they got back up, he was carrying the five-year-old on his back. Without a harness to fit Rudi into, as they hadn't been able to fashion one to take his weight in Izieu, Christophe held him in his arms like a baby. Pierre gave them a disapproving look but didn't comment.

Maureen saw Christophe's energy sap with every step, but the man whose loyalty she'd once questioned kept on putting one foot in front of the other. By nightfall, Christophe was too tired to speak, and Maureen helped him with his socks and even to eat. Her own body was on fire. Her feet screamed with every step and, despite changing her socks, they had begun to bleed. Yet still she kept walking.

Nightfall came, but the trek didn't pause for it. "We stick to the same schedule—a ten-minute rest every two hours."

Christophe put Rudi down, and the boy walked alone for a few hours as darkness closed around them. Maureen's mind was blank. She was too exhausted and in too much pain to think. All she could do was concentrate on placing her foot in front of her again and again. The only thing in the entire world was following Pierre. Her life had devolved into nothing more than that.

The temperature plummeted during the night, and Maureen wrapped a scarf around her neck to keep out the chill while still able to taste the salt from the day's sweat on her lips. Night enveloped them like they'd fallen into a hole. The path wasn't more than a couple of feet wide, and a cross step might mean a broken ankle—a death sentence up here. She followed Pierre, squinting to make out his back in the darkness.

The dawn came like an angel over the horizon, painting the

sky with beautiful orange, red, and pink hues. The group sat and ate.

"You can see why primitive cultures worshipped the sun," Christophe said with a mouthful of bread. It was the first time he'd spoken in almost eight hours. She didn't respond.

Otto was falling behind the rest of the group. He walked through their breaks to catch up and had no choice but to keep going once he caught up to them if Pierre had already left. Falling behind meant death.

They walked through the morning, only taking a more extended rest for an hour at noon. They all slept, but soon Pierre roused them, and aching limbs were called into action again.

The boys were out of tears, and Rudi was on Christophe's back as the afternoon came. The scenery must have been stunning, but Maureen didn't notice a thing. All she saw was her feet and the back of Pierre's head bobbing up and down in front of her.

Another agonizing day turned into night. They didn't shelter anywhere because there was none to be found. Their guides seemed tired but not overly perturbed by what had reduced the rest of them to jelly. Thoughts of home began to fire into Maureen's mind as the darkness arrived again. She longed to see her family but knew there was still much to do here. She turned to Christophe as dawn broke. He was carrying Rudi on his back, hunched over and huffing and puffing like an old steam engine. They took a break.

"Next time I choose where we go on vacation," Christophe said with a smile as he sat beside her. She laughed for what seemed like the first time in years. "Will you take the boys back to America?" he asked.

"I don't know," Maureen responded. "I can't think that far ahead."

Heinz was beside them. Otto was with the boys, making sure they ate something.

Maureen didn't answer. Christophe was too tired to continue the conversation and was now lying on a patch of grass a few feet away. She found herself unable to tear her eyes away from him. The thought of never seeing him again shredded her insides.

They ran out of food a few hours later, but then, as if out of nowhere, the winds lessened, and the gradient beneath their feet began to flatten out.

A winding road ended to reveal a flatbed truck. "End of the hike," Pierre said, but all were too exhausted even to cheer. The guide and his son sat in the front. "We're still in the forbidden zone, but past most of the patrols. We should be okay from here."

Maureen looked at her watch. It was 11:52 a.m. on the 4th of August. They had just over three hours to get to the port in Barcelona. Too tired to talk, Maureen sat in the truck, putting arms around Adam and Rudi. Otto limped around the corner with Heinz, who'd helped him much of the way. They collapsed onto the back of the flatbed truck, and soon they were moving without walking—something that had seemed impossible just a few minutes before.

Maureen looked at her watch again after what seemed like seconds, but 45 minutes had passed. Everyone in the back of the truck was asleep, passed out on top of each other. She banged on the window to the driver's cabin.

"We have to get to Barcelona by three o'clock," she said with all the energy she could muster.

The truck slowed to a halt. Maureen saw a village in the near distance. Pierre got out and walked around to where they were sleeping. Maureen repeated herself.

"You can't be serious," Pierre replied.

"The steamer is at three. They have to be on it, and I need

them to help with the boys," Maureen said pointing to the sleeping figures of Otto and Heinz.

"You're crazy. Look down there, That's the village of Espolla. None of you are in a fit state to travel anywhere past it. We have beds for you, and warm baths."

"No," Maureen said. It even hurt to shake her head. "We've come all this way. It's only two hours to the port. We can make it."

"You're insane," Pierre said. "It's impossible in your state."

"She doesn't like that word," Christophe said, reaching into his pocket. He drew out a wad of cash and handed it to Pierre. "Will that make a difference? Take us to Barcelona, and it's yours and more besides."

Pierre looked at the money and then the prostrate sleeping figures of Otto and Heinz. "If we're stopped, you'll both be arrested."

"We'll take that chance," Maureen said.

Pierre took the banknotes in his hand. "I'm taking this now," he said. "And I'm dropping my son off before we leave."

"I'm too exhausted to argue," Christophe replied.

Pierre got back into the front of the truck and started the engine again.

Christophe fell asleep, and Maureen soon succumbed too. The boys were lying on each other like cats at her feet.

19

Sunday, August 4, 1940

S he dreamed of the ocean, vast and blue—the biggest thing she could ever imagine, and it was dotted with ships. She was on a steamer. All the people from Izieu, past, present, and future, were on board with her and smiling in the sunshine. But something was wrong. Missing. She dove off the side into the water and began swimming back to shore, but it was too far, and soon the ship was a dot on the horizon.

Pierre's voice woke her from what seemed like seconds of rest. "We're here," he said in his gruff voice. None of the others stirred. They were parked on what seemed like an ordinary street in a city she presumed was Barcelona. The sun was high in the sky, and the smell of the sea filled her nostrils. She looked at her watch. It was 2:45. She nudged Christophe and the two German dissidents awake.

"Where's the port?" she said in the loudest voice she could manage.

"A few minutes away," Pierre responded. She wondered how

he was still able to keep awake. "Do you know what dock the ship is sailing from?"

"No idea. Just get us there now!"

"I hope you're feeling lucky," the guide responded and put his foot on the gas pedal. The stone buildings of the city blurred on either side of them as they sped the remaining few blocks down to the harbor. The Mediterranean was just as it had been in her dream, and several ships were visible departing on the sparkling azure water.

Pierre seemed invested in their cause and stopped to point out the terminals where the ships were docked. "Now, which one is about to depart?" He drove down to a checkpoint, where a Spanish policeman stood.

"Which ships are about to depart at three o'clock?" The policeman looked at his watch and then back at Pierre. "We're in a hurry. Please!"

"There's one three o'clock sailing, to Lisbon, but it's just about to leave. It's too late, they're just about to pull up the gangway."

"Let us through," Pierre said. "Give us a chance!"

The policeman raised the barrier, and Pierre drove through, overtaking buses and several trucks winding down toward the ships. He almost hit several people, honking his horn as they scattered in front of them. Dozens of people stood on the dock waving the steamer off, and Pierre pulled up behind them. Maureen jumped onto the concrete, her legs stiff as steel wires, her feet bloody, her body almost beyond redemption. The port workers were pulling back the gangway. She ran to them, shouting in French.

"We're passengers on the ship!"

The two men looked at each other. "Be quick," one of the men replied in French. "It's leaving in five minutes."

"We need tickets for the children," Heinz said. "And for you too, Maureen."

"You can get them on board," the port worker said.

"We made it!" Otto said and clutched his friend in a tired, feeble embrace.

The boys were too tired to realize what the moment meant. Maureen bent down to them. "This ship will take us to safety."

"And we won't have to worry about the Nazis coming after us," Rudi said to his brothers. They nodded in agreement.

"I've never been on a steamer before," Adam said.

Pierre scratched his head behind them. "Miracles do happen," he said.

The ship was over two hundred feet long and flew the free French flag. The passengers were lined up along the railings, ready to say goodbye to their loved ones standing on the pier.

Christophe stood alone, outside the group. "It looks like this is farewell. It's been interesting, Maureen Ritter."

She threw her arms around him. "Thank you. I can never repay you for what you've done."

"Time to go!" the port worker shouted.

"That's your cue," the Frenchman said. "Have the most wonderful life—everything you deserve."

Maureen felt Otto take her hand. "I'm sorry, but we have to go," the German dissident said. Christophe stood still as she turned toward the gangway. The porters glared at them, ready to pull it back as soon as their small group boarded the ship. Maureen's heart was breaking again. It seemed like she couldn't win. Christophe deserved so much more than this. The night in Marseilles when he'd almost proposed jumped into her mind, and she wished things could have been different.

Heinz walked up the gangplank with the boys. It was about thirty feet long, and they were on the ship in seconds. They took a place by the railings to gaze back as Otto joined them. Maureen trudged up last. The man she loved stood alone on the dock, watching as the port workers removed the gangplank.

The ship's horn sounded, and the men on the pier began untying the heavy ropes that bonded it to the land.

Maureen got down on her haunches and hugged the boys.

"It's okay," Rudi said. "You don't have to come with us."

"What?" she said and stood up again.

"Heinz and Otto will bring us to England."

"No, you're my responsibility."

"You've brought them far enough," Otto said. "Go back, before it's too late."

"I can take them to England," Heinz said.

"What?" Maureen said.

"I owe their father that much. The man saved my life. I'll make sure they find a home and help them search for their mother."

"She must be.... gone," Maureen said.

"Not necessarily," the German dissident replied. "And you can't return home to America with them, anyway. They couldn't join you without visas. You'd be alone in England, away from your mission. And him." He pointed at Christophe.

"You'd look after the children?" she said to Heinz.

"Until we find their mother. I'll make sure they're taken care of. You can count on that."

Maureen bent down again. The boys looked filthy and exhausted.

"Is it okay if I stay?" she asked. "Go back to the other children in Izieu with Christophe?"

"Can we write to you?" Adam said.

"Of course. Please do!"

Maureen realized that no matter how much she'd wanted to be the boys' aunt or big sister, she was only their caretaker. She'd done enough for them, but the fight in France was only just beginning. Perhaps the time had come to prioritize her happiness or at least place it on the same level as everyone else's.

The dock workers were untying the last of the ropes, and the ship was ready to leave. Christophe held up a hand to wave. Maureen didn't want to live without him.

"Will you write me when you get to England?" she said to Heinz.

"The moment we arrive."

Maureen hugged each of the boys again, holding each of them for as long as she could. "You be good for Heinz and Otto," she said through a flood of tears. "Rudi, look after your brothers."

The young boy nodded in response.

"Thank you," Heinz said.

"For everything," Otto said.

She pulled most of the cash from her money belt and handed it to Heinz. "Look after them. Make sure you write. I have to go now," Maureen said and ran toward the gangplank. She looked back toward her boys one last time. The steward at the gangplank gate was irate, but she didn't care. "I need to get off," she said.

"It's too late," the man said. "The ship's leaving. Next port is Gibraltar."

Christophe seemed to notice something was happening. Pierre was still standing beside him, watching the situation unfold with interest.

The steamer was fifteen feet above the edge of the dock—too far to jump. She had only one chance, or else she was stuck until they reached Gibraltar.

"Please!" Maureen said. "I don't have a ticket or the money to pay for one."

The steward's face changed, and he yelled out they had a stowaway on board. The ship's whistle sounded again, and disgruntled dock workers scuttled into place to throw the ropes they'd just untied back over the railings. It took about two minutes before the angry steward laid out the gangplank again. Maureen's apologies fell on deaf ears.

Christophe stood at the end of the gangway, shaking his head with a wry smile. She tramped down toward him with her tiny bag.

"And you're meant to be the decisive one?" he said.

"Oh, shut up and kiss me, would you?"

He took her in his exhausted arms and held her against him. They kissed as if it would be the last time. Exhilaration surged through her, and she took his face between her hands.

"I'm sorry I almost left you," she said.

"Okay, but you only get one chance!" he said with a smile before kissing her again.

They both turned to wave to the boys, who were jumping up and down. Maureen cried as the ship left, and she and Christophe stood together until it faded to nothing on the horizon. They were sitting on the dock, unable to stand any longer, when Christophe turned to her.

"How does a five-star hotel sound? Two rooms of course."

"Amazing," Maureen said. "I feel like I could sleep for a week."

"How about a ride into the city?" Christophe asked Pierre, who had stayed the entire time. He nodded and smiled. A few minutes later, they were back in the truck again. The French guide dropped them off in the city outside a swanky hotel Christophe knew, wished them the best, and drove away.

"He doesn't realize he hasn't seen the last of us," Christophe said. "We still have to get back over the mountains into France!"

Maureen looked down at her filthy clothes, laced with mud and grime. Her hair was knotted and smelled like a wet dog. Her hands were covered in tiny cuts, and her entire body ached. Walking was almost beyond her, and Christophe had to help her up the steps to the hotel. The clerk behind the desk almost had them thrown out until Christophe produced a wad of cash and mentioned that he knew the concierge. The clerk appeared with Christophe's friend a moment later. The concierge didn't recognize him until he spoke.

Moments later, they were on the second floor. Christophe had booked them rooms next to one another. Maureen pushed her door open to reveal luxuries she couldn't have imagined the previous night. The bathroom was her first port of call, and soon the water in the tub was the color of the dirt she'd scrubbed off herself. She climbed out and finished with a shower, taking a few minutes to get the knots out of her hair. Putting on a robe, she limped back toward the bed, but just as she was about to collapse onto it had a second thought.

She walked back out into the hallway. Christophe's door was ajar, and she pushed it open. He was asleep on the double bed, the drapes still open and blowing a fresh summer wind on his exhausted body. His hair was still wet from the shower, and he wore new pajamas from the hotel. She lay on the bed beside him, the back of his head in her face. Putting her arm over his sleeping body, she whispered in his ear. "I love you, Christophe. I'm sorry I ever doubted you." He didn't budge, but she got up and closed the curtains before falling into a deep sleep on the bed beside him.

~

Thursday, May 25, 2006

The sign for Denver came into view as Amy pressed stop on the tape recorder. It took her a few seconds to speak. Her grandmother's story was mind-boggling. It was hard to believe she'd been through all that—the old woman with the flower garden in the south of France who sent her cards for Christmas and her birthday. Maureen seemed exhausted by reaching into her memory and settled back on the pillow propped up against the window. Amy determined not to pester her too much but still had some questions she couldn't keep to herself.

"Did Christophe ask you to marry him again when you returned to France?"

"No. He almost proposed on that balcony in Marseilles, but I didn't want to marry while the war was still raging. I didn't want to settle down until the guns and bombs were silenced. I had no idea how long that would take." Maureen stopped for a second as if she was gazing into the past. "I often wish I had said yes to him. I suppose I would have if I knew what our future would bring, but none of us know that."

"Did the boys make it to England?"

"Yes," Maureen said with a smile. "Heinz and Otto took good care of them. They found a family in Oxford to take care of them, and they lived there in safety for the duration of the war."

"And was their mother....?"

"Dead? No. She survived the war. She brought them to Canada in 1947. They grew up in Toronto. The last time I saw them was in '58. They were grown up by then."

Amy was bursting with follow-up questions but knew the answers were coming. She took some breaths to calm herself, resolving in her mind not to push the older woman. Her grandmother settled down to nap.

Amy still hadn't called Ryan to tell him she was coming because she hadn't made up her mind to see him yet. He was in the Four Seasons downtown, just a few minutes away. His ex-wife had been to the funeral the day before, but Amy didn't know how long she'd be hanging around. All she was sure of was that she didn't want to see her. Maureen still had no idea of

Amy's true intention in taking her here, but she'd understand. Ryan had made mistakes in the past. Who hadn't? But wasn't love worth fighting for? All she had to do was call Ryan, and they could rekindle their relationship. Perhaps he'd agree to reveal their love. She wouldn't have to be alone. Maureen shifted a few inches, distracting Amy from her thoughts.

"What would you do?" Amy asked aloud.

Her grandmother stirred a little and closed her eyes again. Then the answer hit Amy like a fist.

"You would delete him from your phone and never call him again," she said, shaking her head. "What am I doing?"

A red light interrupted her thoughts, and she pulled her phone out of her bag. She flipped it open and began to type a text to Ryan. He'd told her he loved her the night before. She replied to that. *I'm in Denver. I was here to see you, but then I realized I don't want to be the type of person who crawls to you or anyone else. You stole my work and had me fired. Then you lied about it and told me you loved me. I don't need you. Never contact me again.*

She hit send and felt a whoosh of exhilaration flood her veins. Her phone buzzed seconds later. Ryan was calling. He never called. Amy rolled down the window and threw the phone out. She was the great Maureen Ritter's granddaughter and would honor that for the rest of her life.

Her grandmother woke up.

"I must have dozed off," she said.

They were about ten miles from the city, and the white peaks of the Rockies filled the horizon.

"Grandma, are you ready to fly back to New York now?"

Maureen smiled. "I think so."

Amy considered telling her about Ryan but knew she didn't need to now.

"There's just one more place I'd like to visit with you, but that's back home."

"I'll go anywhere with you, my dear."

Amy reached across and took Maureen's hand. They found a hotel downtown and went out for dinner together.

She returned the rental car the next day, and they flew back to New York. Maureen slept with her head on Amy's shoulder for the entire flight. It felt wonderful.

20

St John's Cemetery, Queens, NY, Sunday, May 28, 2006

The last place they needed to visit together was only a few miles from Amy's apartment. It was a fine day. The sun was high in the sky above their heads. Maureen was wearing a black blazer and matching pants, making Amy wonder if she'd brought them for this purpose. They stood at Amy's parents' grave in silence for several minutes. Maureen cried a little, and Amy held her. It was good to be here with someone else. Amy had come here alone so many times. Having someone here to share her grief, who knew her mother and father so well, was an astonishing comfort.

It was just after three o'clock when they left the graveyard. Visiting felt like cleansing her soul. Amy was upbeat as they sat down for coffee afterward.

"Sorting out the rest of my life doesn't seem like much in comparison to what you did in crossing the Pyrenees with a three-year-old on your back!" Amy said with a cappuccino in her hand.

"Don't compare yourself to me or anyone else. People seem

to think life is some constant competition with others. The only person you need to compete with is yourself. I did what I had to in 1940. I couldn't let those boys down, could I?"

"I just don't know if I would have had the strength or courage to do that," Amy said.

"Oh, Amy, I wish you could see yourself through my eyes. I see so much strength in you. It's like a sword in a scabbard on your hip. All you have to do is draw it out when you need it." She reached over and put a wrinkled hand on Amy's leg. "It's time to stop blaming Ryan for your unhappiness and let that time in your life drift away. I know it might not seem like it right now, but you're a young woman. Look at me, I'm old. I should know."

"I don't know what I would have done if I'd been in your situation."

"You would have done the same had you been in Izieu in 1940," Maureen whispered. "It's just your battles are different than the ones I faced. Be thankful for that."

"I am, Grandma, but not nearly so much as I am for you," she said. Amy leaned over and hugged her grandmother. "I can't believe we wasted so much time."

"It's the most precious thing we have. It's taken me a lifetime to understand that. It's the reason I'm here."

"Do you have to go home?"

"To France? I think it's almost time."

Amy reached across and took her grandmother's hand. "I'm going to miss you so much."

"Why don't you come over and visit? It's so beautiful in June, and I haven't even spoken to you past 1940 yet."

The figure of Christophe appeared in Amy's mind. It was strange that she was thinking about a man from her grandmother's past, but she felt she knew him now. Still, asking any direct questions about him didn't seem right. She'd let her grandmother reveal the answers in due course.

"I would love to come over in a few weeks. I haven't been to your house in so long."

"It's a date, then," Maureen said, and the two women hugged again.

∼

Friday, June 16, 2006

The words flowed like nothing else she'd ever written. It had taken a few days to listen to the tapes. Her grandmother's tale was even more enthralling the second time. Her shorthand had come in handy as she jotted down notes. Then, before she was ready because she knew if she waited that long, she'd never start, Amy began to write Maureen Ritter's story—the first part at least. The hours melted away as she typed. Words piled up, and soon she had 50 pages, and then 100. The regular calls she and her grandmother shared helped to shift any logjams that did come, although they were few and far between. Choosing to write the story in the style of a novel, Amy fleshed out characters Maureen couldn't remember while staying true to the core of her grandmother's incredible story. The days melted away, but Amy found she didn't care. All that mattered was the book.

She'd already booked her flight to France for the end of June. The thought of summering in Provence with the person who'd become the most important to her filled her with joy. Her tape recorder and notebook were ready, and she could hardly wait to hear the rest of her grandmother's history. The war and everything she went through was alive once more in what she'd written, and she was proud of that.

Amy reached across for the cup of coffee on her desk. It was cold, but she drank it anyway. Her phone buzzed beside her.

She knew it wasn't Ryan. He didn't have her new number. He was still peppering her with emails but deleting them wasn't difficult. She found herself caring less and less when they arrived. It was Sara. *How about you tear yourself away from the computer for a few hours and join me for drinks?*

She took a moment to finish the paragraph and took a deep breath before replying to the text. *Where and when? I think I've earned a break.*

It must have been well after midnight, but Amy didn't bother to check the time. Sara, her husband, and several other friends were standing with her, and she turned to order another round. The mirror behind the bar was obscured by the rows of bottles in front of it, all white glass with amber, clear, and even blue and green liquor. The handsome bartender with slicked-back black hair and bleached white teeth greeted her with a grin. She didn't return it, just asked for drinks instead. A smooth-talking 25-year-old was the last thing she needed right now. Sara turned and handed her a vodka and cranberry juice.

"The office isn't the same without you," she said with sadness. "Do you miss it?"

Amy pondered the question for a few seconds. It wasn't easy to think with the music blasting. "I miss the mission more than the job. The deadlines and the pressure of getting the story aren't something I long for. I'm happy writing. Making enough money to live will be the trick!"

"Don't I know it?" Sara replied.

"I miss you and my other friends."

She told her friend about her grandmother's history for a few minutes. Sara was eager to hear the rest.

"You'll have to read the book."

"Whatever happened to Christophe?"

"I don't know yet, but I intend to find out."

Someone tapped Sara on the shoulder. "Look who it is," she said, and Mike Nugent's smiling face appeared.

He kissed Sara on the cheek before reaching forward to do the same to Amy.

"What are you doing here?" Amy asked in a more accusatory tone than she'd intended.

"It's a bar, Amy. I'm here with some friends," he responded, shrugging it off.

Sara excused herself to the bathroom, and Amy was alone at the bar with Mike.

"How have you been?" he asked. "We miss you at the paper."

She thought to tell him the full truth about Ryan but went halfway instead. "I'm better. I took some time with my grandmother, driving across the country, the west at least."

"That was real?" he said with a smile. "I thought you were just blowing me off!"

"No, I drove from LA to Denver with her. It was incredible."

"I remember you told me she was 90. How did she do it?"

"She's quite a woman. I'm writing her biography now. You wouldn't believe the things she did during the war in France."

"You're writing! I can't wait to read it. If you ever need someone to proof it for you, or just to offer an opinion...."

"Thanks, I might just take you up on that."

Maybe it was the vodka, but he looked better than she remembered, and his smile was infectious. It dawned on her how little she knew about him.

"Where do you live?" she asked.

"In Murray Hill. I managed to snag a rent control place passed on by my aunt."

"But you're from Pennsylvania? Why did she live here?"

"She was the black sheep. Every family has one."

"Are you her replacement?"

"My parents are still on the fence about that."

"Why journalism?" she asked.

"I was a lawyer but it wasn't for me. I saw who my work-mates were becoming and it was exactly who I didn't want to be. I've always wanted to write, always been obsessed by the news. I'm sure you're the same."

Amy wasn't in the mood to waste time. Her brain was loose and fluid, and she spoke the words as they came. "Why aren't you married? How old are you?"

"I'm 31," he said with a smile. "I didn't realize this was an intervention."

"Oh God," she replied with a tinge of embarrassment. "You don't have to answer that."

"I was married for a while, but she died." He looked at the bar and then back at her before finishing his beer.

"I'm sorry."

"It's okay," he said. "It was cancer. Three years ago. I can talk about it. It wasn't easy for a while, but things change."

Amy almost said the standard line that she couldn't imagine how he must have felt, but the truth was different. Still, she didn't want to bring the focus back onto herself. "Is that part of the reason why you changed careers?"

"Yeah, after Lucy passed, I evaluated where I was going. I realized that even though she was gone, I was still here, and that the rest of my life was in front of me. I decided to pursue something in the news and was lucky enough to bluff my way into the newspaper."

"I guess you know a little about starting over too."

"You could say that."

"Her name was Lucy? How did you meet?"

"In college. I went to Temple in Philly."

"What was she like?"

Mike seemed surprised by the question. He looked up, scratching the stubble under his chin before he began. "She was beautiful and so fun. You would have loved her. I could see her now in this bar, and she'd have us all in stitches. I never met someone who could make me laugh quite like her. They say when you meet the one you're meant to marry, you know it right away." Amy thought about when she first met Ryan but dismissed the rogue thought in seconds.

"Was that true for you?" she asked.

"The second I saw her. And when we first talked—it was like someone had sprinkled magic on my entire life. I never thought I was the type to marry at 24, but it was the only logical choice with Lucy. It didn't seem like any other life existed but being with her. And that was all I wanted."

It was hard to imagine someone so different than Ryan.

"I can't think of anything else to say but I'm sorry," she added.

"So am I, but as I said, she's gone and I'm still here. I do intend to be on this planet for the next 50 or 60 years so I need to buck up and get on with things, don't I?"

"Cheers to that," Amy said, clinking with his empty beer glass. "Can I buy you one?"

"I'll get it," he said. He asked the rest of the group if they wanted one and turned to attract the bartender's attention.

Sara offered a sly smile behind his back that Amy didn't know how to respond to. Amy still didn't know what she wanted from this man, and the scar tissue Ryan had left in his wake was still deep, but she was happy with Mike at this moment.

He turned around with another drink for her and Sara and reached for his beer.

"We all have our pasts to deal with, don't we?" he said.

Amy decided to take the opportunity he'd presented to her. "My parents are dead," she said. "They died in a car accident in Montauk when I was 24." His face dropped. "I'm sorry, I shouldn't have said that."

"No, I'm glad you did—I mean, you can talk to me about anything."

"I'm not telling you so you feel sorry for me. I'm not about to break down sobbing here by the bar."

"I wouldn't expect you to."

"You have family?"

"I still have both my parents—I think I'll call them tomorrow. And my brother and sister are still in Pennsylvania too.

Sara appeared over Mike's shoulder. "Time to go, Amy. My friend's on the door at that new club I was telling you about. But he can only squeeze four of us in."

"You're leaving?" Mike said.

Amy didn't want to but knew it was the right thing to do. She wasn't ready for anything serious, and that was all it could be with someone like Mike.

"It was great talking to you," she said and kissed him on the cheek.

He nodded his head. "Maybe I could text you about the state of journalism in America sometime?"

"Again? Okay, but not that. But yes, call me," she said despite herself.

And she left the person she wanted to get to know to go somewhere she had no interest in being.

EPILOGUE

Monday, August 12, 1940

After luxuriating together in Barcelona for a week to recover, Maureen and Christophe crossed the Pyrenees again with Pierre as their guide. The trek was grueling, but anything was easier than carrying the children over. It seemed she'd earned Pierre's respect on the previous trip, as he was much more gracious the second time. After traversing the mountains and avoiding the German patrols again, the couple returned to Perpignan to pick up their cars and thank an amazed Madame Camara. The network of safehouses was in place now, and stranded Allied servicemen, political dissidents, and others were using it.

Otto and Heinz had sent a telegram from London that day. It was only a few words, but they and the boys were safe. It was all Maureen needed until the letters began to arrive. She'd reflected on her decision to let them go many times in the eight days since they'd left. And while she missed Rudi, Adam and Abel she realized she had a separate life to live.

Gerhard had been released from prison the day before. But

even so, the German was a marked man now and had decided to disappear underground for a while.

Maureen parted from Christophe outside the safehouse in Perpignan with a kiss and a promise to see each other in Izieu, six hours away.

Rationing was set to begin in a few weeks, but they'd filled their tanks, and had jerricans to spare in the back of both cars in anticipation of any problems. She would reach Izieu, but soon the vehicle would become useless in transporting refugees across the broad swath of southern France. Perhaps she'd need to invest in a coal-powered car. Without it, they would become even more reliant on trains and buses and the papers ordinary citizens required to use them. Maureen dreaded a country where bread, meat, cheese, and chocolate were soon to become restricted items but knew that far worse sacrifices would have to be made.

She laughed as she thought about the latest letter from her father in New York and pulled it out to read it one last time before she left.

MAUREEN,

TO SAY I WASN'T SURPRISED BY YOUR DECISION TO STAY IN FRANCE WOULD BE AN UNDERSTATEMENT ON PAR WITH CALLING HITLER NOT A PARTICULARLY PLEASANT MAN. BUT I UNDERSTAND YOUR DECISION. I, TOO, KNOW WHAT IT'S LIKE TO HAVE UNFINISHED BUSINESS THAT GNAWS AWAY AT YOU. IT CAN CONTROL ALMOST EVERY CHOICE YOU MAKE. I'D ADVISE YOU TO TAKE A STEP BACK ONCE IN A WHILE TO TAKE STOCK AND FIGURE OUT THE MOST PRUDENT COURSE FOR YOU AND THOSE YOU LOVE. THAT ADVICE, WHILE EASILY GIVEN, MIGHT NOT BE SO SIMPLE TO FOLLOW. BUT I'M YOUR FATHER, AND IT'S MY JOB TO GUIDE YOU, HARD AS THAT MAY BE FROM 3,000 MILES AWAY.

I AM PROUD OF YOU FOR THAT INSANE MISSION TO TRANSPORT THE BOYS ACROSS THE MOUNTAIN RANGE INTO SPAIN. THEY'LL BE SAFE IN ENGLAND. I'M ALSO GLAD YOU DIDN'T TELL ME ABOUT IT IN ADVANCE, AS I THINK I WOULD HAVE HAD A HEART ATTACK. I AM SO PLEASED, BUT PLEASE DON'T DO ANYTHING LIKE THAT AGAIN. EVEN CATS ONLY HAVE NINE LIVES. I THINK YOU'VE ALREADY GONE THROUGH ALL OF YOURS.

DO YOU REMEMBER HOW I USED TO REFER TO OUR TIME IN BERLIN IN THE 30S AS BEING IN THE "LION'S DEN?" THAT PERIOD AFFECTED US ALL, BUT PERHAPS YOU THE MOST. SEEING INJUSTICE ALL AROUND YOU FLOURISHING IN HITLER'S GERMANY, YOU RESPONDED TO IT WITH GUSTO. YOU'VE DONE SO MUCH FOR OTHER PEOPLE SINCE THEN. IF WE LIVED IN THE "LION'S DEN," YOU ARE MY "LIONESS."

PLEASE WRITE AGAIN SOON. WHO KNOWS WHEN WE'LL HAVE TO START CODING THESE LETTERS TO BEAT THE CENSORS.

YOUR LOVING FATHER,

SEAMUS RITTER

Maureen folded the letter up and placed it into her bag. Christophe loved the nickname her father gave her and had taken to calling her "The Lioness" these last few days. When she told him it made her sound like a spy, he'd just turned his head and said that perhaps someday that would be her code name. Her? A spy? She couldn't keep a secret from her friends, let alone the Nazis. She started the car and left the city.

She drove along the south coast and was stopped several times by French police demanding papers. Thankfully she didn't meet the same man she'd smuggled the children past on her way to Perpignan back in July and didn't even have to undo any buttons on her blouse this time.

It was early evening as the mountains behind the houses in Izieu came into view. The gravel on the dirt road that led to her home was bumpy and uneven, but it lent a certain calm. This was where she was meant to be—with her second family. Her bag was stuffed with cards sent by the children wishing her a speedy recovery from crossing the Pyrenees twice. All the time she was away, she'd longed for the fields that led to the river with the backdrop of the massive peaks that formed the border between France and Switzerland.

Christophe's car was parked outside the house, and in typical fashion, he had gathered everyone outside to greet her. Several kids ran to her as she got out. Looking around, Maureen felt the absence of Rudi, Adam, and Abel but drew comfort from the fact they were safe. Maureen laughed as little boys and girls attached themselves to her legs. The adults applauded. Her embarrassment increased when Christophe lauded her as "the lioness of the Pyrenees." But before she knew it, she was laughing along with him. They walked inside together, surrounded by the children they'd rescued, the smell of fresh stew wafting through the hallways. With no time to celebrate, Maureen walked into the kitchen with the other adults. There was still so much work to be done.

The End

A NOTE TO THE READER

I hope you enjoyed my book. Head over to www.eoindempseybooks.com to sign up for my readers' club. It's free and always will be. If you want to get in touch with me send an email to eoin@eoindempseybooks.com. I love hearing from readers so don't be a stranger!

Reviews are life-blood to authors these days. If you enjoyed the book and can spare a minute please leave a review on Amazon and/or Goodreads. My loyal and committed readers have put me where I am today. Their honest reviews have brought my books to the attention of other readers. I'd be eternally grateful if you could leave a review. It can be short as you like.

ALSO BY EOIN DEMPSEY

ACKNOWLEDGMENTS

Writing this book was made all the easier by all the wonderful people who helped me along the way. Firstly, massive thanks again to the two patron saints of this book, Carol McDuell and Cindy Bonner. I can't thank you two wonderful ladies enough. Also to Maria Reid, Richard Schwarz, Frank Callahan, Ave Jeanne Ventresca, Cynthia Sand, Preston Taran, Fiona Grant , and Michelle Schulten who went above and beyond.

As always, much love and gratitude to my mother, sister, Orla and my brothers Brian and Conor. And of course, my gorgeous wife, Jill and my three boys, Robbie, Sam, and Jack.

PRAISE FOR EOIN DEMPSEY

Praise for *The Hidden Soldier*:

"A heartfelt trip into two entangled time periods that fans will want to read in one sitting. Engrossing and surprising at every turn, the book is yet more proof that Dempsey is a master of the historical fiction genre."

— LYDIA KANG, BESTSELLING AUTHOR OF A BEAUTIFUL POISON AND OPIUM AND ABSINTHE

"The Hidden Soldier is a poignant page-turner that will leave you breathless. Gorgeously written, Eoin Dempsey carries you back in time and inserts you into the heart of this tragic, pivotal moment in history. Part thriller, part love story, I was completely enthralled from beginning to end."

— SUZANNE REDFEARN, #1 AMAZON BESTSELLING AUTHOR OR IN AN INSTANT AND HADLEY AND GRACE.

""I didn't see that coming! Or that!" I yelled across the house as Eoin Dempsey's wonderful World War II book raced to an utterly satisfying wallop of a finale. His spare, dialogue-driven style, matched with his strong knowledge of the war and masterful ability to dance between two time periods, made for one heck of an enjoyable read."

— *BOO WALKER, BESTSELLING AUTHOR OF AN UNFINISHED STORY.*

Praise for *The Longest Echo:*

"...a chilling page turner that explores a shocking, little-known episode in history and manages to include a touching love story."

— HISTORICAL NOVEL SOCIETY

"A beautiful, heart wrenching novel that captivated me from the very beginning. This is historical fiction at its absolute best, and one of my favorite reads of the year."

— SORAYA M. LANE, AMAZON CHARTS BESTSELLING AUTHOR OF *WIVES OF WAR* AND *THE LAST CORRESPONDENT*

"Based on the true horrors of WWII Monte Sole, this story tugs at the heartstrings while delivering authentic, engaging champions and page-turning scenes that continue beyond the war."

— GEMMA LIVIERO, BESTSELLING AUTHOR
OF HISTORICAL FICTION

Praise for *White Rose, Black Forest* (A Goodreads Choice Award Semifinalist, Historical Fiction):

"*White Rose, Black Forest* is partly a lyrical poem, an uncomfortable history lesson, and a page-turning thriller that will keep the reader engaged from the beginning to the end."

— FLORA J. SOLOMON, AUTHOR OF *A
PLEDGE OF SILENCE*

"There is much to praise in Eoin Dempsey's *White Rose, Black Forest*, but for me it stands out from the glut of war fiction because of its poetic simplicity. The novel does not span a massive cast of characters, various continents, and the entire duration of the conflict. It is the tale of one young man, one young woman, and the courage to change the tide of a war. Emotional, taut, and deftly drawn, *White Rose, Black Forest* is a stunning tale of bravery, compassion, and love."

— AIMIE K. RUNYAN, BESTSELLING AUTHOR
OF *DAUGHTERS OF THE NIGHT SKY*

"Dempsey's World War II thriller is a haunting page-turner. The settings are detailed and the characters leap off the page. I couldn't put this book down. An instant bestseller."

— JAMES D. SHIPMAN, BESTSELLING
AUTHOR OF *IT IS WELL* AND *A BITTER RAIN*

"A gripping story of heroism and redemption, *White Rose, Black Forest* glows with delicate yet vivid writing. I enjoyed it tremendously."

— OLIVIA HAWKER, AUTHOR OF *THE
RAGGED EDGE OF NIGHT*

"Tense, taut, and tightly focused, *White Rose, Black Forest* is a haunting novel about courage and compassion that will keep you gripped from the very first page."

— COLIN FALCONER, BESTSELLING AUTHOR
OF *THE UNKILLABLE KITTY O'KANE*

ABOUT THE AUTHOR

Eoin (Owen) was born and raised in Ireland. His books have been translated into fourteen languages and also optioned for film and radio broadcast. He lives in Philadelphia with his wonderful wife and three crazy sons.

You can connect with him at eoindempseybooks.com or on Facebook at https://www.facebook.com/eoindempseybooks/ or by email at eoin@eoindempseybooks.com.